# MASSACRE AT JUTLAND

# MASSACRE AT JUTLAND

## Duncan Harding

severn House

This first world edition published in Great Britain 2006 by
SEVERN HOUSE PUBLISHERS LTD of
9–15 High Street, Sutton, Surrey SM1 1DF.
This first world edition published in the USA 2006 by
SEVERN HOUSE PUBLISHERS INC of
595 Madison Avenue, New York, N.Y. 10022.

British Library Cataloguing in Publication Data

Harding,  Duncan,  1926-
    Massacre at Jutland
    1.    Great Britain. Royal Navy - Fiction
    2.    World War, 1914-1918 - Secret service - Fiction
    3.    Jutland, Battle of, 1916 - Fiction
    4.    War stories
    I.    Title
    823.9'14 [F]

    ISBN-10:  0-7278-6343-6

Typeset by Palimpsest Book Production Ltd.,
Polmont, Stirlingshire, Scotland.
Printed and bound in Great Britain by
MPG Books Ltd., Bodmin, Cornwall.

# Extract from *Naval Heroes of the Twentieth Century**

When Sir de Vere Smith, VC, DSO, DSC (and bar), OBE (mil. div.) died at his country house in Gloucester in 1990 at the age of 95, his service record gained him an obituary in the London *Times*, the *Daily Telegraph* and other British broadsheets. After all, he had been a national hero, winning the DSC at the age of twenty and then, four years later, Britain's highest honour for bravery, the Victoria Cross.

In middle age, he had come out of retirement to rejoin the Royal Navy to become a distinguished destroyer skipper and flotilla leader in World War II, fighting at least two vital convoys across the North Atlantic with German Admiral Doenitz's wolf packs seemingly out to get him personally.

But it was pretty obvious that the anonymous writers of 1990 were somewhat puzzled by such an active man who appeared to have spent much of his life doing little but dairy farming, shooting in winter and sailing his beloved Ketch, the *Dulciebella*, in the summer. Why had such a renowned sailor not been employed again in the service after the Second World War, the writers must have asked themselves. Why, too, had he lived in some kind of semi-retirement in the twenties and thirties? In particular, what had young de Vere done in 1913/14 which had led him to leave the service so abruptly in 1918 at the end of the First World War?

His brief entry in the British *Who's Who* gave the obit. writers few clues to his activities prior to and immediately after that 'war to end all wars'. All that standard work records

* Capt. Robert N. Herkheimer, US (retd.): *Naval Heroes of the Twentieth Century: Jellicoe to John F. Kennedy*, Stein & Day, NY 1991.

1

state is that he spent most of his time 'travelling'. But there is no indication of where Sir de Vere Smith travelled, how he won his Victoria Cross and the host of foreign decorations for gallantry recorded in *Who's Who* – from Greece, Belgium, Yugoslavia etc, etc. Why he was even awarded the *Croix de Guerre avec Palmes* from post-war France, a country not renowned for giving awards to aristocratic Englishmen in the interwar years.

The then *Times* obituary writer contented himself with 'De Vere Smith spent the twenties on government service in Europe and Asia Minor.' The *Telegraph* man went a little further, but not much. He wrote: 'The twenties greatly resembled our own time. The German and Russian Imperial empires had collapsed. Europe was in a state of flux. New countries were springing up on all sides. Throughout Central Europe there was war and strife. It seems from what evidence is available from that time, young de Vere played a role in helping those emerging countries which were friendly to Britain to keep their newly won independence.' How, the man from the *Telegraph* didn't explain.

It was only after his death that de Vere's papers came to light. These are a collection of handwritten accounts of his exploits, mainly in the twenties and thirties, which, at a time when the British Secret Service – ie MI6 – didn't exist officially, could not be published. These 'adventures', as de Vere entitled them, are not particularly well written, and his grammar is definitely shaky for someone who went to a leading British public school, Harrow, as a boy (for instance his use of the apostrophe is very haphazard and he mixes his 'to' and 'toos', as well as his 'there' and 'their'). But these days, if he had been prepared to use a ghostwriter, de Vere would have made a fortune. Publishers and so-called 'literary' agents would have been lining up at his door, cheque books in hand. TV and 'Tinseltown' wouldn't have been far behind either.

For after the First World War, de Vere had really led an amazing life: gun-running to the new Poland; helping to stop the Turks massacring the Greeks in that war-torn country under Kemal Attaturk; giving a hand to the German authorities in

2

their first attempt to crush the upstart Austrian Adolf Hitler and his Nazis. In these years, 1919 till 1930, when he was officially retired from MI6 (though this might well have been just another cover for some top-secret task still to be revealed by the British Public Record Office at Kew) de Vere seems to have popped up in every trouble spot from Berlin to Baghdad.

However, as laconic as these 'adventures' are, de Vere does reveal something of significance which gives a clue to how he, as a teenage midshipman in the Royal Navy, first became involved in what his type of patriotic upper class Englishman once called 'The Great Game'. For the first time, he mentions a fellow old Harrovian and pre-war teenage midshipman 'Dickle' Bird and how the two of them, 'damned fools that we were back in '13, nearly got ourselves dismissed the service . . . just before the best adventure of them all, the Great War, which the two of us wouldn't have misse for all the tea in China.'

We know little of Lt. Commander 'Dickie' Bird, DSO, DSC, save what he wrote in his 1950 autobiography, *Down to the Sea in Ships Again* (Maritime Press, Portsmouth). In it the long-dead commander said of de Vere, his old friend and shipmate, 'I would describe him as an Englishman of the finest type. That is to say that he regarded the "old country" as the best, most just and superior spot in the whole wide world. Naturally de Vere didn't force his opinions down foreigners' throats. For him it was simply a fact of life. And if the other chap, the Hun, the Bolshevik, Johnny Turk and the like didn't agree, well that was his funeral. Naturally, if the other chap became "uppity," de Vere often ensured that he'd be carried out feet first in a box, PDQ.

'For the two of us it started almost disastrously after we'd read *The Riddle of the Sands* and had met that old gentleman-firebrand in Queen Anne's Gate with the monocle . . . But I have been warned by the powers that be that, even at this distance of time, I must not write any more about that particular crucial meeting in 1913. So I will desist. All I will say is this. That meeting was the start of many weird and wonderful adventures all over Europe and Asia Minor when de Vere and

I risked our necks on half pay and dare not tell even our loved ones what we were up to, unless we wanted to be sent to the Tower.'

The 'Tower' that Dickie Bird mentions was the British 'Tower of London', to which spies and traiters were sent traditionally in those years. It and the 'gentleman-firebrand in Queen Anne's Gate' tell us how two mere boys in uniform were obviously recruited into the British Secret Service *prior* to the First World War. For Number 22 Queen Anne's Gate, near London's Green Park, was then the headquarters of MI6.

But what was the significance of *The Riddle of the Sands*, written by the Anglo-Irishman Erskine Childers, who was later shot by his fellow rebel Irishmen during the troubles that followed that country's independence in 1922? That is a damnably awkward question to answer. In essence the *Riddle* is an adventure novel written before the First World War, set in the area of the Dutch-German Frisian islands located off the north-west coast of those two countries. It is concerned with two young yachtsmen from Great Britain who uncover a 'dastardly German plot'. At the time, with anti-German sentiment rising in Britain, the novel was something of a sensation. Even young Mr Winston Churchill, the rising politician, as he was then, had praised the book rapturously. It was said that the Admiralty had taken its fictional revelations very seriously and that senior figures in the British War Office had taken active steps to ensure that Childers' 'dastardly plot' should never be be carried out in reality.[*]

But what could that fictional plot have had to do with the mysterious activities of two young midshipmen which nearly caused them to be 'dismissed the service'? Here all that we can mention is the name of de Vere Smith's beloved boat, on which he sailed the Solent throughout the years of his supposed retirement. It was the *Dulciebella*: the same

[*] Interestingly enough, when Ian Fleming, creator of 'James Bond', worked for British Naval Intelligence in WWII, he too visualized carrying out a similar scheme off the German coast as had Childers' two young adventurers. *D. H.*

name that Childers had given to the craft his two fictional protagonists had crewed in that now forgotten novel of 1909.

# Come!

Sons
Of the Islands, rise!
The German guns
Bellow to the skies

And rain their shell
Like Hell . . .

They
Had sworn to come.
They had sworn to come.
They drank 'unto the day',
For years prepared the way.
Now hear the shrapnel hum . . .

*George Weddell, Hartlepool, December 1914*

# Author's Note

'You can allus trust a toff,' my grandad 'Stoker' Harding always told me when I was a short-assed kid. He'd hawk, spit out a gob of thick brown spittle from his old pipe and tap the silver plate at the back of his head for luck. 'Toffs in them days when I was in the 'Royal' allus used to talk pound-notish and look at yer lower-deck matelot as if he was a bit o'muck. But when the shit started to fly, yer knew you could rely on 'em. It was that there public school tradition o' theirs, like.'

Even as a kid I was always surprised when the old buffer began talking like that. After all, ex-stoker third class Harding had voted Labour since the days of Kier Hardy and he thought the conservative *Daily Mail* was the work of the devil – 'Not even good enough for arse-paper in the lav, Dunc!' Still, as we sat on the bench at the prom, with the old man hoping the sea breeze would whip up the girls' frocks and allow him to spot their knickers (he was always a glutton for what he called 'frilly French knicks'), he'd never let a bad word be spoken against his 'toffs', especially if they had been serving officers on the quarterdeck of one of the ships he'd been on.

Naturally, as I grew older, I didn't take his praise of the upper classes at face value. He'd say something like, 'Them days the toffs knew their duty to King and Empire,' and I might retort, bolshy like most youngsters are, 'But Grandad, your bloody toffs went and lost that bloody Empire you're always waffling on about.'

Well, that'd set him off coughing and choking, as if he were going to snuff it on the spot there and then. But when he'd recovered he'd snort, 'That's yer modern toff, Dunc. A lot o' pansies who don't know their arse from their bleeding elbows.

7

In my time you had a different breed o' swells. They was let down by yer working class in '45 and them blokes in Westminster, who talk water an' drink wine. Bloody bunch o' lawyers and schoolteachers – and yer can't trust that kind.'

Probably he'd pause for breath about then and have a quick look up the prom in the hope that some girl'd get the breeze up her miniskirt and flash those celebrated 'knicks' that the old boy was always lusting after, before coming out with his usual plaint. 'The toffs in them days was let down by that fat Welsh git giving yer working classes free glasses and false teeth. He lashed out with the money the Empire needed like a man with no arms, as yer poor dead old granny used to say. In the end, Dunc, it was either the Empire or false teeth for yer old bags – and the toffs could do nothing about it. *That's* how we lost the Empire, me young feller-me-lad.' And he'd suck at the end of his filthy pipe as if he'd said the definitive word on post-1945 Britain and what we were taught in my council school to call 'the New Elizabethan Age' – and there's a joke if I ever heard one.

Just before Suez in '56, when the old boy was visibly failing – 'Dunc, I can't even see their knicks proper when the lasses flash 'em' – I got my first job on the local rag while I was waiting to be called up for what they called laughingly 'National Service' (I'd volunteered for the blood and thunder of the Royal Army Pay Corps, naturally). With my first week's pay packet, I bought the old boy a pair of cheap Jap binoculars – of course, I daren't tell him they were Jap. He would have had a fit.

He never got to use the new glasses though. He died at his 'post' on the prom with them still in their case on the day that the US President Eisenhower – 'Ike' of the ear-to-ear grin – ordered the Anglo-French troops out of Egypt – or else. So much for the 'special relationship' between Britain and America that our politicos are always waffling on about.

In a way, it was good that the old boy never experienced that day of shame, especially as it was his 'toffs' who were in charge in London and who tamely accepted Ike's dictate. God knows what he'd have made of it all. Perhaps it was better that he passed away then, with the binocular case

8

unopened in his big-veined stoker's hands. I don't think he'd have lived down the shame of it all. What would he have thought of his toffs, who could always be trusted, then?

Me, old hack that I am, I didn't really care one way or the other. All the same, I was curious about them then – and still am all these years later. I know naturally that they were brought up to command, imbibed their feeling of superiority with their mothers' milk, even before their public schools put the final touches to their overbearing arrogance: that stuck-up look they once had, as if they were Jesus about to walk across the water.

All the same, despite their privileged backgrounds, they seemed to have been tough babies, especially the young naval officers my grandad admired so much. The Royal Navy grabbed them when they were still babes-in-arms, at fourteen, even thirteen in some cases. For years thereafter they lived in conditions that no self-respecting 'lifer', with his gym and choice of menus in one of Her Majesty's prisons, would tolerate for an instant these days. If my old grandad's 'toffs' were arrogant devils who thought the world was their oyster, I suppose they'd earned their privileged status over all those hard years before they officially were granted the status of 'officers and gentlemen'. And when the crunch came and they. went to war, the 'toffs' proved themselves. They *could* be trusted, as my working-class grandad always maintained.

Thus when my publisher, the one who knocks back the French red wine at twenty quid a bottle in those posh London 'eateries' he frequents, suggested *we* should try something new, involving the 'Great War' as he's now started calling that forgotten conflict, I thought I might tackle the project. 'The punters are sick of World War Two, Duncan,' he stated after the third bottle of his 'Mouton' something or other. 'They've had enough of the *Kelly*, the *Warspite* and the like.[*] What about a naval yarn set during that war. There must be some good tales about,' he rabbited on. 'Deeds of derring-do, that sort of thing.'

[*] He meant my 'plumbing books', as I call them because they are all entitled *Sink X* or *Sink Y* etc etc.

It was no use telling him that the great British reading public were no longer interested in tales of 'derring-do'. These days, those of the current generation who manage to leave school with the ability to read in the first place seem to prefer stories in which nothing happens, by Jap authors who live in the exciting swashbucking world of Hampstead or similar exotic locations. Still the good man, carried away by all that Mouton red, was offering a generous advance – well, generous for him – and I needed the money, *urgently*. My new lady friend is causing a major cash crisis in the Harding household (I'm thinking of trying to get her banned from Marks and Sparks before the bailiffs make their appearance) and at that moment I would have written advertising copy for the labels of HP Sauce, as long as the purveyer of that great asset to British cooking paid me for the task.

I accepted. But what to write? Where to start?

It was about then that I remembered Grandad, 'Stoker' Harding, and these days on the windswept prom, where he indulged himself in the glorious past and his pop-eyed search for young girls' 'knicks', which excited him so much. Once during those years he had told me what I thought, even as a gullible kid, a far-fetched tale. It was about two of these young 'toffs' of his, who, single-handed, had tried to prevent the Battle of Jutland back in 1916.

I didn't believe much of his story then, and still have my doubts to this day (after all, the battle took place nearly a 100 years age now and all of those who took part in the tale are long dead). Yet; all the same, I couldn't dismiss it entirely. In a way, the old man's yarn was much too involved for the simple brain of a one-time three-badge stoker who'd left school at 12. He couldn't have just made it up. Especially as, at that time when he told it, the miniskirt had just come in and Grandad's mind and imagination went running wild every time one of 'them dolly birds', as he called the teenage girls, bent down carelessly in front of him.

Naturally the heroes of his yarn were two of his celebrated toffs, whom you could 'allus trust'. They had to be. I mean, what lower-deck sailor in his right mind would ever have tackled such an impossible mission as the one described by the old man?

Indeed, gentle reader, I think it's best to leave the judgement to you. But I'd just like to add this bit of – er – poetry, which I found in the diary of Lt Commander 'Dickie' Bird, DSC, RN (ret'd)*, one of the two toffs supposedly involved. The doggerel of that time nearly a century ago reads as follows:

> We'll pay in full the debts we owe.
> Though red with blood the rivers flow.
> Yet once again, our foes shall know
> That blow for blow is Britain's way . . .
> And what Britain owes she'll surely pay . . .

That debt in blood, I have discovered, actually took place. But did those two toffs, barely out of their teens in 1916, actually repay it at Jutland, this time in German blood? Yes, there's the rub. How do we separate fact from fiction all these years later? Still, it's a good yarn, set at a time when Britain was 'still full o' piss and vinegar', as 'Stoker' Harding would have put it. Let's believe it, eh?

*D. H.*
*Withernsea, E. Yorks and Hamburg,*
*Germany, Spring '05*

---

* Courtesy of the Imperial War Museum, London.

1913

# One

Somewhere off the Dutch coast, a foghorn sounded mournfully. On the shore itself, seagulls swooped and dived, crying shrilly like lost babies calling for their mothers. Raindrops dripped miserably off the fishing smacks stranded in the deep, stinking mud of the *wad*, now the tide was out.

Midshipman de Vere Smith, dressed in the shabby 'slops' that he had worn since they had set out on what he called a 'ripping adventure', shivered and cursed, 'Heaven help a ruddy sailor on a night like this, Dickie.'

'Dickie' Bird, his old chum from their Harrow School days together and now his fellow midshipman, forced a grin, as he stared out at the stretch of mud that seemed to go on for ever until it reached the North Sea. '"Twas brillig, and the slithy toves, did gyre and gimble in the wabe,' he quoted Lewis Carroll, for some reason known only to himself.

'Oh shut up, Dickie,' De Vere snapped, 'and don't be such a silly ass. This is serious, you know.'

'I know, de Vere, old chap. But as the late and unlamented Oscar Wilde is supposed to have said, "Life is too serious to be taken seriously," what!'

De Vere, tall and handsome in a languid, upper-class English fashion, snorted, 'All right, put a sock in it, Dickie.' He raised the home-made sledge which he and Dickie had fashioned back in the cabin of the little boat. 'Let's get cracking. We can assume that the good Dutch folk have gone to bed with the chickens as usual. I think no one will spot us anyway in this damned murk.'

Dickie, a grin seemingly set on his wide-open, handsome, freckled face, nodded. 'I agree, old bean. Anyone out now in

15

this dreadful weather needs his head seeing to.' He raised his own sledge. 'Into the fray, what?'

'Into the fray, Dickie.'

Together they let the rough metal sledges drop into the mud of the *wad*. Gingerly they lowered themselves on to the home-made devices, taking great care to place their upper bodies on them, as beneath the sledges the thick goo quaked and bubbled as if it were a live thing, resenting this attempt to cross the wide and dangerous expanse of the *wad* to the sea. For, as carefree and silly as the two of them were, they knew they were about to risk their lives. If anything went wrong, the thick grey mud of the *wad* might well swallow them up as easily as the deadly quicksands they read about in their monthly copies of *Blackwoods*.

Side by side, moving very slowly at first, they started to propel themselves with their gloved hands towards the sea and the great secret that they believed they would discover there: a secret that, if it was there, they, two humble 'snot-ties', still in their teens, were expected to report immediately to that strange old firebrand with his sharp tongue and monocle located in that rabbit warren of a building behind London's Green Park . . .

'This way, gentlemen,' the old servant in the rusty black tailcoat, adorned with the ribbons of the Boer War on the right lapel, had croaked. He had held out his skinny claw to the two puzzled midshipmen as if they were favoured guests at some high-class restaurant who were liable to tip well. Adjusting his wing collar around his scrawny neck, he ushered them into the new-fangled lift, which bore no indication of what lay on each floor. De Vere looked at Dickie Bird signifi-cantly, but if the old servant caught the glance, his own lined face was like a mask, revealing nothing.

Number 22 Queen Anne's Gate might have been a decrepit, cold rabbit warren of a place, but the lift was ultra-modern. It sped them upwards noiselessly and at high speed. In seconds they seemed to have ascended several floors to be deposited in a narrow passage. Indeed, it was so narrow that a modestly fat man would have had difficulty passing through it.

'This way, gentlemen,' the servant croaked once more, and

started to creak audibly down the passage. The two young men guessed that one of the old servant's legs had to be artificial, the wooden part hinged to the limb by leather straps and springs. De Vere told himself that the servant fitted in well in this strange place to which they had been summoned from their base on the North-East coast so surprisingly.

Slowly they progressed deeper into the building along narrow winding corridors, lit by low-watt naked bulbs, which threw their shadows on the dirty walls and which provided cover for the rats scrabbling and scratching on both sides as they passed.

Behind de Vere, Dickie shuddered dramatically and whispered, 'Oh my sainted aunt, this place really gives me the creeps, de Vere.'

Up in front, the old man seemed to have surprisingly good hearing for his age, for he said, 'Not much further now, gentlemen.' He paused to open a massive steel door which had suddenly barred any further progress. Moments later they were passing over a rickety iron bridge which seemed about five floors up and which linked the roof of the Georgian house with that of its neighbour.

Once more they entered a network of passages. Time passed leadenly, though both the young midshipmen felt their nerves tingling with excitement mixed with apprehension. When they had accepted the strange invitation, which had come completely out of the blue, they had accepted the free trip and accommodation with alacrity. After all, as Dickie had remarked when they had signed the telegramme the Post Office boy in his side-cap had brought, 'Anything to get away from this ruddy North Sea end of the world – in winter.' Now the strangeness of the place was beginning to make them think differently. What had they let themselves in for?

Finally, at long last, the old servant stopped in front of a door, covered with a thick leather screen, which bore no name on it, though, strangely enough, the door did have above it a coloured bulb the like of which the two midshipmen had never seen.

Gently the servant tapped on the leather-covered door. The sound was barely audible and for a moment the two young

17

men thought the tap hadn't been heard. They were wrong. Suddenly the bulb above the door started to blink an urgent bright green. In his usual creaking manner, the old servant opened the door and then, surprisingly, he winked and said, 'Don't take his nibs so serious, gents. He don't half go on sometimes.' With that he creaked away, disappearing into the shadows of the corridor like some ancient ghost.

Gingerly the two of them entered and, although they weren't in naval uniform, they clicked to attention. The middle-aged man who had risen from behind the big desk that they would find out had once belonged to their hero, Admiral Nelson himself, was obviously a senior officer in mufti.

'Ah,' he said in a deep plummy accent. 'The two young sacrificial lambs, eh?' He indicated the two hard-backed wooden chairs in front of the big old desk. 'Sit ye down. There's scotch and glasses to your left. "Don't be vague, ask for Haig",' he quoted the current slogan of the whisky firm, plastered all over London at the moment. 'Help yourself, if you want a snort.'

Firmly the two young men shook their heads in unison and Dickie said, perhaps tongue in cheek. 'Don't touch the stuff, sir. But thank you for the offer.'

The man peered at him through his monocle as if he were some strange sort of animal life. 'That is not what I have heard from the current captain of destroyers about your conduct while you were serving in these new torpedo boats at Portsmouth.'

Dicke flushed red and was about to answer. But the man behind Nelson's desk held up his hand for silence and turned to the papers on the desk, leaving them to stare about the place in a somewhat awed daze. The office was tiny but terribly cluttered. In addition to the mountain of official-looking files on Nelson's desk, there was a smaller table shoved in a corner, littered with maps, models of submarines and the new-fangled aeroplanes which had just been introduced into the Royal Navy back in 1911. Behind it on a blacked-out window sill there was a row of opaque glass bottles with their labels in Latin, which suggested either a chemist's shop or some sort of scientific investigation. For de Vere, the strange bottles

18

with their Latin names and the even stranger-looking chemical equipment that went with it only heightened the overpowering atmosphere of mystery that hung about this tiny office at the top of the old Georgian house. The very air, stale and smelly, added to the strangeness of the place. Again he wondered what they had let themselves in for when they had sent that telegramme of acceptance from their remote Reserve Fleet base on the North-East coast.

Finally the man behind the desk raised his balding head and stared hard at them through his gold-rimmed monocle. 'Young men,' he said slowly. 'I like what I read about you – ' he tapped his files – 'and I like what I see in front of me now.' Suddenly, almost startlingly, his stern countenance and eagle eye behind the pane of glass melted into the friendliest of smiles. 'You must be puzzled by all this. Well, I'll tell you as much as you need to know. I am called C. Don't ask why and never reveal that initial to anyone, even your nearest and dearest. If you do, you will find yourselves in serious trouble, very serious trouble indeed. But as you both signed the Official Secrets Act when you joined up, I think you can understand. His eyes twinkled. 'And I might add that I am head of an organization which doesn't exist officially. Parliament knows nothing of us. We are funded secretly and even if you ever do betray that secret, not even the King-Emperor himself, King George V, would be able to save you from the Tower of London.'

'Do you mean, sir,' Dickie blurted out, 'that we are to belong to your organization, whatever it is?'

'Yes, Mr Bird, in a way you will, if you accept the task that I have called on you to undertake.'

'And what is that, sir?' de Vere, like Dickie, was unable to restrain himself, feeling new excitement surging through his lean, hard body.

C held up his hand. 'Hold your horses, Mr Smith,' he ordered. 'Let me explain a few things first.' He glanced at the open file he had sought for a moment, holding on to his monocle in case it dropped out of his eye, and an excited de Vere guessed C didn't need the pane of window glass really. It was all part of the strange man's cover. 'Now, the two of

19

you have been keen small boat sailors, I see, ever since you left Harrow-on-the-Hill to join the Senior Service. It says here that the captain of *HMS Britannia* thought highly of your seamanship even as young cadets, though he didn't think so much of your private Sunday afternoon grudge fights in the nearby quarry, Mr Bird.'

Dickie actually blushed.

'Now, both of you know from *The Times* that currently there is a naval race going on between ourselves and the Germans. Their crazy emperor and his admirals are determined to match the strength of the Royal Navy in a few short years. Indeed they are almost there now.'

The two of them nodded their heads gravely, as if both of them perused *The Times* every morning after breakfast, instead of the *Sporting Pink*. That seemed to be the only thing that young midshipmen read, apart from more shady periodicals which were illustrated with comely French ladies in various states of undress.

'But what are the Germans and their mad emperor going to do with their fleet once they have achieved parity with ours?' C answered his own question, leaning forward over Nelson's desk in his eagerness to do so. 'I shall tell you. The Huns will definitely attempt to test their strength against us in the Atlantic, or more probably in the North Sea, closer to their bases in the Baltic and North Sea.

De Vere gasped, caught completely by surprise. 'You mean . . . *war*, sir?'

'I certainly do, Smith.'

For a moment the three of them were as if frozen. The thought of another war had obviously shocked even this mysterious C, who looked as if he had seen several wars in his time. Finally C broke that heavy brooding silence. 'I doubt it, gentlemen, but if we were able to uncover the dastardly Hun plan to start this new war – which, I am sure, would set the whole of Europe ablaze, with us and the French and probably the Russians too against Germany and Austria and their Central European allies – we might, with luck, stop any war.'

'How, sir?' de Vere ventured hesitantly.

'Make the Hun plan of attack known to the world – in particular, to the United States. That might do the trick.' He dismissed the matter with a snap of his finger and thumb. 'But first we must find out what that plan is.' He looked hard at the two young midshipmen, as if he were seeing them for the first time and etching their features on his mind's eye for reasons known only to himself. 'And this is where – if you are prepared to help me and the old country of course – you two young men come in.'

Patriots that Dickie and de Vere were, brought up in the public-school tradition of unquestioning loyalty to the Empire and the King-Emperor, they snapped in unison, 'What do you want us to do, sir?'

C's hard face cracked into a wary smile, as if he were pleased with their response, yet hesitant about committing them to an enterprise that might well endanger their young lives. 'It could be dangerous, you realize, very dangerous. The Hun, I am afraid, wouldn't hesitate to take – er – very serious measures, if they caught you doing what I have in mind for you.'

'What is it, sir?'

C hesitated no longer. He rose from his chair and limped to the large map of Western Europe that was fixed to the wall behind him. He slapped it with his hard hand. 'The German Empire,' he announced. 'Clustered here to the North-West are the main bases of the German Imperial Navy: Cuxhaven, Bremerhaven, Emden etc, and in particular, Wilhelmshaven, where their High Sea Fleet is based. You probably know about that from your studies at Dartmouth?'

The two of them nodded, but said nothing. They were too fascinated by C's exposé and what it had to do with them.

'Now, to the west of those German naval harbours are the East Frisian islands, where, if I recall correctly, our worthy Germanic ancestors came from. They became civilized here. Unfortunately, their fellow countrymen they left behind didn't.' Presumably the comment was supposed to be humourous, but his two listeners didn't laugh. 'These islands from Spiekeroog to Borkum on the Dutch border are located in shallow and treacherous water, which we have always supposed couldn't be navigated by ships with a large draught, such as the German High Sea Fleet. For that reason, in case of a war with Germany, their Lordships at the Admiralty have always planned to mine the main channels leading from Wilhelmshaven and the like to prevent the Huns from getting into the North Sea. You understand, gentlemen?'

'Yessir,' de Vere agreed. 'That wouldn't tie up our own Grand Fleet, and would leave us ships over for any hostilities in the Med, and possibly the Far East, the China Station and the like too.'

'Exactly. But there's a catch in their Lordships' plan. It is this.' He lowered his voice, as if he half-suspected that someone might well be listening at the leather door outside. 'What if the Hun has found some way of navigating in these treacherous waters to the south of the East Frisian islands? They'd dodge our minefields and be in the North Sea before you could say Jack Robinson.' He looked at them. 'It could well mean the surprise destruction of our own Grand Fleet and leave us defenceless against any German attack on our beloved island. Gentlemen,' he concluded solemnly, 'it could mean the British Empire would lose the war before it had started . . .'

# Two

For over three days now, the two young midshipmen had been observing the comings and goings of coastal shipping around the East Frisian islands from what they thought was the safety of the Dutch Frisian island of Rottumeroog, just across the Dutch border. De Vere had reckoned no one of the solid Dutch burghers in their wooden *klompen* and baggy trousers would ask questions of two English 'milords', who had time and money to play with fancy boats when normal people were fully engaged in catching the herring or tilling the newly won land behind the island's dyke.

He had been right. Even in the little *kroeg*, the local drinking house where the locals spoke their own Frisian dialect and sat stolidly drinking their rum punches or a strange mixture of black tea and some kind of spirit, no one paid much attention to the two foreigners. Instead the islanders sat there in a kind of morose silence, puffing steadily at their long clay pipes, speaking only when they wanted another drink or excused themselves to go outside and urinate noisily in the yard.

The locals' lack of curiosity had suited the two youths fine, even more so when they had been hammering away, making their tin sledges in the cabin of their little craft. Back at their base on the Yorkshire coast, the natives would have started asking questions right away. 'What tha up to, lad?' they'd have queried. 'Tha's mekkin' a reet old noise with yon hammering.' Not on the Dutch island. Here they could get on with their self-imposed task with all speed, unbothered by awkward questions and curious glances.

For they had discovered that the vast expanse of mud, the *wad*, had made it virtually impossible for them to identifty the craft passing between the islands and the land with any real accuracy, even with their binoculars (which they didn't dare use often in case anyone on board the passing shipping spotted them and reported the watchers to the German naval authorities). They had to get closer and they had soon realized that the only way to do that was to reach the North Sea beach and observe the coastal craft from there. On the second day after they had come to that conclusion, they had ventured out on to the *wad*, as soon as dusk had fallen and the locals were already preparing to go to sleep in their *kojen*, the narrow bunks, enclosed in wooden shutters to keep the warmth in and the draft out.

They hadn't got far. Within minutes they had been fighting for their lives. Floundering in the mud, up to their waists in the goo, they had been panting and gasping, almost at the end of the tether before they had managed finally to reach the firmer sand, to lie there exhausted, like great muddy fish on the point of dying. It was that same evening, when they had fortified themselves with a full litre bottle of the potent local genever, that they had dreamed up their idea of the tin sledges, which they would fashion from the tin drums sold at the local ship chandlers.

Now, as they fought their way forward yard by yard across that dangerous waste, with the seagulls diving and screeching at them, they knew that they were going to do it, even though it was getting progressively darker. But that fact didn't worry them. With the dusk would come the evening high tide and, as they were both powerful swimmers who had braved a mile or so swim in the North Sea in winter, they reckoned they could cope with that problem. Indeed, it might well prove to their advantage. For, as de Vere had gasped to Dickie, now that they had almost reached the sea shore, 'Anything's better than this ruddy *wad* paddling. I ruddy well ache all over.'

'Me, too,' Dickie agreed. The words died on his lips.

To his left, an old coal-burning freighter, very low in the water, as if it were very heavily laden, was slowly coming into view, trailing clouds of thick black smoke behind it.

De Vere caught on at once. 'She's pretty close,' he said, pausing near the water's edge. 'You'd think that an old tub like that, plying these coasts, would know the dangers of low and high water, Dickie.'

Dickie, pausing next to him, looked puzzled. 'Yes,' he agreed, 'and why's she running without lights? The local fishing fleets from the islands out for the herring will be sailing soon. It could be damnably dangerous for them if they ran into that old tub. She must displace at least two hundred tons. She'd soon make mincemeat of these fishing boats.'

For a moment or two they lay there on their tin sledges, ignoring the cold wind now blowing off the North Sea, studying the strange craft, which couldn't be making more than five knots, as if her skipper had all the time in world, instead of making all possible speed and heading for the warmth and fiery clear alcohol of one of the island's snug little inns. Finally de Vere broke their silence with, 'You've got better eyesight than I, Dickie. Can you make out her flag?'

Dickie shook his head. 'I've already looked. She hasn't got one.' He shrugged. 'Their skipper must be damned careless, running without navigation lights, so perhaps he isn't particularly worried about flying a national flag.'

'You'd think he would, so close to the German-Dutch border. Perhaps he's a smuggler. That's why she's so close to the shore.'

Again the two young adventurers fell silent as they watched the old tub, which seemed to be slowing down even more, so that she appeared to be hardly moving at all now, as she came parallel with them. They turned their heads into the wind so that they could hear better, for both of them thought they heard voices on board the craft, now that the thud-thud of her engines had died away almost to nothing.

Despite the muting effect of the mist beginning to creep in from the sea, now they definitely could hear voices. De Vere strained hard to make out the language spoken. He knew that in both the Dutch and German Frisian islands they spoke a similar Germanic dialect which most other Germans couldn't understand.

But as far as he could make out the men on board weren't speaking that local dialect. Was it then Dutch or German? Both were guttural languages, but as he had already established from

25

the time they had spent on the little Dutch island, the local pronunciation of the letter 'l' clearly distinguished between the two languages. Now, however, as the old tub came to a complete stop, he didn't need that 'l' sound to make him realize that the men on board were speaking German. That harsh command, followed by the sound of a boat being lowered from the ship, told him all he needed to know. It was '*Achtung!*' He whistled softly and whispered, 'Did you hear that, Dickie?'

'I certainly did, old fellow. *They're Huns!*'

'Yes,' de Vere added hastily, 'and they seem to be coming this way.'

'Crikey!' his comrade exclaimed. 'Do you think they've spotted us? And if they are smugglers, I don't think, de Vere, they're going to be overjoyed to know that we've got a grandstand seat, what?'

De Vere didn't reply. For, although it was obvious that the little rowing boat was coming closer to their observation post, it was not heading in their direction with any haste. Indeed, after the first few yards, the boat stopped, the two men in civilian clothes resting on their oars, while a third man balanced himself and tossed a line into the shallows.

For a moment the two observers were puzzled by the civilian's action. Then they tumbled to it. 'They're not smugglers, Dickie,' de Vere hissed.

'That's for certain . . . But if they're not smugglers, what in heaven's name are they? And what are they up to?'

De Vere answered at once. 'Dickie, I think we've cracked it. It's just as C thought. They're Huns, and you know what they're doing . . .?'

But before Dickie could answer that overwhelming question, a harsh voice demanded in German, '*Wer da? Wer versteckt sich da?*' And then in Dutch, '*Waar is dat?*'

De Vere didn't hesitate. He knew instinctively they were in danger. The German's voice was full of menace. The Huns were up to no good. 'Back-peddle, Dickie,' he hissed urgently. 'Let's do a bunk while we're still in one piece.'

The young midshipman had guessed correctly. They were in real danger. For, the next moment, the civilian, if he really was a civilian, dropped his plumb line. Scarlet flame stabbed

26

the foggy darkness and, as the two of them started to propel themselves backwards as fast as they could on their tin sledges, a bullet splashed into the *wad* only yards away.

'Oh my sainted aunt!' Dickie exclaimed. 'The bugger's actually firing at us . . . Real bullets! Why, he really wants to kill us, de Vere.'

In years to come, after the two of them had been fired upon more times than they could count, the old friends would laugh at Dickie's surprise on the occasion of their first time under fire. But not this evening. The man's reaction to finding them there spying on him was too frightening. It only made them redouble their efforts to get away before the German improved his aim.

Now a searchlight of some sort clicked on aboard the old tub. An icy finger of silver light started to part the foggy dusk. Slowly but surely it started to close on them. 'Quicker,' de Vere urged. 'For God's sake, Dickie, get a ruddy move on. If—' Again the civilian standing upright in the little rowing boat fired. A bullet whined off the tin plating of Dickie's sledge. Dickie yelped with pain as a splinter of the metal struck him on the left cheek. Blood started to pour from the wound, and now the two of them really realized for the first time that the German in the rowing boat was out to kill them. Why, they didn't know. But there was no denying the fact. If they didn't get out of the *wad* soon and out of range, they'd be dead. Furiously, with every last ounce of their strength, they started to paddle backwards, their breath coming in great gasps, their upper arms burning electrically with all the effort.

But then the German did something foolish. Perhaps he didn't realize that only feet from where the water lapped against the little sandy beach, the treacherous thick grey mud of the *wad* commenced. Even as they paddled with all their might to escape, they could hear the splash as he went over the side of the rowing boat and into the shallow water, crying as he did so in German, '*Halten Sie an* . . . Hold it there . . .!'

His feet splashed through the water and then he was on the beach. They could hear the stamp of his nailed waders as he crunched over the little patch of shingle. '*Los!*' he cried. '*Oder ich schiesse—*' His cry ended in a sudden, startled curse. The next moment that sharp order was changing to an urgent plea for help. '*Kameraden, ich bin zum Knie im Schlamm . . . Zu Hilfe!*'

The two young men, their breath coming in harsh, hectic gasps as if pumped by a cracked leather bellows, knew instinctively what had happened. Unaware of the grave danger, he had plunged straight up to his knees in the start of the *wad* and now, in his panic-stricken struggles, he was sinking ever deeper by the second into its treacherous, clinging mud. Still they did not stop their frantic paddling. Summoning all their energy, hearts beating crazily as if they might burst out of their ribcages at any moment, they kept up the pace, knowing that their lives wers still in danger. For, now, that icy beam had left the water's edge and was approaching ever closer to where they fought to get away; and by now they had no illusions about the Germans in the old tub. They were out to kill them; and if one of them was armed, as the man now sinking in the mud to his waist, his arms flailing the air in abject panic, had been, de Vere and Dickie were certain he would use his weapon for that very same purpose.

But then luck turned in their favour. As if by magic the fog swept in from the sea in full force. In an instant, the old tub, the rowing boat, and that dangerous searchlight, which only seconds before might well have threatened their young lives, had vanished, swallowed up by the thick grey gloom, which deadened even the cries of the German trapped and sinking rapidly in the mud of the *wad*. They were saved . . .

Half an hour later they were stripped naked and shivering in the tight little cabin of their vessel, washing themselves down in buckets of lukewarm water, drinking a powerful mixture of Camp Coffee, well laced with the last of their scotch. But despite the cold and their goose-pimpled nakedness, the two old friends were full of high spirits, as they went over the exciting events of that late afternoon, relating them time and time again, as they attempted to make some sense of what had happened; and the fact that, for the first time in their young lives (but it wouldn't be the last) someone had tried to murder them in cold blood.

'So they were Germans,' de Vere said once again, his voice slurred slightly as the scotch started to take effect.

'And the Huns tried to bump us off,' Dickie repeated his part of their tipsy litany.

'Why, Dickie. They weren't smugglers. That was for certain.'

'Besides, old bean, smugglers don't shoot people. Well, not these days at least. It's agen the law.'

'Exactly, Dickie.' De Vere took another swig of the hot but dreadful-tasting mix of Camp Coffee and strong scotch. He shuddered as he swallowed it. Thickly, he said, 'Nor do smugglers test the depth of the water as the Hun chap who went into the mud did – God rest his black soul, if he ever had one. For that's what he was obviously doing with that plumb line.'

Dickie dabbed his wounded cheek, which had started to bleed slightly once more, and winced with pain as he did so. Hurriedly, he too took a drink of the revolting mix from his chipped enamel mug, which bore the crown and anchor of the Royal Naval College at Dartmouth. 'So, what can we conclude, my dear Dr Watson, eh?'

De Vere assumed what he fancied would be the grave appearance of the great fictional detective's confidant, thumbs clasped in a non-existent waistcoat. 'This, Holmes: C was right. The Huns are trying to find a channel from their naval harbours, which their Lordships, our penny-pinching admirals in Whitehall, appear not to be able to afford to mine in the case of a war between ourselves and the Huns.'

'My thinking exactly, Watson.' Dickie chartled, finishing the rest of the disgusting mixture in one gulp, the tears springing to his eyes as he did so. He laughed, ignoring the pain. 'Well, there we are, up a gum tree, as the Aussies say.' Suddenly and surprisingly, he burst into song, full of the exuberance of youth, relieved in a way that their undercover mission had not been for naught. '*We're poor little lambs who have gone astray, baa, baa, baa . . . Little black sheep who have lost their way, baa, baa, baa . . .*'

Carried away by relief at the success of their mission, de Vere, who was not normally given to the enthusiasm of Dickie, joined in heartily too, so that the little cabin rang to the sound of their young, innocent voices, '*Gentlemen matelots, all are we doomed . . . from here to eternity . . . God have mercy on such as we, baa, baa, baa . . .*'

Engaged as they were in the old song they had sung often enough at Dartmouth, the two of them, happy and probably full of whisky too, didn't hear the hesitant knock on the porthole of their little craft, which looked out on to the top of the ill-lit little jetty.

It was only when the tap came again and a soft voice said, '*Mevrouw de Waal . . .*' that they realized someone was there outside.

They stopped abruptly. They knew no one on the island, save for the ship chandler who had supplied them with the material for their tin sledges, which were now safely over the side in the deeper water of the tiny harbour, and the keeper of the inn where they had eaten the terrible salt herrings of the Frisian Islands straight from the barrel, washing them down with weak Dutch beer. 'Who in God's name is calling at this time of the night?' Dickie began, but he was out off by a soft voice calling in accented but good English, 'Have you a moment, gentlemen . . . Please? I have a message for you, *please*.' They sensed the urgency in what was obviously a female voice. Still, they were cautious after what had happened to them only a a few hours before out on the *wad*.

Carefully de Vere pulled back the little curtain which covered the porthole. It revealed in the flickering blue gaslights which illuminated the jetty a pair of slim ankles clad in sheer black silk stockings unlike the floor-length dark dresses and wooden shoes of the local women. Whoever was out there, asking to see them, didn't look as if she came from the little island, to judge by the expensive stockings and well-polished shoes with their silver buckles. He flashed a look at his companion. 'What do you think, Dickie?'

Dickie shrugged his shoulders and winced with pain again. 'Search me, old fellow. But let's be careful. You never know with these foreigners, woman or not.' He reached for the steel starting handle they used to fire the little craft's unreliable engine. 'Let her enter.'

'Come in,' de Vere called.

'*Dank u*,' the unknown female replied, and even the coarse, guttural Dutch sounded charming when she spoke it. Moments later she was clattering down the little steps on and into the craft's cabin.

Dickie exclaimed something under his breath. Later de Vere thought he'd said, 'Golly, what a beaut!' But at that moment he was too entranced himself by their surprising visitor to listen to what his old friend had to say. For the slim woman, who was a little older than they were – perhaps twenty or so – was strikingly beautiful in an un-English way. Indeed, she didn't look at all like the other rather homely and well-built Dutch girls they had seen so far. Her face was delicate and, underneath the brief veil that she wore, her cheekbones were broad in an attractive manner, which seemed more Slavic than Germanic.

But the strange girl, *Mevrouw de Waal*, as she called herself – though the two bemused youths couldn't spot any wedding ring on her slim fingers which would entitle her to that form of address* – gave them no time to consider her beauty. Instead she said urgently, 'You are the English gentlemen who ventured out on the *wad* this afternoon.'

Before they had time to deny they were, she went on rapidly to say, 'You have disturbed dangerous people . . .'

'What kind of dangerous people?' Dickie managed to cut in.

She ignored the interruption. 'There is no time to waste! She must sail now while the tide is high.' She fluttered her delicate white hand like someone trying to shoo away importuning infants. 'They must not find you here, gentlemen. Your lives are at risk.'

'*Who . . . What . . .?*' de Vere asked a little helplessly.

But it was obvious that she was not prepared to answer his questions. Instead she tugged the little black veil down lower

---

* Married woman.

31

over her beautiful face, as if she wished to hide it, and pulled up the fur collar of her expensive-looking coat. 'I must go. You must flee . . . *Now!*'

And with that she was gone almost before the two of them had realized. Hastily de Vere sprang to the little porthole and ripped back the curtain. He caught a quick glimpse of Mevrouw de Waal in the hissing blue circle of the jetty's gaslights, and then she vanished, as if she had never been there in the first place. He turned and faced Dickie, who was just as surprised by this sudden departure as he was. He scratched the back of his blond head in bewilderment and muttered, 'Well, that's a turn-up for the books, Dickie. Now what?'

It seemed to take his old pal a long time to react, but in the end he did so, saying, 'Well, she seemed serious enough . . . I suppose we'd better do as she says . . .'

# Three

'And what happened then?' C asked. 'After this Mrs de Waal gave you her warning about – presumably – the danger from the Huns.' He paused momentarily, as if he were considering whether he should tell his young listeners any more. 'And by the way. I don't think the pretty young lady's real name was de Waal. But I'll tell you more about that a little later when I've heard your account of what happened that night.' He signalled the waiter, holding up his matchbox in the upright position, the old India hand's signal for a large scotch.

The three of them were seated under a palm tree in the far corner of the great lounge of York's Railway Hotel, with the noise of the LNER's locomotives passing back and forth in their journeys to London and Newcastle, muted by the thick grey stonework of the great pile in the centre of the ancient Roman city.

De Vere sipped the half pint of mild-and-bitter he had ordered and said, 'Well, sir, everything went well as we started out on the high tide. The islanders had long turned in – they'd even turned out the gas jets on the jetty.'

'A thrifty people, the Dutch,' C said with a half smile as the waiter deposited a large scotch and the siphon of soda water in front of him. 'Some might even say damned mean. But carry on, Smith.'

'We used our engine till we'd cleared the harbour and then we hauled up our sail to save fuel. We were running low and, after what the girl had told us, we decided to make for Texel before refuelling, just in case.'

Dickie said, 'Besides, sir, we were getting short of the readies.' He looked at the older man, who had come up specifically to meet them here in the sleepy provincial city away from what C called the 'prying eyes' of the capital. 'Midshipman's pay is pretty poor, sir, as *you* know.'

C caught his meaning and said swiftly. 'Never fear, young man. I'll see to it that our slush fund reimburses you forthwith for any outgoings on your part – and a little extra as well.'

Dickie didn't know what a 'slush fund' was, but he knew what that 'little extra' meant. He smiled and said, 'Thank you, sir. Sorry to bother you with the filthy lucre business.'

C waved his hand to dismiss the matter. 'Please carry on, Smith.'

'Well, sir, as I was saying. We cleared the little harbour with no problem. Then we got busy with the sail because the sea had become choppy and we had decided it might be safer after what had happened that afternoon to sail without navigation lights.'

'Very wise. But . . .' C added, face suddenly very shrewd, 'but it didn't work, did it?'

'No, sir,' de Vere replied.

'It certainly didn't, sir,' Dickie chimed in, face grim as he thought of that night just outside the little harbour when out of nowhere there came the sudden, startling roar of high-speed engines and they spotted the 'white bone' of an unlit craft surging through the waves at a tremendous speed, heading straight for their little boat. 'There was no doubt about it, sir. They—'

'The Huns?' C said swiftly.

'Well that was our guess, sir,' de Vere agreed. 'After what had happened that afternoon and Mrs de Waal's warning. My God, sir, it was really nip-and-tuck for us. Frankly I thought that our number was up. We hadn't the speed or the ability to get away from a craft moving at that lick. And it was certain that she was about to ram us and send us to the bottom.'

'So how did you avoid being sent down to – er Davy Jones' locker, Smith?'

'Sheer luck, sir, and Dickie here and his strong right arm.'

'Yessir. I don't even know now, how I did it. But the winch we used to start the engine was still close by. I suppose it was

34

instinct really, sir, and the fact I used to play cricket for the first eleven at Harrow-on-the-Hill. But I let go with the handle with all my strength, and God knows how I did it, but I managed to hit their lookout on the foredeck. He must have been directing the cove on the bridge. He went over the side. We heard his splash and cry for help – in German – and all of a sudden, the Hun craft was slowing up and was off course. Whether it was because they were blinded without the lookout or whether the Hun skipper slowed down to pick him out of the briny, I don't know.' Dickie licked his lips, which were abruptly very dry at the memory and the long explanation. Hastily he picked up his glass and had a swift drink of the warm beer. 'But it gave us the chance that we needed.'

'It certainly did sir,' de Vere took up the story. 'We ski-daddled back for the coast toot-sweet. We assumed that even with the Hun's craft shallow draft, she wouldn't be able to tackle the bits closer to the edge of the *wad*.'

'And?'

'We'd almost made it when she opened up with a machine gun, sir.'

Even C, the veteran, was surprised. 'I say, that was a bit thick. First time under fire for you young chaps, too, I suppose.'

Dickie nodded. Adventurous and ready for anything as he and de Vere were, he hadn't liked the steady pounding of the Hun machine gun one bit, as the bullets had chipped their woodwork and ripped holes in their sail.

De Vere finished the last of his beer as the newspaper boys who had collected the latest dailies from the London-to-Newcastle train came into the hotel to deposit them on the reception desk. He flashed a glance at the headline of the *Morning Post*. It read, 'Kaiser Issues Warning. Will Tolerate No Further Foreign Interference in the Balkans.'

C sniffed. 'I see Kaiser Bill's up to his old games. That man's mad. One day he'll set the whole bloody continent of Europe alight. Anyway, you are here safely, young men. Thank God. In my time I've sent some very good men, true Englishmen, to their deaths. But it's never been easy, I can tell you. It has weighed on my conscience greatly. I am sure I'll have a lot of explaining to do when I meet my maker. But no matter. Now let me tell you my news – and I'm afraid it's not good.'

The two of them leaned forward eagerly as the string quartet struck up and launched an attack on 'In a Monastery Garden'. Thus, it was against the strains of that Edwardian oldie, played not too well by four beaming middle-aged ladies in old-fashioned teagowns, that they heard what C had to say about the reception of their findings in London.

'Their Lordships were not at all receptive, I am afraid,' C said. 'Indeed, I think they were bloody-minded, very much so. They said they accepted your findings that the water off the Frisian islands between them and the coast proper was much shallower than they thought, and that their own Admiralty charts were definitely out of date. So far so good, I thought. Then came the crunch. Agreeing with you that the Hun was up to something fishy there, they couldn't see what it was. All right, so they could get their lighter craft through that way and dodge the minefields. But what good would they be against our capital ships of the Home Fleet? Even if they did circumvent the minefield we would lay off Wilhelmshaven and the like in case of war, what could light craft, smaller than the smallest Hun destroyer of the *Mowe* class, do against our battleships and lighter battlecruisers?' He paused and took an angry pull at his scotch as if he were trying to eradicate a bitter taste in his mouth.

In the lounge a prosperous-looking fat man in a bowler hat, linked up to a pretty young girl with rouged cheeks, who certainly wasn't his wife – or his daughter either for that matter – glanced at the headline of the *Morning Post* and snorted in a thick Yorkshire accent, 'That bloody Kaiser. Him and his Huns'll ruin our export trade. Yer'd think them ministers in London'd do summat about it before all of us up here end in t' bankrupt court.' They passed on and C continued with, 'In a way their Lordships are right. All the same, the Huns are not going to all that trouble up there on the coast of Holland for nothing. I mean trying to kill you two young bloods. But what are they up to?' He looked at the two younger men, as if he expected them to come up with an answer. But they had none, for they too realized their Lordships had a point. Even if the German light craft with their shallow draught *could* dodge the minefield by using the channel between the islands and the North Sea coast, what use would they be against the might of the British battlewagons with their 15-inch guns and massive armour-plating? Presumably they wouldn't be capable of carrying torpedoes weighing up to a ten and half. If they did, they'd probably lose the advantage of their shallow draught.

'So,' C broke their silence as the quartet scraped away merrily, the middle-aged ladies beaming inanely, tossing their heads from one side to the other, their light silk teagowns fluttering wildly with the motion, as if they were in the throes of some demented sexual excitement. 'In essence, the Admiralty is going to sit on its thumbs and do nothing. Indeed, I personally have been ordered not to undertake any more – er – work in that area. We don't want to upset the Hun, apparently. More importantly, the Dutch government in the Hague has protested about our activities in that area. Not about the Huns, naturally,' C added somewhat bitterly. 'But the Huns are their next-door neighbours and the cheeseheads' best trading partners.'

He clicked his fingers at the waiter as if he was back in the mess at Simla, signalling to the turbaned mess steward. He reached for his wallet to pay, saying, 'Oh, and by the way, the lady you call Mevrouw de Waal, who attempted to save you from the dastardly Hun—'

'Yes?' they said in unison, concealing their disappointment at the apparent failure of their 'adventure'.

'Well, that pretty lady is neither a 'Mevrouw', nor a de Waal, and for that matter not Dutch either.'

'Well, who and what is she, sir?' Dickie was first off the mark, for he had been quite 'smitten', as he put it in his youthful fashion, by the beautiful young woman.

'Her real name is Freifrau von Hoofstra-Mecklenburg – she is distantly related to the Dutch House of Orange and, I believe, also to the German prince consort of the present Dutch Queen. Hence the Dutch part of her name. But take it from me, she's German all right, through and through I would guess.'

'*German?*'

'Yes, German Kleinadel, impoverished small aristocracy, as the Hun calls them.' He took a ten shilling note out of his wallet and offered it to the waiter, saying, 'Take thruppence for yourself as a tip, my man.' He waited till he had disappeared back to reception to get the note changed before adding, 'Oh, in case I forget, I think I ought to tell you she's also a spy.'

Dickie's mouth dropped open stupidly. 'A spy, sir?'

'Yes, for *Kapitan zur See*, Prinz Klaus von Bismarck of German Naval Intelligence. A blackguard and a rotter through and through.'

'You mean *those* Bismarcks, sir?' de Vere asked sharply.

'Correct, I think he is a distant relative of the Iron Chancellor, von Bismarck, whom that madman the Kaiser sacked some twenty-odd years ago. At least, when he has leave from German Naval HQ at Wilhelmshaven, he spends a lot of time at the Bismarck estate at Friedrichsruh just outside Hamburg.'

Dickie whistled softly. 'Who would have thought it – a nice girl like that. I say, that is a turn-up for the books.'

'Quite possible, Midshipman Bird,' C said coolly, pocketing his change from the ten shilling note as a bowing waiter pulled back his chair. 'Oh, and another thing, the pair of you. She's also suspected of being this von Bismarck's current mistress.'

Together they walked across to the station towards platform three, where C would catch his train back to London before they turned in the opposite direction and caught their own to Scarborough and their base. The little man standing next to the newspaper kiosk, under the great station clock, lowered his copy of the *Yorkshire Evening Press*, dating from the previous day, and watched carefully as the three Englishmen stood there, waiting for the London express to steam into the Victorian station.

C was in a reflective, perhaps even a depressed, mood, unusual for a man of his experience and temperament. He said, as the third-class passengers started to pick up their brown-paper parcels and shabby cardboard suitcases ready to board the approaching train (naturally, in his position and with his background in the Brigade of Guards, he wouldn't have

38

been seen dead carrying anything save his customary black Malacca stick with its silver horsehead handle), 'Our work together, young fellows, has ended in something of a failure, I am afraid to say. However, I still think we're on to something, whatever the gentlemen in Whitehall say to the contrary. No matter. We shall be vindicated in due course. Of two things I am certain, we shall be at war with the Huns before very long and we shall be vindicated then.' He tipped his bowler to them and waited till the porter had opened the door of his first-class carriage for him. He forced a tight smile. 'Never fear, sooner or later we shall be all working together once more.' With that, he entered his carriage, sat in the overstuffed red plush seat and looked out of the opposite window, as if he had forgotten the two young midshipmen already.

The little man with the day-old copy of the *Yorkshire Evening Press* had seen enough. He fumbled in the pocket of his greasy waistcoat for change and then he crossed over to the telephone operator and, speaking in the purest cockney, asked the girl at the exchange. 'Miss, get me the German Embassy in London, please . . . Naval Attaché section . . .'

1914

# One

'Prince von Bismarck would turn in his grave,' the head gamekeeper whispered out of the side of his mouth to his assistant as they stood there on the frozen grass, collars of their green loden cloaks pulled about their ears. For this December was proving exceedingly cold, though for the aristocratic hunters the icy temperatures were proving useful. They were bringing out the wild boar and the deer, which roamed the great forest of Sachsenwald, which stretched virtually from the Bismarcks' great house at Friedricharuh to the outskirts of the port of Hamburg. All the same, the head gamekeeper, who was responsible for the number of animals to be shot by the family and their official guests each season, didn't approve one bit of the manner in which the great man's distant relative was going about the business of bagging a wild boar this particular November day.

The fat von Bismarck, who had to be helped climb the rickety steps of the *Hochstand** this morning, had obviously not had the patience to wait for an animal to venture out of the forest's dense undergrowth to be shot. He wanted a quick kill so that he could add an 'eight-pointer' to his collection of trophies.

Instead, the fat, middle-aged naval officer had scattered precious turnips (for already, due to the British blockade, foodstuffs were in short supply in Northern Germany and turnips were now part of the peasants' normal fare instead being reserved for the animals) in a trail leading from the forest. Obviously the hunter, crouched in his *Hochstand*,

---

* A raised wooden blind for hunting, common in Germany.

sipping cognac from his silver flask, high-powered rifle with its telescopic sight at the ready, hoped the turnips would lure a wild pig out of its hiding place so that he could fell the animal easily with a 'shoulder shot'.

The head gamekeeper sniffed at the illegal and unsporting manner of bagging a prize *Wildschwein*. 'Someone ought to report the fat bastard to the Hunters' Association so that they could take his licence to shoot away.'

Next to him his assistant, who was still of military age, whispered, 'Not so loud, *Oberjägermeister*. A rotten pig like Kapitan von Bismarck could get me called up to the Army by a click of his fingers. I don't fancy the trenches in Flanders at this time of the year. *Scheisskalt!*'

'Yes,' his boss agreed. 'Shit-cold indeed. All right, let him get on with it so we can get back to the house and get warm. I'm freezing.'

Five minutes later a huge bristly wild pig emerged from the undergrowth, head low, as it sniffed the beets, occasionally stopping to turn up the hard ground with its snout, as if the animal suspected the food was hidden there. Then it spotted the first of the frozen turnips. It dashed forward with surprising speed for such an awkward, short-legged animal. Watching, keeping well out of the wild pig's scent range, the head gamekeeper whispered, 'That's a real porker. Bet you it's not much less than two hundred pounds.'

'*Jawohl, ja*,' his assistant agreed, his breath fogging on the icy air. 'Make a nice roast for somebody, *Chef*.'

'But not for you, my friend. That'll be reserved for the gentry—'

The sharp crack of von Bismarck's rifle broke into his words. The wild pig staggered. It went down on its knees. A sudden dark red patch began to stain its bristles. The head gamekeeper watched tensely, hand falling instinctively to his curved knife, with which he would slit the animal's throat. But that wasn't to be. The wounded animal staggered to its feet. Shaking its great tusked head, it turned, ignoring the beets now, and began to trot hesitantly into the bushes from which it had emerged, as von Bismarck, cursing audibly, began to reload his hunting rifle.

He didn't make it. Just as he pumped the first bullet into the chamber, the pig, leaving a trail of bright-red blood on the frozen grass behind it, disappeared into the undergrowth.

He reached the ground, his fat face lathered with sweat despite the biting morning cold. Breathing heavily, he ordered, 'You'd better shoot the damned thing before someone complains about the Bismarcks leaving a wounded animal in the forest. These days the world is full of busybodies meddling in other people's business.' He gasped and reached for his silver flask of cognac as the two keepers hesitated to carry out his order. He paused with the flask held to his fat sensualist's lips. 'Well, man,' he addressed the head gamekeeper, 'what in three devils' name are you waiting there for? Get on with it.'

The head keeper went red-faced with embarrassment. 'But you know wild pigs, *Durchlaucht*,' he stuttered. 'They are dangerous when wounded, especially in undergrowth. They can turn on a man—'

'Get on with it,' he cut the man short. 'The front is in urgent need of men, you know, even older men like yourself.'

The threat worked. The head gamekeeper unslung his hunting rifle and, turning to the other man, who was equally reluctant to enter the forest and face a boar weighing a couple of hundredweight and savage with pain and the sense of being trapped. He had seen what happened to keepers who had been foolish enough to do so and had not had the time to get off a killing shot before the beast charged. Their guts had been ripped out by the pig's tusks and left hanging down their bloody bellies like steaming grey-green snakes.

Prince von Bismarck dismissed them with, 'Damned impertinent peasants! They need to feel a navy lash across their bare backs.' He finished the drink and turned back for the Bismarck manor, stumping up the incline with difficulty, breath coming in short sharp heavy gasps. But the gross-looking prince, who had achieved the rank of naval captain with difficulty, despite the von Bismarck name, was no fool. He came from the impoverished line of the family. He and his family didn't possess any of the great farms of the 'Iron Chancellor's' descendants in East Prussia, or these newer ones in Schleswig-

Holstein, where Otto von Bismarck had commenced his unification of Germany back in 1864 and had been amply rewarded by the Prussian king for doing so. One day, he would have to live off his naval pension and he had expensive tastes, especially in women. He grinned momentarily at the thought. But the nubile young mistresses would be out if he didn't make at least rear-admiral before retirement. He had to retire to that boring, remote farm on the border with Russia, eeking out an existence, growing maize and potatoes, drinking cheap corn spirits and, with luck, tumbling the fat ugly daughters of his serfs.

Today, however, there was a chance that he might make the next step up the ladder of promotion if his scheme was accepted. He had been working at it for over a year and believed the stuffy fleet admirals, steeped in conventional naval tactics, might well accept it, especially after their recent defeats at the hands of the hated English off Heligoland and in the Falkland Islands.[*]

He entered the house and stamped the earth off his big boots. The noise brought one of the valets rushing immediately out of one of the side rooms, bowing and scraping, though the prince knew the servants didn't really respect him. Awful snobs that these Northern German servants were, they kowtowed to him as a relative of the master. But in reality they looked down on him as a 'poor relative' and that angered him. He took off his grey-green cloak and deliberately dropped it on the floor before the valet could take it from him. *Let the swine pick it up. Good for him to learn to dirty his hands*, a nasty little voice at the back of his mind rasped.

With the white-gloved hand poised delicately above the dropped garment, the servant said, 'There is – er – a lady to see you in the drawing room, *Durchlaucht*, and the naval gentlemen called from the railway station at Aumühle to say that they are proceeding by motor vehicle to here, sir. They should be here in a matter of half an hour.' He sniffed and looked at the cloak once more, as if he was considering whether he should pick it up or not.

[*] Both in autumn 1914.

46

'Good,' the prince snapped, knowing that he must hurry now. He didn't want to keep the damned self-important admirals waiting. 'See there's coffee, brandy and cigars – good Havana cigars, mind you – waiting for them in the library. Ensure that there's a good fire in there, too. The oven is not sufficient.'

The servant again gave that haughty sniff of his. He said, 'All has been prepared already, sir.'

But von Bismarck was not listening. Sussi von Hoofstra-Mecklenburg was waiting for him with the information he needed before he met the admirals. Besides, his face lightened a little at the thought he might be able to squeeze in a little bit of fun after she had reported. She knew his ways; she wouldn't object, especially if she wanted to live in the style to which she was certainly not accustomed.

Quickening his pace and wishing he had time for that delightful white powder that always added a little something extra to his sexual encounters with young women half his age, he entered the downstairs room that his fop of an uncle had allotted him for the duration of his stay at the von Bismarck pile.

She was waiting for him, standing next to the grand piano covered with silver-framed portraits of the members of the senior branch of the family, with, naturally, the Iron Chancellor in uniform, complete with winged, burnished helmet, making up the centrepiece.

She turned. Looking as beautiful as ever, she whispered, 'Klaus.'

He crossed to her, heart beating faster as he took in the splendid figure of his agent-mistress, and, raising her dainty hand to his lips, kissed it, saying, '*Küss die Hand*,' in his most gallant manner. For her part, she sniffed, as her nostrils took in the smell from his balding head, covered with spots filled with pus.

'Now, my dear, what news have you from Holland for me?' He rubbed his big hand idly over her firm left breast and felt the nipple harden under her thin lace blouse. He licked his lips. Fat and middle-aged as he was, a woman's body always excited him, even without the drugs. Already he could sense

47

that old delightful thickening of his loins. 'What is with these English North-Eastern ports?'

'I have two contacts, Axel,' she answered in that professional manner of hers, though most casual observers would have taken her for a slightly silly young woman, whose main interest was young men and clothes. 'A Dutch skipper who sails the route between Rotterdam and Hull.'

He understood and nodded his approval, gaze fixed on those splendid breasts of hers, clearly outlined through the thin material of her expensive blouse. Obviously his touch had excited them.

'And a Belgian soldier, allegedly wounded at the front, who is being taken care of by the English in Scarborough. They are turning the hotels there into emergency hospitals for their wounded, English and Belgian.'

'Good, and what do these contacts report, my dear?'

'That stretch of the coast is virtually undefended. In Scarborough, for instance, the Belgian maintains that the only coastal artillery dates back to a war the English fought against the Russians in the middle of last century. Muzzle-loaders firing cannonballs.'

'Excellent. But go on. Sea defences?'

'They are a little more formidable, Klaus,' she replied, as from outside came the crunch of solid rubber car tyres rolling over the frozen gravel of the drive up to the grand house. 'There are naval stations at all the minor parts along that stretch of coast, including Scarborough.'

He nodded. 'That was to be expected. The English will have to protect their coastal convoys. So naturally they'll have small patrol craft and minesweepers stationed there. Now, minefields. What does your Dutch skipper report? The English will naturally have had to warn him where they were in that stretch of the North Sea if he sails back and forth to the coast's major port, Hull.'

'Yes, Klaus,' she agreed. 'The Dutchman says there are two main areas of mines that he knows about. He has the information from the English Admirality's official notification.'

'Go on,' von Bismarck urged her, feeling the tension in his loins grow apace. It was nearly four days now since he had

48

enjoyed a whore in the Reeperbahn, Hamburg's red-light district. He really needed a woman if he was going to function correctly, especially now when his nerves were being stretched to the limit.

'One minefield extends from the Farne Islands to the Tees.'

'And the other?' he asked eagerly. For that particular minefield was of no interest to him.

'From somewhere called Flamborough Head to the Humber Estuary. Both, according to the Dutchman, are not covered at all by enemy warships, or very lightly, Klaus.'

'Excellent, excellent, my dear.' He pressed her breast again, feeling very excited now. 'I shall ensure that there'll be a little bonus ready for you at the end of the month. No doubt you will spend it easily on some fine clothes for yourself in Amsterdam, perhaps even those naughty little pieces of underwear you favour, ah?' He licked his thick red lips and she knew what he was after. She had long got the measure of Klaus von Bismarck and she didn't like what she knew of him and his filthy sexual habits. But with no money, she knew, there was no future for her. All the young men she knew had gone to the front or had been killed already. The old ones were already married and would only want her as a mistress on call for an hour or two in some shady, shabby hotel when they could escape their wives. After that the only work opportunity was to grow old as some dried-up governess in black, teaching the spoiled naughty children of the rich.

'*Jawohl*, Sussi. I might take a Christmas leave if all goes well, and we could spend it in the Berlin Adlon with champus and proper food. Then –' he licked his fat wet lips again, sliding his tongue from one side of his mouth to the other, as if he was already savouring the food at the capital's finest hotel – 'you could wear those frillies you'll buy with your extra money, eh?' He leered at her hopefully.

'Yes—'

She never finished, for she was reacting too slowly for the impatient spymaster. Abruptly he seized her. For such an unhealthy fat man, who sweated and panted a lot even during the slightest physical exertion, he was surprisingly strong. 'Klaus!' she gasped. But he was no longer listening. He turned her round so that she was caught off balance and was forced to grab the grand piano for support. It was exactly what the lecherous von Bismarck wanted. He threw up her skirt to reveal the silken bloomers below. With one hand he fumbled with the ribbons that tied the slit at the back. With the other he ripped open his flies to reveal his member, ugly, swollen and red, protruding like the rubber clubs the police carried.

'Klaus!' she hissed urgently. 'Somebody might come in.'

'Let them!' he gasped through gritted teeth. Next instant he had thrust himself into her with such force that he pushed her against the piano. She gave in. What did it matter if anyone came in? She had lost her soul and her honour long ago. This was all she was good for: to be bribed and taken by a man who didn't respect her one bit – a mere piece of female flesh to be used and abused. She was no better than a cheap Reeperbahn whore, selling herself in the Herbertstrasse.

# Two

'*Guten Morgen, meine Herren.*' Von Bismarck opened the door of the library and clicked his booted heels together sharply, hoping the eau de cologne he had just splashed hurriedly over his face would take the smell of body odour and sex away.

They were all there, the three admirals, bearded and stiff in the Prussian fashion, enjoying their good cigars and brandy in front of the roaring fire beneath yet another portrait of the Iron Chancellor. Beyond, clustered around the green-tiled stove which reached the ceiling and which didn't give off as much warmth as the open fire, were the senior advisors, chatting quietly among themselves, tugging now and again at their high stiff collars – 'father-stranglers' as they called them in the Imperial Navy – waiting for the summons to give their advice or suggestions.

Admiral von Ingenohl, the senior admiral present, bearded, stiff and patrician, who was wearing a black ribbon around his arm in memory of the dead from the recent battles of Heligoland and the Falklands, lowered his glass of cognac. 'Good morning, Captain,' he said in his low measured tones. For he wasn't the usual naval firebrand, charging into action without thinking. He was a careful tactician who weighed up all the pros and cons before he put his plans into action; and ever since the defeat of the Imperial German Navy earlier that month, he had been working on a plan to make the perfidious English pay for their victory. 'I hope that you have been successful in obtaining some good news for us? We need it. Morale in the fleet is bad. These damned socialist agitators are at work again after Heligoland.'

Acting Admiral, Kapitan zur See von Reuter, the senior

captain who commanded the battleship *SMS Derfflinger*, looked von Bismarck up and down sharply. Von Bismarck knew why. He was still in mufti and he suspected there might also be a stain on the front of his breeches where he had taken Sussi only minutes before. Before the bearded acting admiral could ask why he was not in uniform, von Bismarck said quickly, 'I have been talking to one of my agents who resides in Holland. She has brought us excellent news about the English North-East coast.'

Von Ingenohl, who had dreamed up the new plan and had already submitted it to 'Old Electric Whiskers', Admiral von Tirpitz, the Prussian Minister of the Navy, for approval, said eagerly, 'Pray tell us this good news, von Bismarck.'

Swiftly the spymaster sketched in the details of the British naval defences of the North-East between the Tees and Scarborough, north of the area's major port, Hull. 'So you can see, sir, on the face of it we will not be threatened by either shore batteries or major naval forces.'

'Excellent, excellent,' the Admiral said thoughtfully, stroking his neat pointed beard, while the others waited for his reaction. 'But are you sure that your informant has given you bone fide information about the Tommies' minefields? We can't run any risk from mines, especially with some five or six capital ships being involved.'

Von Bismarck smirked, suddenly pleased with himself. 'If I may say so, sir, I have been concerning myself with the problem of enemy minefields since long before this war broke out.'

'Yes, yes,' von Ingenohl waved his manicured hand – which looked more like that of an artist than the calloused one of a sailor who had trained in the old-fashioned sailing ships – impatiently. 'I have already taken your good work in the Frisian islands into consideration. We'll come to that later. Please continue.'

Von Bismarck explained what Sussi had found out about the two major minefields off the North-East coast, and the bit she had found out about the larger one off the Frisian island of Terschelling.

The admiral listened attentively before saying, 'We know

about the Terschelling island minefield. But you have the solution for that, don't you, von Bismarck?'

'Yessir,' he replied proudly and was about to explain the results of his work in the Frisian Islands back in 1912 and 1913.

The admiral didn't give him a chance, saying, 'We'll discuss that later, von Bismarck.' He turned to the others. 'So, gentlemen, this is the general plan.'

As one, the staff officers took out their notebooks, as von Ingenohl began with his exposé. 'Our nation needs a victory after our recent defeats at sea. In particular the Navy needs one. Morale is bad, especially in our larger ports: Kiel, Hamburg and Wilhelmshaven and the like. The Reds are at work there, spreading their damned subversive socialist ideas around the lower deck.'

There was an angry murmur of agreement from his listeners.

'So, we can attempt to achieve a minor moral victory over the English and show their people and the rest of the world, in particular the Yanks, that Britannia doesn't rule the waves any more – or we can do that, *plus* gain a major strategic victory over them.'

Even von Bismarck, the sensualist cynic, who was really only interested in his own welfare and not that of Imperial Germany, pricked up his ears at the admiral's words.

'You wonder how, eh, gentlemen. I shall tell you. If this feint of ours is done effectively and we risk staying off the coast of England between – say – Scarborough and Hartlepool long enough, one might expect a large part of the English Home Fleet to venture from their harbours in that part of the world to intercept us. After all, if I remember my English history well enough, it has been over a century since England has been attacked on its home territory by a foreign fleet.'

Several of the officers present nodded their understanding and von Bismarck could see what the admiral was driving at. Feint with the left hand like a boxer, and then hit him hard with one's right. His heart started to race excitedly. This operation was growing larger than he had anticipated. It might well turn out to be a decisive victory for the Imperial Navy. If it did, everyone connected with the plan would be rewarded – if they survived the coming battle. And he, Klaus von Bismarck, intended to survive. God in heaven, he might well become a rear-admiral sooner than he had anticipated.

'Now,' von Ingenohl continued, 'the English have wireless stations the length of that particular coast, including at Scarborough. Let us say we bombarded Scarborough, which, according to von Bismarck here, is poorly defended and presents no danger to our capital ships, that wireless station would undoubtedly summon help from further north. What would the English up there do?'

He paused, as if he expected an answer. In the event, however, he answered his own question. 'They might send help down to the place. But I doubt it, *meine Herren*. On the contrary, I think they would attempt to cut our ships off, pushing them back to their minefield at the Frisian island I've already mentioned. Thinking themselves very clever, the English milords would believe they had our ships between the hammer and the anvil. In fact, gentlemen –' he smiled coldly – 'it would be the English who would be trapped.' He gave that cold smile of his yet again, as if he were savouring the thought of those superior English naval gentlemen who thought their fleet ruled the world and might well find now that they had been deluding themselves about their superiority for far too long. He nodded to von Bismarck. 'Thanks to Captain von Bismarck here, we need not fear the English minefields. When the time comes, he will ensure that any enemy-laid minefield will not hinder our ships one bit. For their paths will have already been swept and the English milords will find to their surprise that we have a clear and open door to do just what we like.'

Von Bismarck returned the Admiral's cold smile with one of his own, his fat, sweaty face beaming with pride. Now he was sure that his promotion was already certain. All he needed now was the signature of the 'All Highest, His Imperial Majesty, the Kaiser' and he'd be a rear-admiral at least; and he would achieve that rank without even risking having a single shot fired at him. He'd leave that to those who surrounded him now, discussing the trap, eager for some

54

desperate glory, even if it meant sacrificing their lives on what they called foolishly 'the field of glory'.

Finally the admiral had heard enough. He took out his pocket watch, glanced at the time and announced, 'Gentlemen, I think we could allow ourselves a toast on this splendid winter morning.' He looked around at their excited faces, as if he wanted to etch their features on his mind's eye for ever. 'I'm sure it will speed us on our way to victory.' He nodded to Von Bismarck.

The latter nodded back his understanding. Outside, a group of servants were carrying in the head gamekeeper on a makeshift stretcher seemingly made of a shed door. He was writhing with pain and leaving a trail of bright blood in the sparkling hoar frost on the frozen grass of the great house's lawn. Von Bismarck told himself the fool of a peasant clod-hopper had allowed himself to be surprised by the wounded wild pig and gored. It served the idiot right. He forgot the wounded gamekeeper and clapped his hands to summon the servant. He appeared immediately, as if he had been poised behind the great door waiting for the summons. 'Cognac – the best French from the cellar.'

The servant bowed. '*So fort, Durchlaucht,*' he said in a sombre tone. 'May I say that *Oberjägermeister* Hansen has been—'

'No, you may not,' von Bismarck cut him off sharply. 'Get the cognac.'

The servant fled.

A few minutes later, glass in hand, the admiral rose from his chair at the fire. Automatically the others did too, holding their glasses level with the third button of their tunics, forearm set at a right angle, as naval etiquette prescribed.

Patiently the admiral waited for them to ready themselves for the toast. He raised his own glass. '*Meine Herren,*' he said very solemnly. 'Let us drink to victory at sea and damnation to our enemies. *Gott strafe England!*'

'*Gott strafe England!*' they echoed as one.

'*Ex!*'* the Admiral ordered.

---

* Literally 'out'.

'*Ex!*' came back their cry. As one they downed the fiery cognac and then, as custom prescribed, they dashed their empty glasses one after another into the fireplace, where they shattered in an icy rain.

Outside now, her warm cloak thrown over her thin shoulders, Sussi von Hoofstra-Mecklenburg was startled by the noise of the shattering glass. But then she recognized it for what it was: men, military men, drinking a toast to something or other in the harsh, brutal Prussian fashion, which smacked more of their pagan Slavic forebears than the Protestant Christians they purported to be.

She continued her walk, glad to be out of the house, despite the biting cold and away from the loathsome caresses of her lover. For she guessed that he would want her again before she travelled back to Holland. When he had been drinking, as he was obviously doing at the moment, he was particularly demanding sexually. At such times, it pleased his cruel sadistic nature to humiliate her. She didn't dare even think about the awful things he had forced her to do in the past, even when she had been virtually innocent, when her knowledge of sex had been gained by listening to older women who had just borne babies, and the carefully worded pieces in *Brockhaus* and such texts. So far she had never once experienced the 'love' that the female scribblers gushed about in the fifty *pfenning* romances that the servant girls drooled over.

To her front a young deer was cropping the short grass at the edge of the Bismarcks' forest, its breath coming from its nostrils in the icy air like twin jets of steam. To her, the young deer looked so peaceful and gentle, so remote from the vicious world of men and their demands on her. Her heart went out to the animal, as he paused there. She asked herself a little helplessly why she couldn't lead such a simple, unspoiled existence.

The deer raised its graceful head, soft brown eyes abruptly alert . . . It sniffed the air, nostrils twitching from side to side, as if it had scented danger. She prayed the animal hadn't spotted her. She wanted it to remain there so that she could continue to feast her eyes on it: a source of calm and gentleness in this rotten world in which she found herself.

In vain. The deer turned its head in her direction. It was alarmed. It scampered a few paces closer to the protection of the fir forest. Again it stopped. She prayed it would not move out of sight. At that moment it seemed all-important that it should remain where it was.

That wasn't to be.

'*Sussi,*' that hated drinker's voice called out sharply into her reverie. It broke the spell. '*Sussi, mein Schatz, wo bist du?*'

It was Klaus. His hoarse rasp broke the spell. The deer moved off at great speed. It covered the distance between the frozen meadow and the forest in amazing frightened bounds. She caught one last glimpse of the white patch of the tail and then it was gone for good; a rustling in the undergrowth, the cracking of the frozen white twigs under its weight, followed by a silence, broken only by von Bismarck's heavy tread and harsh breathing as he spotted her and hurried in her direction.

She turned slowly, head hanging slightly.

Von Bismarck beamed at her. 'Excellent news, my darling!' he gasped, out of breath as usual.

'Yes,' she said dully as he clutched her, hands falling automatically to her breasts.

'We'll have that Christmas break in the Adlon for certain now, darling. Those admirals think highly of me. There'll be promotion for me, I am sure. And for you.' He squeezed her breasts painfully with his big hands. 'There'll be a nice little bonus.' He looked at her knowingly. 'You'll be able to buy those naughty frillies of yours all right.'

'Thank you . . . thank you very much, Klaus,' she breathed, the scheme unfurling itself there and then inside her brain like some dangerous snake preparing to strike. 'But I'd . . . have to go back to Holland.'

His smile broadened. He thought she was going to pander to his wishes, as perverted as they were. Perhaps at last she was going to enjoy what he did to her. As he had often told a reluctant Sussi, 'Just relax and enjoy it, my darling. At first it is painful, I understand that. But once you have got used to it, you'll like it – enjoy, perhaps beg me to do it to you.

After all, that way does not present any complications in the matter of that stupid phrase – the patter of little feet.'

'Of course, you shall go back to Holland,' he said.

'Thank you, dearest,' she said as tenderly as she could. For now her brain was racing with the scheme that had just come to her with the instant clarity of a vision. 'You are so kind.' She attempted not to wince as he pressed her breasts even harder.

'One thing, however,' he cautioned her as they started back for the house. Now the sky was darkening and a chill wind had commenced blowing straight from Siberic – or so it seemed. It looked as if it might begin to snow soon.

'What is that?'

'You must be back in Germany by December sixteenth, darling.'

'Why is that, Klaus? Is that when you can take your Christmas leave?'

He shook his head. 'No, that is something totally different. No matter. Soon thereafter I shall be in a position to take my leave in Berlin. Don't you worry your pretty head about it. But remember – back by the sixteenth. Now let's forget time, Sussi. We have a whole afternoon in bed together. We must make the most of it. It will be an age before I see you again.' He pressed her to him roughly and gave her a wet kiss on her forehead.

'Yes, an age,' she agreed, her mind on her plan. From what seemed a long way away, she heard herself say, 'I shall miss you greatly, Klaus . . .'

# Three

The little British craft rolled to and fro with the swell just off the mouth of the Humber. Another sea fret was coming in and soon it would be as dark as night. Then de Vere knew he'd have to break off the patrol, signal the new Sub-lieutenent Dickie Bird to join him so that they could make their way back to their little base at Scarborough further up the coast. He shivered with cold and pulled the collar of his greatcoat higher. Now he knew why, as most of his crew of cockneys complained, 'East Yorks is the arsehole of the world and the Humber is right up it.' A hot rum toddy would be just right at this moment, but that wasn't to be just yet. The tide was all right for incoming vessels and anyone trying to smuggle in contraband, especially the kind he and Dickie were seeking, might well use an opportunity like this – working on the assumption that the Royal Naval patrol vessels would give up their watch and sail home – to run in their illegal cargo, human or otherwise.

For, ever since the start of the war, more and more neutral ships had been sailing into Hull from Sweden and Holland, bringing in vital supplies needed for the home and fighting fronts, plus another import that C in London didn't welcome one bit – spies and agitaters!

According to C, the Dutch were the worst. 'Never trust a cheesehead,' he always maintained in that no-nonsense manner of his. 'They'll dance to any bloody piper's tune as long as the bill gets paid in full. And the Huns are prepared to do that all right.'

Now de Vere was prepared to intercept a Dutch freighter which Dickie had spotted further out in the North Sea, and which he had lost once it had disappeared into the sea fret. Despite the fog, the Dutch ship had been sailing illegally without navigation lights: always a sign that a neutral skipper was up to no good. Thus, despite the freezing fog, his empty stomach and his urgent need for a stiff, hot drink, de Vere was keeping a keen lookout for the missing Dutch freighter. For he knew any skipper who knew the mouth of the Humber would keep to the Spurn Point side of the Humber entrance, and there, unless the Dutchman was capable of disappearing altogether, he'd spot him.

Some five minutes later, as the buoy anchored in the middle of the channel tolled its funereal warning, he heard the first steady chug-chug of an ancient engine and knew instinctively that this had to be the missing Dutch freighter.

Now de Vere forgot the bone-chilling cold, the fog and his general weariness after a long boring patrol. 'Stand by the searchlight!' he called from the bridge. 'Ferguson, stand by your Lewis gun.'

'Ay, ay, sir,' the ratings' cries came back at once. They too were eager to get the patrol over with, swallow their 'tot' and, if they were lucky enough to have shore leave, go into Scarborough and its pubs in the normal matelot's search for 'wimen and free wallop'.

Then there she was: a dark outline sliding without light through the grey mist, proceeding so slowly that she hardly raised a white bow wave to mark her progress. De Vere strained his eyes and took in the huge Netherlands flag painted on her side, and her name: *Op de Polder – Rotterdam*. He hesitated no longer. He raised his megaphone to his lips and ordered, 'Hello, Skipper, *Op de Polder*! Royal Naval Patrol here . . . Heave to, please. We're coming aboard!'

Nothing happened. Like some ghost ship, fated to sail the seas for eternity, the rusty old tub continued at its slow speed, with not a crew member in sight.

De Vere flushed in sudden anger. Like all new sub-lieutenants, he took his rank seriously and expected his order to be executed at once. He waited a moment longer before repeating his command. Out of the side of his mouth, he ordered, 'Turn on the beam. Let her see who we are.'

With startling suddenness, the icy white finger of brillant light swept the length of the freighter's rusty, buckled plates and came to rest on the bridge.

Still the Dutch ship didn't heave to. Just as Dickie's sleek little craft came into view, heading forward to block the freighter's progress, de Vere lost all patience with the Dutchman. 'Gunner, fire a burst of tracer across the cheeky bugger's bow!' he yelled.

Ferguson, the ship's cook from Liverpool who acted as a gunner on such occasions, didn't hesitate. He jerked up the heavy, ugly-looking Lewis gun, grinned and pressed the triggcr.

White and red tracer sped across the water, glowing on the sea's surface as it hurried towards its target. Whether Ferguson intended it or not, de Vere could hear the bullets howling off the bow of the freighter, before plunging with a hiss into the water beyond. Ill-aimed or not, that sudden burst of machine gun did the trick.

An angry voice called from the freighter, 'Hey, you bloody fool Englishman, what do you do?'

De Vere grinned as a fat figure popped up from the bridge's housing. In his best Senior Service manner, he called back through his megaphone, 'Just heave to, Captain, please. That's all. We'll soon have you underway again, if you comply straight away.'

The skipper cursed in Dutch, but gave in. The search could begin.

De Vere and Dickie, who joined his old friend a little later, thought this would turn out to be the usual routine thing: a little bit of contraband, some smuggled cigars or perhaps Dutch gin hidden away in a locker to be sold at knock-down prices in Hull's thriving Preston Road black-market pubs. Indeed, they soon found the kind of contraband they anticipated finding. Behind the dirty panelling in the captain's own filthy cabin, they discovered several score boxes of fine cigars, while the Dutchman watched them sullenly, drinking *genever* and puffing moodily at his own cigar.

But that wasn't all they discovered. Ferguson, the Liverpudlian, wise to the ways of the petty crook, which he had once been himself before he had joined the Navy, soon made the discovery, which altered the situation altogether. It was a map of the East Yorkshire coast pinned behind the flyblown portrait of the Dutch queen, the cabin's only adornment save for a picture of a hefty female in tight drawers, minus her chemise.

Immediately the two officers realized they had hit on something more than the customary contraband: something which made it quite clear why the Dutch freighter had veered from the prescribed course for neutral shipping sailing into the Humber. Abruptly the tight smelly cabin was heavy with tension. For what was revealed by the hidden chart had changed the situation totally.

The chart was covered in red chinograph marks, which clearly had been placed there recently: marks indicating new defences and naval obstacles, which should not have interested a merchant seaman, especially one who looked so stupid as the drunken, dirty sot of a Dutch skipper, who was now no longer blustering about reporting this 'illegal' search of his ship by the 'English Imperial Navy'. The Dutchman was obviously connected with some sort of espionage and, as Dickie Bird remarked afterwards as they tied up in Hull, 'One doesn't need a crystal ball, old bean, to guess who our fat cheesehead is working for, what.'

To which de Vere answered, 'No, Dickie, old chap. The Huns. He's in the pay of the enemy all right!

'He's been at it for a while now, gentlemen, working for the Germans, I mean,' the hard-faced detective from the Special Branch said, as the three of them sat in the pub next to Hull's Central Law Courts that same evening. 'And he's got the wind up.' He chuckled, though there was no warmth in the sound. 'Especially after I told him they could string him up for spying.'

'He's working for the enemy then?' Dickie asked.

'Yes, that much he's admitted. He says he's been black-mailed into it. The Squareheads found out about him running in contraband and threatened to tell our authorities about it if he didn't work for them. If he did work for them, then he'd get a nice back-hander.' He sniffed. 'I don't believe him, of course. He's been working for them right from the start of the war – strictly for the filthy lucre.' He rubbed his big hands together and de Vere shuddered a little at the gesture. He could guess that the big policeman wouldn't hesitate to use those hefty paws on a suspect if they didn't cooperate, as he would put it.

'What next?' Dickie asked, finishing his pink gin.

'Well, so far, Lieutenant, I've played Mr Sweet with his nibs.' He jerked a thumb like a hairy sausage in the direction of the jail where they were holding the Dutch skipper. 'And it's worked. But I haven't got all he knows out of him yet. It's time for Mr Sour.'

'Mr Sweet and Mr Sour?' de Vere asked, puzzled.

'God bless yer, sir,' the policeman said. 'That's the way we call it in the trade. Mr Sweet is being nice to 'em, making 'em promises if they cough up the dibs. Mr Sour's the opposite. He's a bad bugger. Bash yer head in as soon as look at yer.'

'I'll give him five more minutes of Mr Sweet. After all, I did pay for fish and taties out of my own pocket for his supper. But if he don't give me what I want, it's Mr Sour . . .' He smashed his big fist into the palm of his other hand with a loud noise. And with that he was up and gone, leaving the two young friends staring at each other, thinking they knew so very little about the way the other half lived.

But, as Dickie said, 'I suppose the working classes are used to that sort of thing, de Vere, what.'

An hour later, when de Vere and Dickie had decided already to stand the crews down and book a hotel for the night, the big tough Special Branch detective returned, rubbing his knuckles but still with a smile on his face. He nodded to them as they ordered fresh drinks just before the pub landlord prepared to ring his bell and the shore patrol peered round the door of the Four Ale Bar looking for sailors who were overstaying their passess. 'I didn't have to play Mr Sour for long, gents,' the detective announced and took a grateful drink of the scotch they had ordered him.

'Did you find out who is behind our Dutch friend?' de Vere asked.

'I certainly *did* – and that gentleman in the Big Smoke who doesn't exist officially will be in for a big surprise when my chief informs him who it is, gents.'

The two of them knew he was referring to C, for Special Branch and the two London-based Intelligence agencies worked hand-in glove; they knew that by now.

'Can't you tell us who?' Dickie asked eagerly.

'Suppose I could. We're both on the same team in a way, Lieutenant, and you did give us the lead we needed.'

'I can assure you that his name wouldn't go any further if you did,' De Vere said hastily.

'I am sure of that, Lieutenant.' The big detective's grin broadened, as he prepared to spring his surprise on these two toffs of naval officers, who he suspected hadn't a clue about the harsh realities of the world in which he lived professionally.

'But it's not *his* name,' he said, 'it's *hers*.'

They looked puzzled.

He waited no longer. 'There's a woman in Holland behind all this, not a man. A German woman, if you can believe our Dutch skipper. And I think we can trust him, now that I've told him a few home truths about what he'll let himself in for if he lies to me.'

'A woman . . . what kind of a woman?' Dickie stuttered, somewhat foolishly.

'According to his nibs, she calls herself something posh, Can't get my tongue around it rightly. Double-barrelled name. Very foreign. Hoofstra—'

'*Hoofstra-Mecklenburg!*' De Vere beat him to it.

'That's right, sir. How did you guess?'

De Vere didn't answer the Special Branch detective's question. Instead he turned to his old comrade and exclaimed, 'Did you hear that, Dickie? It's her. Mevrouw

64

de Waal . . . From the islands last year. Now, what do you make of that, old bean?'

But the new sub-lieutenant Dickie Bird had no answer for that particular, overwhelming question . . .

1915

# One

'What a damnable mess!' C exploded, unable to control his anger at the events of that first wartime Christmas. 'First we give them the information about the situation off the Frisian Islands, then the name and location of the Huns' principal agent in Holland, and they do nothing but sit on their thumbs and allow harmless British civilians to be slaughtered off the North East Coast, with the Navy barely able to stop the slaughter. What a tremendous bit of propaganda for the Huns!' He slammed his fist down on Nelson's table so that the bits and pieces which littered it jumped up and down.

De Vere and Dickie knew who 'they' were – the senior admirals up the road in Whitehall. But, wiser now after the terrible events at Scarborough which had caught them, too, by surprise, they refrained from expressing an opinion, leaving that to a red-faced C, who looked as if he might have a stroke at any moment.

Outside, another draft for the front was marching through the snow, singing their hearts out, still full of that patriotic confidence which had led hundreds of thousands of young civilians to volunteer to fight for 'King and Country'. Catching snatches of the popular song 'Tipperary', muted by the falling snow, de Vere felt for those unseen young men marching so bravely to their deaths. For they wouldn't last long in the Flanders trenches. Now they were on to another favourite. *'Pack up your troubles in yer old kitbag,'* they sang lustily, *'and smile boys, smile.'* He shook his head and told himself that they wouldn't be smiling much longer; then he dismissed the marching soldiers and turned his attention back to C.

'Then, to top it all,' C was ranting, 'only last week the bloody British passport officer in the Hague has another chance of getting more information about the Huns and their intentions and he fluffs it totally. My God, if I had my way, the chap should be horsewhipped for such gross dereliction of duty. You can believe me when I say I am actively working to ensure the damned fool is sent back to his regiment, which is currently serving at the front in France, and I, for one, will shed not a single tear if he doesn't come back.'

Dickie Bird opened his mouth as if he wished to ask what heinous crime the Hague passport officer, the cover for one of C's own men, had committed. But C didn't give him a chance to do so. Instead, calming himself a little, the head of the Secret Service asked, 'But pray, gentlemen, don't let me get carried away. Tell me what happened when the Huns attacked at Scarborough just before Christmas. I'd like to know the exact details.' He leaned back in his chair, as if he had calmed himself, but de Vere could see that his hands were still shaking slightly with suppressed rage.

'Well, sir,' Dickie commenced. 'We thought we'd done a fair job in that business of the Dutch freighter off the Humber and decided, as we weren't allowed any home leave for Christmas, to treat ourselves to a slap-up Christmas in Scarborough itself.'

'Well, as far as anyone can have a slap-up time in that godforsaken bit of the coast,' de Vere chimed in with a malicious smile on his handsome face. 'Believe you me, sir, it takes imagination and plenty of coin of the realm to do so. The natives *do* take their pleasures sadly.'

'Oh do shut up, de Vere. Let me get on with it,' Dickie said. 'Well, sir, we booked a pretty expensive table at the Grand for the night in question, and no expense spared for the midday Christmas dinner. Good job we booked in there, because the other seafront hotels were going to get a right pasting in due course, when the balloon went up. Still, I'm afraid we never did get our Christmas dinner, sir. But that's another story.'

Since the summer and the declaration of war, things had changed a great deal at the old Victorian seaside resort. The local territorials, the 5th Battalion the Green Howards, who had been a feature with their weekly drills on the promenade, had gone to France. Many of the young men who had remained behind before Lord Kitchener had asked for volunteers for the front had then followed. So the town had become devoid of young men, save the newcomers in khaki and naval uniform.

Food for the poor had become difficult to find, especially as the less fortunate elements of Scarborough couldn't afford the inflated wartime prices, though the rich, staying in the hotels and the great rented Victorian villas, knew no such shortages. Still fish was plentiful and cheap and easily available, until the local trawlers started being called up for naval service and became more afraid of venturing far out for the cod. For the wildest rumours had now commenced circulating. German U-boats were lurking everywhere along the coast between Scarborough and Bridlington, just waiting for the unarmed fishing trawlers – and even German dreadnoughts had been sighted further out to sea, carrying out unspecified mystery missions.

De Vere and Dickie Bird knew better. Indeed, they would have been delighted to have spotted a dreadnought and tackled it, lightly armed as their craft were. Why, they would be the heroes they dreamed of becoming in their youthful imaginations. Unfortunately, search as they might on their boring routine missions, they were unable to sight even the smallest German battleship.

Once, however, they had been forced to watch impotently as a German zeppelin sailed in majestic silence overhead, bound for the Humber and, further up the river, for the old garrison town of York. They possessed no form of anti-aircraft weapons, save for the ratings' rifles, and they didn't dare waste precious ammunition on a target they hadn't a hope in hell of hitting.

So, November had given way to December 1914, and with the excepton of their apprehension of the Dutch freighter, they had so far passed a boring war, limited, it seemed, to boring patrols that seldom brought any reward. That had been till Wednesday December 16th, when they had forgotten the war, busy with their preparations for what they called their 'slap-up Christmas binge' and the festive party they were organizing for their two crews, ensuring that there was enough John Smith's beer for the ratings, whose thirst seemed insatiable.

That December morning at Scarborough had dawned as cold and foggy as usual, with the same middle-class residents walking their silly little dogs along virtually deserted beaches and the odd elderly fisherman, too old for military service, digging up lugworms as bait, plus a schoolboy peering out to sea through his cheap telescope, hoping to catch a glimpse of those mysterious 'Jerry dreadnoughts' rumoured to be sailing back and forth along the north-east coast.

It had all seemed very normal as the men of the small naval craft, anchored in the shelter of Scarborough's ruined castle on the top of the cliff went about their routine duties, shivering in the cold breeze, complaining about the lack of sugar in the morning porridge, whistling or singing the same old boring ditty of 'the girl I left behind me', who succumbed to the 'mate at the wheel who had a bloody good feel'.

That normalcy had been shattered by the banshee howl of a shell ripping the still air. Next instant it had exploded just below the ruined castle, the first missile to explode there since the English Civil War. But that December morning no one was thinking of that conflict of nearly three centuries before. Now death and destruction were in the air and Scarborough reacted with both defiance and dread.

Suddenly the air-raid sirens were wailing their warning all along the coast. Minutes before the naval wireless station on the cliff top was hit, the coverage signallers were sending out their message to all other stations all along the coast. '*The Germans are attacking us!*'

They were. As the abruptly panicked civilians hurried to find some sort of shelter and the middle-class visitors to the seafront hotels suddenly found their grilled kidney and sausage sprinkled with glass splinters from the shattered picture windows looking out to sea, the shocked naval crews below, still drinking their mugs of cocoa, were shocked to spot the first lean grey shapes of the German battleships emerging from the mist, their great 11-inch cannon belching scarlet flame and thick black smoke.

'Holy mackerel!' de Vere yelled as he seized his telescope

72

and focused madly on the first enemy ship. 'It's the *Derfflinger* – all bloody twenty thousand tons of her.'

'And that's the *Von der Tann* behind her,' Dickie joined in. 'And the smaller one's the *Kolberg* . . . It's the whole bloody German fleet . . . and they're shooting at us, de—' The screech of another salvo of German shells passing overhead drowned the rest of his words. With a hellish roar they slammed into the seafront houses, splattered the front of the hotels with shrapnel, shattering the huge plate-glass windows and leaving the serving maids dead and dying among the mess of the breakfast crockery and trays.

'*Why?*' Dickie cried. '*Why Scarborough?*'

De Vere had no time to answer questions now. The three German ships had turned broadside on and were preparing to fire salvoes from all their nine cannon at the virtually defence-less seaside town, with the smaller of the three German ships, the *Kolberg*, heading south in the direction of Bridlington and Flamborough Head. Instinctively de Vere knew why. The German attackers would head that way, once they had finished with Scarborough, and thus avoid the British minefields to the north. The German fleet had come well briefed by their Intelligence officers. Someone had betrayed the British defences to the Germans and even at that moment of extreme danger de Vere could guess who.

But there was no time to dwell on that fact now. He knew that he and Dickie had to do whatever they could to deflect the great German ships from slaughtering the seaside town. As another massive salvo slammed into Scarborough, he yelled, 'Dickie, let's get underway – at once.'

Behind them, Ferguson, already seated behind his Lewis gun, shook his cropped head in wonder and said to no one in particular, 'Christ Almighty, what we gonna do – throw frigging stones at 'em!'

But in his haste and anger de Vere had no time to consider what their flimsy little wooden craft, armed only with machine guns and one single torpedo apiece, might do against the might of the German Imperial Navy. They were of the class and background of that time who felt it their duty, if necessary, to fight and die against what might seem overwhelming odds.

Ten minutes later, with the *Kolberg* disappearing again into the morning mist, heading southwards to recce the other ships' escape route, the two small craft were closing fast with the German battleships, which for the time being didn't seem to notice their approach. If they did, they were not reacting. Thus it was that the two brave skippers and their bemused and not a little apprehensive crews closed with the German ships, which towered above them like great grey steel cliffs.

De Vere didn't hesitate as he lead the attack in. Balancing at the wheel, twisting back and forth wildly, for he knew the Germans would spot their craft sooner or later, he shouted at the torpedo mate braced in front of him on the deck, 'I'm going to steady her in half a sec. Don't wait for my order. Launch the fish *then*. Clear?'

Under his breath the pale-faced torpedo mate cursed, 'This is gonna be a real bloody lash-up.' Aloud, he said confidently, 'Ay, ay, sir. Steady as we go.'

High above them, scarlet flame winked off and on. They had been spotted! Tracer zipped towards them in a lethal morse. The torpedo mate didn't hesitate. As de Vere suddenly steered a straight course, ignoring the bullets slamming into his craft, showering him with wooden splinters, the torpedo mate pressed his button. There was a hiss of compressed air. Smoothly, like a porpoise, the one-ton torpedo slipped into the water. A mad flurry of bubbles. De Vere tensed. He felt the cold sweat running in an unpleasant trickle down the small of his back. Would the 'fish' go under? She didn't. She set off streaking towards her target. Instinctively de Vere broke to the right as he had been trained to do.

The little craft's mast came tumbling down. A salvo of machine bullets ripped the length of the hull. Ferguson cursed wildly and fired a crazy burst at the dreadnought. The machine gun on the upper deck ceased firing abruptly. De Vere tensed. He counted off the seconds it should take the torpedo to reach the enemy ship. *Nothing happened . . .* 'God damn and blast!' de Vere cursed angrily. They had missed the target. Now it was up to Dickie.

# Two

'It didn't work, eh, old chap?' C commented with unusual kindness for him.

Dickie shook his head, mouth bitter. ''Fraid not sir. We were out of luck. Instead of heading for the Hun ship, the tin fish decided to explore the bottom of the North Sea.'

'Oh, bad luck. But you tried . . . did your best against overwhelming odds. There wouldn't be many who would tackle two dreadnoughts like that in a couple of frail wooden craft, armed only with a single torpedo.' He smiled. 'But if it's any consolation to the two of you, I've heard from my sources in Whitehall that His Majesty personally has ordered you should be awarded decorations for bravery. I agree with him – and as an old sea dog himself, His Majesty should know – you two richly deserve an award.'

Dickie looked at de Vere. He didn't say a thing. But the look on his face said everything. Barely out of their teens and they were being awarded a decoration for bravery on the order of the King-Emperor George V personally. No one in their year at Dartmouth could boast of that honour so far. De Vere managed to say, 'Thank you, sir.'

C's smile broadened for a moment. 'Don't thank me. It is I – and the whole nation – who should thank brave young fellows like yourselves.' His smile vanished. 'Now then, this business on the North-East coast. You can imagine the impact it has had on the Empire, and more importantly on the Yankees. Here we are, the possessor of the greatest naval fleet in history, bigger than any two navies of the major nations together, and we can't stop the Huns raiding our coastal ports and slaughtering our defenceless citizens. I am sure the anti-British press everywhere is having a field day at our expense.'

The two young officers nodded their heads gravely. They understood well what C meant. The Royal Navy was the envy of the world. But envy brought with it hatred too. The Yankees especially were jealous of the Senior Service, just as the Huns were. Now the latter had cocked a snout at the Royal Navy and in certain quarters there'd been rejoicing at the fact the British had been taken down a peg or two. The Germans had avenged their defeats in the Falklands and off Heligoland, and had shown the jealous foreigners that the British Navy was not so good as it was thought to be.

'Remember,' C added, 'no foreigner has done this kind of thing in British waters since the Dutchman van Tromp swept up the Thames in the seventeenth century with the broom stuck on his masthead to indicate that he had cleared our fleet from the sea. We cannot afford to have that sort of thing happening too often. It is a question of prestige . . . and we don't want to lose face in front of the blacks and browns. It might well cost us our Empire one of these days.'

The two young officers sat in silence, listening to C's angry outburst, but knowing he was right. The natives, especially in India, were restless as it was. Such incidents as the bombardment of the north-east coast on that Wednesday played right into the damned agitators' hands.

C calmed himself again. 'So, in a way, we're back where we were in nineteen thirteen, when you did such sterling work off the Frisian islands – not that their Lordships did anything about it. Now they are starting to listen to us.'

'Well, sir,' de Vere said loyally. 'You can understand them. They – we – got it wrong. The Huns weren't going to pass their dreadnoughts through that shallow water. That would have been impossible. Instead they used the Frisian channel to slip their shallow-draught minesweepers through to clear away our minefields and clear the way for their capital ships.'

'Exactly.' He paused thoughtfully before saying. 'But why did the Huns show their hands at this stage of the game? After all, the raid on the north-east coast was exactly that – a mere raid. But now we know how they get out of the West German ports despite the minefields. It seems to me that they can't

76

pull that particular trick more than once.' He looked at the other two enquiringly.

Silently they nodded their agreement.

'Perhaps they just wanted a propaganda victory,' C mused. 'Yet all the same they can't just let their High Seas Fleet rust in their harbours for the rest of the war. Old Kaiser Bill, their Emperor, crazy as a loon as he is, wouldn't tolerate that. In addition, we know that up to the north-east coast raid the morale of their lower deck was bad. So what's their game, eh?'

For what seemed a long while, the three of them simply sat there, listening to the wind and the hiss of the falling snow. It was as if some God on high wanted to blot out the war-torn world below for good.

'There might be one way to find out, sir?' de Vere broke the silence finally.

'What's that?'

'The girl, sir,' de Vere said simply.

'What girl . . .? Oh, I see, you mean your Miss de Waal, or Freifrau Sussi von Hoofstra-Mecklenburg?'

'Yessir. You said she's approached our people in the Hague and our Dutch skipper mentioned her as being behind his spying trips. Obviously she is – was – important in the Hun spy ring. I guess she's reporting primarily to German Naval Intelligence.'

'You guess right, of course,' C answered, a new light in his eyes. 'Go on, Lieutenant.'

'Well, sir, she might know more, even if she seems to be wanting to get out of this nasty spy business.'

C laughed hollowly. 'Remember, yours truly is also involved in this nasty spy business, young man.'

De Vere actually blushed. 'Well, sir,' he went on hastily, to cover his embarrassment, 'she could be of some use to us.'

'If we can find her,' C reminded him. 'We had our chance and that bloody fool of a passport officer fluffed it. Perhaps she's got cold feet now?'

'She might try again, sir,' Dickie suggested. 'For all we know, she's blown her boats and the Huns who run her might have rumbled what she's up to. If that were the case, she'd have no other option than to try again at one of our other consulates.'

C pondered Dickie's words for a few moments before saying, 'You might be right. From what I've heard she has blotted her copybook with her German masters, and Klaus von Bismarck is known for his ruthlessness. There's no saying what he might do to the young lady in question if he finds her.' He gave a little grin. 'Rather piquant in a way, isn't it? Two rival intelligence services after the same young woman, who might well be murdered by one side and imprisoned, at the very least, by the other.'

De Vere was not amused. He looked hard at the cynical old spymaster. 'You're sure of that, sir – that the Huns might well kill her?'

'Of course. I would too if it served any advantage for us . . . Look, I think it's important to find her and discover what she knows, if anything, of the Huns' future plans for their High Seas Fleet. We can't afford another humiliation at the hands of the Germans like that of December 16th – or perhaps even something worse.' He looked directly at the two young officers. 'I know this isn't exactly your line of work. But you've been on the fringe of the Great Game for nearly two years now. You know roughly how my organization works. Are you following my reasoning, gentlemen?'

'You mean you want us to go to Holland and try to find the girl, sir?' De Vere was first off the mark.

'Yes.'

'But where would we start? I mean, I know Holland isn't a very big country, but all the same . . .'

'Look,' C cut de Vere short. 'We don't know where your de Waal woman is. She's certainly vanished from the Hague. If she's going to make another attempt to contact us, it'll have to be through one of our other consulates, especially in those cities close to the Belgian border. We use them a lot to run agents back and forth through that part of the front that the Germans hold opposite King Albert's gallant little Belgian Army.'*

---

* The King of the Belgians, who was defending the narrow coastal strip of his occupied country against the German invaders.

78

'Yes, I understand that, sir,' de Vere protested. 'All the same, it'll be a lot of territory to cover.'

'Agreed. But remember this, you two are the only people on our side who know what the lady in question looks like. We haven't a single photo of her for identification and the description we got from your Dutch skipper is pretty sketchy.'

C saw their hesitancy, but he didn't give the two young officers time to deliberate. He knew he was clutching at straws by sending them to Holland to find the missing girl – it would be like trying to find a needle in a haystack. Still, he had precious few other options open to him, and C, the old hand, was desperate to find out what the Huns might do next; for he was sure the German megalomaniacs had something up their sleeves. 'Just off the cuff,' he went on, 'we could do it like this. The two of you take the newest craft the Admiralty can find at short notice and you use it to impress the Dutch naval cheeseheads. The Huns are always doing the same thing, sailing their small craft down the Maas and Rhine to show off their latest vessels. In your case it'll be sort of showing the flag kind of thing.' He smiled at them winningly, animated by a growing feeling that his ad hoc plan might just work. 'Once at the most convenient Dutch port, let's say Dordrecht for example, you'll take a weekend leave, heading south towards the Belgian border –' he shrugged – 'perhaps you'll strike it lucky . . . and I have a feeling you will. Now, what do the two of you say to my rough-and-ready plan, eh?'

The two of them looked at each other a little helplessly. They knew they were trapped. Trying to find female spies was not what they were trained for and, in essence, both of them knew they were rank amateurs, who would have to be damned lucky to get within sniffing distance of the missing German agent. Still, they had been taught ever since they had gone to their first prep school that duty came first before any personal considerations. Their class had always known that instinctively – imbibed it, as it were, with their mothers' milk. Reluctantly de Vere nodded his head, followed a moment later by a suddenly very solemn Dickie Bird, who said, 'I suppose we've got nothing to lose, sir.'

Now it was C's turn to be solemn, very solemn. He leaned

across Nelson's desk and said quietly, 'Oh yes you have, young man – *your lives*! Don't let yourselves be lured across the border into German-held territory. If you're taken by the Huns, they'll show no mercy. They're different from us. They'll put you against the nearest wall and shoot you out of hand . . . Spies, you know.' And with that he bent his greying head over his papers once more in dismissal, as if they were no longer there.

Silently, trying not to scrape their chairs as they pushed them back, they went out on the tips of their toes. Noiselessly the door closed behind them and the light above it flashed red. Without a word they walked down that narrow corridor, the snow beating against the dirty windows and piling up around the chimney pots, their minds full of C's warning and the knowledge that they were now to become spies . . .

# Three

'You speak pretty good English, sister,' the Yankee sailor said, as he offered her a match to light her cigarette. She was glad it was dark on the dockside so that no one could see she was smoking; people might have thought she was a lady of the night, seeing her smoking, like so many of the Dutch drabs who plied their trade along Rotterdam's docks. As he came close, she could smell the stink of food on the American's clothes and she guessed he was probably a cook or worked in the freighter's kitchens. Cooks, she knew, usually had more money than the average foreign sailer. They made it from the crew's rations or goods stolen on board, which they sold on the local black markets.

'Thank you,' she said, and puffed out a stream of blue smoke, already feeling a little giddy from the strong American tobacco, despite the coldness of the night air. 'I learned English at school.'

'Yeah,' the cook said cynically. 'They all say that, don't they.' He exhaled the rich smoke and added, 'What's it going to cost me, sister?'

Sussi von Hoofstra-Mecklenburg feigned ignorance, though she knew well what the greasy cook meant. If necessary, she would let him have his way with her, just like the other poor wretches who were plying their degrading trade against the walls of the warehouses or inside the derrick housing, moaning and groaning with fake passion to flatter the American sailors who had just come in with the freighters and the other American ships. But if she could avoid his greasy embrace, she would. The very thought of the Yankee touching her body repelled her.

So instead of answering his direct question, she posed one

of her own, hoping that it might lead to her real reason for being here on the wet docks at this time of the night when she should be looking for some cheap place to rest her weary body after her days of running from the unseen danger she knew threatened her. 'When do you sail again?' she asked with assumed casualness.

'Tomorrow on the tide,' he answered, bored. 'The Limeys insist we go out together. Hell, they've got the damned cheek to tell our skipper and the others to do what they want us to do – or else. Damned Limeys!' He hawked and spat on the wet, glistening cobbles.

'Straight back to America?'

'Yeah, back to goddam Boston. Still, it is the United States. That is, if that drunk of a skipper of ours can find the USA.' Again he hawked in his disgusting manner, which turned her empty stomach, and spat on the cobbles. He bent down to her and blew a stream of cigarette smoke at her face. 'So, fancy giving a lonely sailor boy a good time before he risks the perils of the sea? All those days on the ocean in his lonely bunk with nobody to – er – talk to.' He leered at her and grabbed the front of his dungarees to make his point quite clear.

She hesitated. She knew that, if he were to carry out her plan of escape, she would have to submit to him or someone like him. But could she trust him? She knew that all he wanted was sex. But would he be prepared to take the risk of smuggling her aboard even if she offered him her body during the long crossing to the United States? She decided to take a chance. 'I don't want your money,' she said.

'*What?*'

'I said, I don't want your money,' she repeated.

He whistled through his rotten front teeth. 'Jeez, now I've heard everything, sister. Well, what do you want?'

'I would let you do what you want,' she answered slowly, 'if you would take me aboard your ship to America.'

'Hot shit!' the Yankee exclaimed, as if she had just said something completely outrageous. 'You mean as a stowaway?'

She didn't know the word, but she guessed its meaning. 'Yes,' she answered. 'And you could have me during the voyage, too.'

'Have you during the voyage! Hell, sister, the skipper'd have me in irons before my feet touched the ground if he caught me taking a stowaway aboard. Jeez, it's strictly against company rules and if the Limeys caught us, it would be even worse. It'd be the calaboose for yours truly, living off them sprouts and the other crap the Limeys eat.' The Yankee controlled his emotions with difficulty. He laid his soft pudgy cook's hand on hers and drew it to the bulging front of his dungarees. 'Why don't you just make a sailor happy? I'll pay you what you want and then I'll get back on board. I've got to start my shift—'

'No!' she cut into his words, suddenly repulsed by the greasy smelly cook. 'That's enough.' Angrily she pulled her hand away from his flies, which he had already unbuttoned ready for sex.

'Hey, sister,' he responded, 'cut it out, willya. Ain't my dough good enough for ya . . .?' But Sussi von Hoofstra-Mecklenburg was no longer listening. She was already hurrying down the quay in the thin cold rain, which had started to fall, her shoulders bent as if in defeat.

As she walked towards the cheap lodging houses and inns that lined the dingy streets of the harbour area, listening to the snatches of drunken singing from the red-light bars and the high-pitched shrieks of the equally drunken whores and barmaids, she told herself she had planned it wrong right from the start. She should have taken more money from Klaus von Bismarck before she had left Germany for Holland. He had been in a generous mood and would have given her much more. Now she was running out of cash swiftly. Soon she wouldn't have enough to bribe an American to take her aboard and smuggle her to America, so far away from this dreadful war-torn Europe. And she knew it was urgent that she did so. Perhaps even her very life depended upon it.

For she had made a bad mistake in going to the British Legation in the Hague. She had thought the English would have welcomed her with open arms. After all, she had many secrets to sell them in exchange for transporting her safely to some country where Klaus couldn't touch her.

She had known right away that the Passport Control officer

had been the wrong person to approach with her offer of naval intelligence. The Englishman, with his stiff collar and gold-rimmed pince-nez perched at the end of his long red nose, had looked more like a *Gymnasium* teacher addicted to drink than an officer of the famed English Secret Service. His first words had only reinforced that impression.

After she had explained her business there, mentioning names of those in the Imperial Navy's intelligence department, especially that of von Bismarck, he had tut-tutted and quavered, 'That's all well and good, young lady, but we have people coming in here every day offering us intelligence information. I'll have to consult my superiors in London first. Perhaps – and I emphasize the perhaps – I might be able to give you some sort of assistance if you came back in a week or so's time. Naturally I can't offer any assurance—'

'But don't you realize?' she had blurted out, angry but at the same time almost in tears at the bumbling Englishman's manner. 'I'm in danger. My life is at risk. You should know the Hague. It is a diplomatic gossip shop.'

The Englishman had been unmoved at her outburst. He had looked at her over the top of his silly schoolmaster's glasses and said coldly, 'You should have thought of that earlier, young lady. Now I wish good day to you.' And with that he had disappeared back into his cubbyhole of an office, leaving her red-faced and trembling with anger.

An hour later she realized she had made even more of a mistake by going to such a public representative of the English presence in the Dutch capital. She had been walking slowly and miserably down one of the narrow cobbled streets behind the villas of the place's seafront, her mind in a turmoil, hardly aware of her surroundings in the growing darkness, when she had heard the slow growl of a large motor. Instinctively she had pressed herself closer to the far edge of the pavement. Busy as she was with her problem, wondering what she should do next, she sensed somehow that the car behind her wasn't gathering speed. Indeed, it seemed to be slowing down. She turned and stared behind her.

A large car was crawling along, almost filling the breadth of the narrow street, its licence plates obscured by what looked like mud. Suddenly she was filled with apprehension for no apparent reason. It was just that the car, with its two dark outlines in the front seat, seemed somehow threatening, sinister even. She bit her bottom lip. She slowed down even more, but turned her head to her front once more.

Now she quickened her pace, her problems forgotten as she listened anxiously for the car to react, if it was going to. It did. Its motor grew louder. Now she knew defintely that there was trouble brewing. The car was following. Fighting off her sudden panic, telling herself that she was on her own; that it was up to her to deal with what might soon happen.

Ahead she saw the way the street bent and the few sign-posts, including a large one warning, '*Laat op*' – give way. That indicated she was approaching a larger street, perhaps one with people on it, not like this one, without a living soul in sight. She hurried even more. Behind her she heard the clash of gears, as the unknown driver badly mangled his double-declutching. She knew then that, whoever he was, he intended her harm.

She was tempted to run. She forced herself not to do so. She must not show the men in the car that she suspected that they were up to no good. If she could only reach the corner and the main street, she'd be safe. They wouldn't attempt anything bad once there were witnesses about. Gripping her hands into fists, damp with the sweat of fear and apprehension now, she prayed as she had never prayed before that she'd reach the corner before those in the car knew what she was up to.

Now the driver had got his car into gear. She could hear the increased roar of the engine. He was coming at her at speed. The corner was still metres away. Would she make it in time? Wildly she flung a glance to left and right. There was no escape. There wasn't even a doorway into which she could press herself. Her nerve snapped. She started to run. Behind her the driver flicked on his lights. She could see their reflection in the nearest windows. Two baleful gleams of light like leering eyes. God, they were going to kill her! She'd never make the corner into the main street in time. The big car would smash into her, crush her thin body into a mess of broken bone and bloody gore. *'Help me!'* she cried in despair. 'Please God, *help me!'* But, on this late afternoon in the little Dutch capital, God was looking the other way. Now the car was almost upon her. The roar of its engine echoed and re-echoed down the stone chasm of the narrow backstreet. She tensed and almost stopped running. She might as well give in and let Fate have its way with her. She could run no more. She was at the end of her tether. She was finished.

But now Fate gave her a hand. Later she could hardly believe what happened next. It had to be a miracle. Or perhaps God had taken pity on her after all.

In that same instant that she faltered to a stop, her breast heaving frantically with fear and the effort of running, a small courtyard gate opened on the same side of the street on which she found herself. Before she could take in really what was happening her ears filled with the mighty roar of the big car's engine, a little cart pulled by a horse – with a dog yapping at its heels to make it move faster, – emerged on to the street, the peasant-looking owner cracking his whip over the horse's head lustily. Behind, in the wicker-work cart, great milk churns rattled back and forth.

Too late the Dutchman saw the car bearing down on the girl – and him. Madly he jerked at the reins. The horse attempted to rise out of the shafts, its forelegs flailing. To no avail. In that same moment, as she sprang into the courtyard with the last of her strength, the speeding car missed her and slammed directly into the cart. The horse whinnied shrilly and went down on its knees. Blood spurted from its broken flank in a bright red arc. Beneath it the dog howled as it was crushed under the horse's weight. The driver leapt from his perch and slammed into the cobbles, which were flooded instantly with milk from the flying churns.

Frantically the driver of the car hit his brake. There was a screech of solid tyres. The air was filled abruptly with the acrid stink of burning rubber. Helplessly she watched as the driver skidded on the milk. She could see his fear-contorted face quite clearly. But the driver was out of luck. As the horse, trapped between the shafts, struggled in its death throes, its gaping muzzle filled with bubbling froth, the car slammed into the opposite wall.

*Whoosh!* Its petrol tank burst into flame immediately. Like a gigantic blowtorch the blue-red flame seared the wall of the house, right up to the roof, as the two men in the front of the car attempted to escape. Without success. The one next to the trapped driver managed to force open the door and fall on to the milk-covered cobbles, his body wreathed in flames. There was the hiss of steam. He cried out and slumped down, dying or dead already.

Holding her hands in front of her face, she slipped past that terrible scene, trying not to look at the man on the cobbles, his body shrivelling up to that of a charred dwarf in the intense heat. Breathing with difficulty, as the tremendous searing flame drew the very air out of her lungs, she staggered into the main street and nearly collapsed as everywhere people started to run, shouting in alarm, towards the appalling scene.

No one seemed to notice her; they were too concerned with what had just happened. For that she was glad. She just wanted to slip away unnoticed. For the cry of the man who had fallen out of the blazing wreck had been in German; and even in her shocked state she didn't need a crystal ball to know who had sent the two men in the car to kill her. It had been Kapitan zur See Klaus von Bismarck!

# Four

'Cor, ferk a duck, Chiefie,' Tommy 'Soldier' Atkins said enthusiastically, as the engines of the sparkling new motorboat, straight from the Thorneycroft Works, started to pick up speed. 'We're off on our hols to foreign parts.'

Chief Petty Officer Egan, chest ablaze with the ribbons of the South African War and other campaigns, grunted severely, 'Mind your language, Atkins. We're not in the ruddy Marines now, you know.' He raised his voice as he spotted Ferguson, hands covered with grease from the new Lewis guns. 'And you, you Scouse fellah, keep yer dirty paws away from my woodwork or I'll have you on the rattle before yer filthy feet can touch the deck.'

Ferguson, one of the few of the original Scarborough crews to be picked for the voyage to Holland, muttered something about 'ruddy Scottish git' under his breath. All the same he avoided touching the woodwork as he climbed up to the twin Vickers machine guns mounted behind the bridge of the new craft. Egan had a reputation among those who sailed in small craft. They said he'd been in the Royal Navy so long that he'd even served under Nelson, and that even the victor of Trafalgar had been afraid of him.

Watching the ramrod-straight CPO with a face that looked as if it had been hacked out of the granite of his native city, Aberdeen, de Vere and Dickie Bird could well believe it. In truth both the young sub-lieutenants, now transferred on special duty to show the flag in neutral Holland, were not a little afraid of Egan themselves. Still, he did possess the advantage of being able to control such a divergent crew of matelots. For already the two young friends had guessed they would spend a lot of time ashore while they were in the neutral country; and, as C had warned them before they had left London, 'Watch your backs. This Hun Klaus von Bismarck is a devious bugger. I wouldn't trust him as far as I could throw him. He's capable of anything. Your task, gentlemen, is to find that girl and get her out of Holland before the Hun marks you and tries one of his nasty tricks on your persons.'

Now, as they went below to the tiny yet well-appointed wardroom for the traditional pre-dinner pink gin, the two of them were glad to have CPO Egan on board. For they knew already that not only might they face trouble in Holland, but also possibly problems before they reached that country. For, as CPO Egan had explained to them, 'If I may be so bold, gentlemen, yon squareheads'll be looking out for something nice and juicy and small like ourselves. Ye ken, they'll think we're easy meat. My experience on the Dover patrols is that the squareheads will turn up just when ye dinna expect 'em. We'll have to be on guard all the time. And Jock Egan is just the matelot to give 'em a surprise too – when they don't expect it.'

Now as they lounged on the brand new leather sofa, sipping their pink gins, listening to the mournful wail of the ships' sirens in the Humber, both of them considered that eventuality and what they had in the way of defensive armament if they were confronted, as Egan expected, by one of the fast German armoured motor launches.

It wasn't much. Four Lewis guns, two Vickers and two forward torpedo tubes. 'Not much to pit against the Huns, with their fifty-seven-millimetre cannon quick-firers at that, Dickie,' de Vere mused. 'It'll be a question of who gets off the first shots.'

Dickie, as flippant as ever, lowered his glass and said easily, 'Dinna fash yersen, as CPO Egan would say. This is not the Channel. This is the North Sea and we can always rely on the good old Yorkshire sea fret to give us the cover we need.' But as usual Dickie Bird was wrong. This time the 'good old Yorkshire sea fret' was going to let them down.

An hour later they had cleared Spurn Point and were rapidly leaving the coast of Yorkshire behind them, heading north-east into the open sea, bound for Holland. The mood on the brand new craft was good. C had ensured that the little ship had been well supplied with food, despite the shortages which were now affecting even the Royal Navy, and Dickie and de Vere had decided to celebrate their new command: there would be an extra tot of rum for the men of the lower deck. Naturally Egan, who didn't believe in spoiling ratings below the rank of petty officer, had objected, stating, 'The way some of yon matelots look, gentlemen, a sniff of the barmaid's apron might be too much for 'em, ye ken.'

Dickie, as flippant as ever, retorted, 'Now then, Chiefie, they lead hard lives. They ought to have a little treat.' He winked at De Vere. 'Ye ken.'

But humour was wasted on the dour Scot and he went on his way to carry out their order, muttering something about 'spoiling the men . . . They didn't do things like that when I was a young rating . . . More than likely got a taste of the bosun's rope-end.'

So the two young officers settled down in their snug new wardroom, sipping their gin and idly discussing their mission, though, in reality, both of them had little idea of how to go about it. C had called them before they had left Hull and told them the latest he had on the girl. After she had left the British legation in the Hague, an attempt had been made on her life. As he had put it, 'Spy that she might be, she is, after all, a mere girl. It shows you just to what depths that Hun swine von Bismarck will sink.' He had added, 'I can't confirm this. But after the attempt was made to kill her, she took a train to Rotterdam. My guess is that she might well have attempted to get a passage from there – to God knows where. But there is no evidence she did so. At all events, remember this. The Huns know she has attempted to betray them, and if they associate you two young fellahs with her, they'll be after you as well.' And with that bit of cheering news, the head of the British Secret Service had rung off.

'So now,' Dickie said, puffing away at the briar pipe which he now affected to make him appear older and more mature, 'we've only got the whole of Holland in which to look for the lady in question.' He took a larger than normal puff at his new toy and coughed throatily.

De Vere smiled and said, 'Oh for God's sake, old chap, give it up. That pipe simply doesn't suit you.'

'Oh, I don't know. I thought of getting my photo taken smoking it the next time we reach a port. Jaw jutting out, steely-eyed and all that stuff . . . A bit like Captain Kettle, you know. Then I send copies to all my girlfriends. They—' He stopped short, his grin vanished and he stared through the large modern porthole. 'I say, de Vere, what's that?'

'What's what?'

'I thought I just saw something out there . . . in the sky to port.'

De Vere craned his neck and peered upwards at the grey cloudy sky over the North Sea. 'I can't see anything, old bean. It's that ruddy pipe. The tobacco's too strong for you. You're seeing things.'

'I'm not,' Dickie declared stoutly, and took another defiant puff at his expensive briar. 'I swear—'

'*Sir!*' It was CPO Egan, who had tapped at the wardroom door and opened it without invitation, something very unusual in a petty officer who lived by *King's Regulations*.

'What is it, Chiefie? Where's the fire?' de Vere asked, a little surprised by Egan's sudden entrance.

'Up above, sir!' Egan gasped, a little out of breath with running down to the wardroom. De Vere told himself that Chiefie was getting on a bit and ought to be on the beach really instead of serving on one of His Majesty's fighting ships.

'What's up above?'

'An aircraft or something like it, sir. Just caught the noise of motors before it disappeared in the clouds.'

'I told you—' Dickie began, but de Vere didn't give him a chance to finish.

He grabbed his cap and barked, 'Come on, Dickie, let's go and have a look-see – and for heaven's sake, put out that bloody pipe! An enemy could see the bloody flame you're producing all the way from Berlin.'

But as they stood on the deck, there seemed at first to be nothing visible in the cloudy sky to the east. Indeed, de Vere was just about to tell Dickie off (he didn't dare do the same to CPO Egan, naturally) for having dragged him from the snug warmth and pink gin of their new wardroom, when he heard it.

It was a steady faint humming noise, barely audible over the roar of the sea, but very definitely there. De Vere held up his hand, as if to silence any other noise, and commanded, 'Keep it down to a low roar, Dickie . . . But there's something up there. You were right.'

'A plane, sir?'

'No, Chiefie. Not a plane,' de Vere answered. 'They make a heck of a racket. Something else . . . Oh, my sainted aunt,' he cried the next moment. 'Will you take a look at that, Chiefie!'

A dull grey shape had slid from the cover of the low cloud, emitting the soft throbbing sound which had just alerted de Vere, and there was no mistaking that brutal-looking silver-and-grey iron cross which adorned the craft's fabric side.

'A bluidy zeppelin!' Egan exclaimed. 'Yon buggers which raided York earlier this year.'

'Yes,' Dickie agreed, 'and the *bluidy* thing's coming straight at us.'

Dickie Bird was right. The German airship was heading straight for the little craft, as de Vere pressed the alarm button and the crew came tumbling from their hammocks to join the duty watch and help fight what was going to be the uneven battle between the enemy leviathan and their own poorly armed ship.

For already the Germans were lowering their observer, a dimly perceived leather-helmeted and goggled German confined in a tight glass cage at the bottom of what looked like a steel cage, while up above, next to the airship's bridge, other helmeted figures were scurrying to man heavy machine guns.

Now the airship was approaching their craft at speed, the gun crews swinging their massed banks of machine guns round to fire on the ship below, while the observer in his open cage, his scarf flying in the wind, was telephoning the bridge urgently. Obviously it was his task to direct the enemy fire and it was equally obvious that the Germans were going to make a determined attempt to destroy the British ship which had unwittingly ventured into the trap they had set for Allied shipping off the mouth of the Humber.

What now?' Dicke yelled, as the zeppelin came lower and lower. 'Fight or run?'

De Vere hesitated. He knew they were hopelessly outclassed by the huge zeppelin towering above them. Their torpedoes were of no use in this case and all they possessed in the way of firepower were their Vickers and Lewis machine guns. Besides, for all he knew, the Germans might be carrying bombs and mines. The Hun airships operating over Britain usually did. Still, it went against the grain to run away. So he compromised. 'We'll try to hold her off, Dickie. Get Sparks.' He meant the morse-code operator. 'Tell him to raise Driffield Field. They've got Sopwith Camels there. If they can scramble quick enough—' His words were drowned by Ferguson opening fire with his Lewis gun at Egan's order, for the chief petty officer had moved very fast for such an old man. Already tracer bullets were streaming upwards, a lethal white blur.

'And we can hold the bugger long enough, the Camels'll put paid to the Huns. Hopefully.'

Dickie crossed himself and intoned solemnly, 'We who are about to die salute thee,' and then he was off, doubling across to where the operator had his little shack, crying, 'Get a move on, Sparks . . . Shake a leg! The game's afoot, you idle man!'

The next instant the first fifty-pound enemy bomb fell from the sky and exploded in a furious spout of wild white water only yards away from the little craft. The uneven battle had commenced.

# Five

Now de Vere at the wheel handled the little craft with all his skill. He forgot their course completely. He thought it was one way to dodge the great lumbering zeppelin until help arrived from Driffield or any other of the east coast airfields which might have picked up their urgent plea for help.

Unfortunately the captain of the airship, clearly visible on the thing's great bridge, had already guessed he would abandon the north-east course to the Dutch coast some 150-odd miles away. His ship stuck to the British craft like glue. All the while the gunners peppered the sea all around with deadly machine-gun fire, while the four British gunners, armed with their puny weapons, retaliated the best they could. But it was clear to a sweating, red-faced, cursing de Vere that slowly but surely the German skipper was gaining the advantage on him. His bomb-aimers were standing or crouching at their posts beneath the zeppelin waiting for the signal from the observer, suspended in his glass cage, to drop their deadly cargo.

But the Germans had not quite reckoned with CPO Egan, the veteran of many wars, large and small. He had spotted the airship's weakness almost immediately. At first he thought his own gunners might seriously damage the airship's canopy with well-aimed machine-gun fire. But Ferguson, the British ship's marksman and best gunner, had failed to do so. Admittedly he had placed several volleys along the airship's hull. But without effect, and an angry Egan had realized that the zeppelin was impervious to ordinary tracer bullets. They needed armour-piercing or incendiary slugs to set her on fire. But she could still be blinded.

He yelled at Dickie Bird, supervising the gunners' defence, as de Vere flung the agile little craft from side to side so that both of them had to cling to stanchions in order not to be thrown over the side, 'We can blind yon bugger, sir.'

'Blind her?' Dickie yelled back, puzzled.

'Yessir. Knock out the observer . . . That might put her off. At least for a while.'

Dickie understood at once. 'With you, Chiefie,' he cried. 'Give me that Lee Enfield.' He meant the British Army's standard rifle, which was very accurate and which had a range of up to one mile in the hands of a marksman.

At Harrow-on-the Hill and later at Dartmouth, he had been on the rifle team and had won many a prize for the school and the college. But then Dickie had shot for the honour of the school or for a silver cup (which was very probably gilt in reality). Now, as he raised the rifle, tucked the butt into his shoulder and braced himself the best he could on the wildly swaying deck, he knew that this time he was shooting to save human lives, those of his comrades, and the ship. Even as he took aim, he realized just how much of a responsibility that was, and how much depended upon him getting in that killing shot before the German observer telephoned the skipper on the bridge to start dropping the zeppelin's bombs.

Next to him a suddenly tense Egan would have dearly loved to have wished the young officer 'good shooting', but he didn't dare spoil Dickie's concentration. The latter needed to concentrate his whole being on hitting the squarehead before it was too late. So Egan kept silent and prayed in his humble Scottish manner.

Carefully, as if he were back on some peacetime range under perfect shooting conditions – a firm base, a windless sky, a steady target – Dickie Bird prepared himself for the shot of his life. Straight off he dismissed all other considerations from his mind, cleared it entirely, as he tucked the brass butt of the Lee Enfield ever tighter into his shoulder. He swung the rifle round. The foresight neatly dissected the observer in his wildly swinging cage. He eased his breathing, taking in every detail of the German peering down at the speeding little craft, right arm raised, telephone in the other hand, as if he

95

were perhaps guiding the airship on its final run up to bombing the English ship.

Next to him Egan swallowed hard. He knew that he wouldn't survive any sinking. The others were vigorous young men, half his age. If nothing else, if he had to go into the drink – and he had heard dark stories told in the petty officers' mess of the Germans machine-gunning British sailors in the water – the freezing-cold North Sea would finish him off. He redoubled his prayers, praying harder than he had ever done since he had left the crofters' school in remote northern Scotland.

Dickie's finger curled round the trigger of the Army rifle. He took first pressure, squinting down the Lee Enfield's long barrel at his target, knowing that, with luck, the German up there would be dead or dying within seconds and not feeling very happy at the thought. He asked himself how the snipers in the trenches of Flanders could keep on killing their fellow human beings like this day after day. He dismissed the thought, controlling his breathing now with an effort of sheer will power. He took final pressure.

*Crack!* There was a sharp dry noise like a twig being snapped underfoot in a dense wood at the height of summer. The rifle butt slammed against his right shoulder. Automatically, not waiting to see what had happened to his target, he jerked back the bolt and ejected the spent .303 cartridge case. Instantly he thrust the bolt back in the breech. But there was no need to do so.

Next to him Egan cried with unusual excitement for that dour man, 'Ye've hit you squarehead, sir . . . Ye've got him!'

Dickie Bird had. Slowly, but surely, the helmeted figure of the German serial observer started to sink behind the cover of his cage, his blood spurting a bright scarlet over the glass upper part. Dickie breathed out a sigh of relief as, behind the bridge, a gunner opened up with the twin Vickers, sending tracer upwards in an angry lethal morse towards the zeppelin. Naturally his fire had no effect except to rattle the suddenly blinded Germans on the airship's bridge even more. For, without their observer, it seemed the skipper high above them hesitated to press home his attack on the speeding British craft.

At the wheel, de Vere breathed out hard. They had done it. He altered his crazy zig-zag course. Instead he headed straight out to sea, slamming into each wave as if it was a brick wall, feeling the shock in his guts as hc did so, and knowing he might well be sick again afterwards, as most skippers of these fast craft were when they were going all out. All the same, he was determined to put as much distance between him and the airship as possible. Ahead there lay a bank of fog. Once he had managed to reach that, he felt he'd be safe.

But already the German zeppelin commandant had recovered from the loss of his observer, now lying dead in his little shattered cabin, as it swung back and forth like a children's swing in the wind. He put on more speed. The whirr of the great airship's electric motors increased. Up above, the bomb-aimers at their stations prepared to bomb blind, or at least without the aid of the skilled observer.

Now it had become a crazy race between the little craft down below and the gigantic airship; and both sides knew it. As Ferguson blazed away furiously but purposelessly, Egan and a suddenly pale-faced and silent Dickie, who had abruptly realized that he had killed a fellow man for the first time in his wartime career, watched the airship as it started to catch up with the motor launch. It was clear to the two of them that there was nothing that they or the rest of the crew could do any more. It all depended upon de Vere hitting that fog bank before the Germans caught up with them. They realized too that, even without the observer, dead in his swinging cage, the Germans had a good chance of striking them with their bombs; and even a fifty pound bomb scoring a direct hit would suffice to sink their boat, which was made of wood and light alloys.

But if they were overcome by a miserable sense of impotence, de Vere was carried away by the thrill of the chase. Sick as he felt, he was also animated by an exhilerating and reckless excitement, crying to himself as the craft's sharp knife-like prow cleaved the water, 'Come on, you Hun bugger . . . come on and try to catch me, if you can!'

But that was exactly what the Germans were doing. They were gaining on the fleeing ship. Already the bomb-aimers

97

were leaning perilously over the side of their bombing platform slung beneath the airship, craning their necks, hands
clutching the toggle ropes which would release the bombs
when they came level with their target – and that was going
to be only a matter of minutes at the speed the zeppelin was
flying, now that their electric motors were going all out.

Two minutes later it happened, as they had thought it would.
'Moses', as the youngest member of the crew was always
called in the Imperial Navy, jumped the gun. He pulled his
toggle. The bomb fell, released cleanly and immediately.
'*Verdammte Scheisse!*' the petty officer in charge of the
bombing platform yelled angrily. '*Zu fruh, du Idiot* . . . too
early.'

With air surging through the little bomb's fins, making a
banshee-like howl, the fifty pounds of high explosive dropped
from the sky, while the others of the bombing party craned
their necks over the side of the platform watching it fall. Perhaps
the 'Moses' might be lucky, They often were. But the young
sailor, face flushed beneath his leather face mask, wasn't.

The bomb struck the sea some fifty yards behind the fleeing
ship, right in the centre of its wild white wake. It exploded
in a great spurt of dark green. The ship rocked wildly. Madly
the crew grabbed for support. For a moment the screws lifted
out of the water and the craft slowed alarmingly. De Vere's
heart skipped a beat. Had the bomb somehow hit the little
engine room? It hadn't. Next moment the screws slapped
down into the sea once again and they were racing forward
at well over thirty knots, the deck trembling and quivering
under his feet like a live thing.

Still the zeppelin was gaining upon him and the fogbank
seemed as far away as the moon from the earth. 'Come on
. . . come on,' he cursed, his body lathered in sweat, urging
the craft to reach the only cover before the Germans
commenced bombing in earnest. To no real avail. The airship
was catching up with him. He guessed he wouldn't make the
fog bank in time. He changed his tactics. Once more he started
zig-zagging. Almost effortlesly, he threw the craft one way
then the other, the sea pouring over the sides, as the little mast
almost touched the water time and time again.

Now, however, the zeppelin was right above him. A sweat-lathered de Vere tensed. Now they were for it. 'Start praying, old boy,' a hard, cynical voice at the back of his mind warned.

The voice was right. There was the sharp whistle of a descending bomb. Next moment it exploded just astern. Steel splinters, red-hot and razor sharp, flew across the boat as it heeled and reeled under the impact. 'Soldier' Atkins the former Marine, who thought he was off on a 'foreign hol', screamed shrilly like a hysterical woman. He fell to his knees, grabbing at his throat as he choked on his own blood, his shattered face slipping down from his forehead like red molten wax. A second later he pitched to the deck, dead before he hit it.

Another bomb fell to port, even closer this time. The mast came tumbling down in a welter of blue electric sparks. Ferguson ducked hastily as shell splinters, red-hot and gleaming like polished silver, hissed lethally through the air, twisting and turning his beloved guns into gnarled grotesque metal statues like the products of some demented modern artist. 'Holy Christ!' he commenced in an awed voice, and ducked again as yet another fifty-pound bomb exploded even closer by.

At the wheel, de Vere yelped with pain. A sliver of bright steel struck his right hand. For an instant he let go of the wheel. The speeding craft lurched. He caught it just in time. Crazily he swung the wheel to port as another bomb narrowly missed the wheelhouse. Now he knew he had only a matter of moments to live. The very next bomb that came hurtling down *had* to hit his battered craft.

But Fate intervened on their side at the very last moment, when de Vere and the rest of the crew had about given up hope. It came, not in the form of the nippy Sopwith Camels they had hoped for from Driffield, a few miles inland from Hull. Instead, two lumbering twin-engined bombers – perhaps the latest double-decker de Havillands – came right out of the fog bank to their front, the racks of bombs clearly visible beneath their camouflaged wings.

Egan yelled, 'They're ours, lads . . . They really are!'

Some gave a hoarse cheer. It was taken up by the rest of the shaken crew, many of them brushing off the wooden splinters where the deck had been smashed into a crazy matchwood by the enemy's steel bomb shards.

Up above, the skipper of the zeppelin saw the danger. For the two British bombers were climbing now to gain height, despite the fire that the airship's gunners were pouring in their direction. He guessed what they were about. They would attempt to get as much height as possible and then launch their bombs at the airship's vulnerable upper envelope. Once they started a fire, there'd be no hope for him or his ship. Without parachutes they would have to drop over the side; and if the fall didn't kill them, the sea would freeze them to death.

Desperately the zeppelin skipper, bearded, middle-aged, dressed in full naval uniform, complete with old-fashioned collar and ceremonial sword, made his attempt to escape into the fog bank. Below, safe at last, de Vere relaxed. He eased back the throttle and gazed at the spectacle – though he felt no joy as the zeppelin prepared to ward off the British planes' attack. For he knew the Huns didn't stand a chance.

Egan and Ferguson felt differently. 'Give the squarehead bastards a sock in the jaw for me, lads!' the Liverpudlian urged on the planes which were now dropping out of the sky to commence their attack. 'Pay the bastards back for what they've just frigging well done to us.'

And this time CPO Egan didn't look askance on the 'Scouse git's' profane language. 'Ay,' he growled, gnarled old hands clenched into fists. 'They deserve it alreet.'

The two British bombers had split up now. One was coming in from port; the other from starboard. And they were so low that the watching sailors below could clearly see the helmeted bomb-aimer in his open cockpit behind the pilot. Already he had his gauntleted hand on the outside toggle ready to unleash his deadly cargo on the airship's vulnerable envelope; filled with highly explosive gas.

But the Germans were not going to give up without a fight. They all knew, even the 'Moses', what their fate would be if they did. Now they poured a murderous hail at the great lumbering bombers. The two of them seemed to be sailing through a glowing white network of criss-crossing machine-gun fire. But the young pilots, eager to be among the first to down one of the dreaded zeppelins, which held British cities in fear, came on bravely and undaunted. Below, the crew had stopped cheering now. Instead they watched tensely, knowing just what risks these teenage officers and sergeants flying above them were taking.

Suddenly tragedy struck the attackers. The plane in front seemed to stagger and stop in mid-air. Dickie Bird groaned. 'Oh, my God!' he breathed, as thick black smoke started to pour from the bomber's port engine. Its prop stopped abruptly. Its nose dipped alarmingly. Slowly, very slowly, but inevitably the stricken plane lost height. Greedy little tongues of cruel blue flame licked about its fuselage. 'The poor bugger's coming down!' one of the watchers yelled. At the wheel, de Vere agonized, willing the unknown pilot to come out of that dive. That wasn't to be. The port wing, with its dead engine, dipped. It struck a wave. The plane careened round, carried about by the force of the windswept sea. In that same instant de Vere throttled back even more and yelled almost angrily, 'Don't just stand there . . . lower a boat, will you, damn your lazy hides.' 'The plane struck another large wave. In a flash it started to sink. Even before de Vere's angry command had time to register with the awe-stricken deck crew, the bomber vanished beneath the surface of the North Sea. No one got out.

But as, above them, the Germans cheered at their victory, the other bomber came in for the kill, its young pilot throwing it all over the sky as if it were a single-seater fighter. Desperately the German gunners took up the new challenge. This time they were out of luck. The pilot came, braving their murderous gunfire. The plane seemed to bear a charmed life. Time and time again the watchers thought the bomber had been hit, as it disappeared into the smoke puffs of the heavy machine guns. But each time it came through unscathed.

Now the pilot was finally in position. For a moment or two the bomber seemed to hover motionlessly like some giant metal hawk, seeking out its prey. Next moment the bomb-aimer started to release his deadly little eggs. At that range he couldn't miss. The first bomb hit the envelope with an

101

audible thud. Nothing happened. For a moment the watchers thought the bomb's impact fuse was defective. They were mistaken. As the second little bomb followed, the first exploded in a flash of ugly yellow flame and smoke.

In an instant a great flame was searing the length of the zeppelin, as its gas-filled interior exploded. Even at that distance the watchers could feel the intense heat which seemed to drag the very air from their lungs, so that in a flash they were gasping for breath like ancient asthmatics in the throes of some final fatal attack.

Panic-stricken Germans, their bodies burning like torches, were throwing themselves over the side of the airship, which was shrivelling up visibily, as gas tank after gas tank ignited, throwing off that unbearable killing heat. She started to lose height. De Vere turned away, unable to stand the horrific sight any longer. A muffled explosion, the hiss of the envelope hitting the icy water, the last frantic cries of the crew stiffled almost instantly as they went under.

Thus when de Vere brought himself to turn and view the area once more, there was nothing left of the airship, only the bits and pieces of pathetic wreckage bobbing up and down on the waves, and what looked like charred logs floating among it: the bodies of dead men . . .

# Late 1915

# One

'*Seine Allerhöchste Majestät Kaiser Wilhelm der . . .*'
As one, the high-ranking naval officers in their best uniforms turned. At the great double door, the chamberlain in his gold livery rapped down his staff three times and the doors began to open with slow, deliberate ceremony. At both sides, the two gigantic cavalrymen in their silver breastplates and great winged eagle helmets raised their sabres in salute, and somewhere in an inner room a small orchestra struck up '*Deutschland über Alles*'.

Wilhelm the Second swaggered in, his withered useless hand holding the pommel of his sword, the other the field marshal's baton, a rank which he had granted to himself immediately he had taken over the throne of Germany. Eyes blazing fiercely, his moustaches waxed to perfection, he shot a look to left and right and, seemingly pleased with what he saw, he nodded stiffly and said, '*Guten Morgen, meine Herren.*'

'*Guten Morgen, Majestät!*' they responded as one, save for Klaus von Bismarck.

This was the same man who had sacked his famous uncle, Otto, who had unified Germany back in the sixties, when he, the Emperor, had been nothing more than a silly boy who preferred playing with toy soldiers and ships without a thought that his aggressive policies might well lose everything that his one-time Chancellor Otto von Bismarck had worked so hard to build up for his country.

'He has bad blood in him, Klaus, my boy,' he remembered his uncle lecturing him as a youngster back in Friedrichsruh, to which he had been forced to retire by the new Emperor. '*English* blood. Look how Victoria's daughter, his mother, with her stupid English liberalism and silly ideas, fitted him out for life.* Why, she even left him with a withered arm. All these Saxe-Coburgs on the other side of the Channel have something wrong with them; diseased, perverted, whoremongering, puppets of Jewish moneylenders – the damned lot of them.'

Now, as the Emperor faced his admirals for the meeting he had called completely out of the blue, Klaus von Bismarck, in the second row of the illustrious gathering, felt nothing but contempt for the perfumed popinjay who hid his weaknesses under this outward martial display.

'Gentlemen,' the Kaiser commenced, still keeping these admirals and other high-ranking naval officers standing at a kind of awkward attention so that they felt like young cadets again, not knowing whether to stand at ease without orders. 'We are greatly pleased with the success of your raid on the north-eastern coast of Albion last year. It certainly demonstrated to the English just how powerful our German fleet is.' He gave them a stiff little smile, as if his jaw was worked by rusty springs. 'However, we must remember that it *was* only a raid.'

The Admirals looked grave and there was a murmur of approval from the older and senior ones among them, who were fighting the war from their desks in Berlin's Tirpitzstrasse. They naturally wouldn't be risking their lives in any future naval action Klaus von Bismarck guessed the Emperor was going to suggest.

'However, we can't afford to rest on past laurels, gentlemen,' the Emperor admonished them. 'With our men at the front in France dying by their thousands, we can't have a large navy stationary in their harbours, polishing the ships' brasswork. Besides, there are too many of those damned socialist agitators around there trying to cause trouble, and we all know that the Devil finds work for idle hands. So saying, gentlemen, we request you to reveal your plans for a future major naval action against the damned English.' He rattled his ornate sabre with his good arm, as if he already

* The Emperor's mother had been Victoria of England, the eldest daughter of Queen Victoria.

saw himself leading his brave sailors into some derring-do action.

Klaus von Bismarck pulled a face. The Imperial court was a gossip shop. There were still the children of the English princess Victoria, who, although they now had German nationality, might well still feel loyal to their old country. What if some of them were in the pay of the notorious English Secret Service and were passing on information to the English naval authorities? To discuss top-secret naval plans in this manner was tantamount to betrayal, and Klaus von Bismarck knew from his own personal spies in Germany's north-western naval parts – all hotbeds of sedition and radical socialism, that the Imperial Navy would not survive a major defeat at sea; there'd be a mutiny.

Admiral von Hipper, the most senior admiral present, cleared his throat and gave the Kaiser a stiff little bow. 'All Highest,' he commenced, using the traditional form of address to Wilhlem. 'We have a plan.'

'Excellent, excellent!' the Kaiser exclaimed. 'Please enlighten us if you would.'

Von Hipper looked embarrassed. There were still people in the big room who shouldn't be there to listen to what he had to say: the chamberlain, the Kaiser's elegant aristocratic adjutants, all of whom had English relatives, even the two gigantic soldiers of the Garde du Corps. The Kaiser tapped his right foot impatiently and von Hipper knew he would have to continue. 'Sire,' he said. 'We are prepared to challenge the British Grand Fleet itself, although their capital ships outnumber us.'

The Kaiser beamed. '*Grossartig!*' he exclaimed loudly, looking around his fawning attendants as if to display his confidence in these brave naval men who were going to challenge the greatest fleet in the world.

Inwardly Klaus von Bismarck groaned. How long had he worked on preparing the plan for von Hipper and his fellow admirals? Perhaps ever since 1914! Now a simple indiscretion on someone's part here in this room – and there were plenty of candidates – and his whole carefully prepared plan would be in ruins. God, what a world!

'*Majestät*,' Hipper went on. 'The problem is that the English capital ships outnumber ours.'

'I know that, *Herr Admiral*, but ours are more modern and better armoured than those of the English. As they say in that terrible country, our craft can run rings around the British ships.' Hipper looked puzzled at the phrase in English and inwardly von Bismarck groaned. The Emeperor hated the English passionately, yet when he had to explain something succinctly, he used a saying in the English language because he didn't know the German equivalent. The Emperor really had to be mad, as von Bismarck's dead uncle had always maintained he was.

'Well, sire, the plan which has been put forward to us is to draw off the bulk of the English so-called Grand Fleet, mostly made up of their older ships incidentally, and then tackle their newer vessels. The estimate is that we shall be roughly of the same strength, with our ships being the superior ones. We haven't got comparable fire-power but we have better armour, as you say, sire, and better trained gunners and crews.'

The Kaiser's eyes lit up. 'I take your point, Hipper. We shall be able to achieve a victory in that manner over a much superior fleet in strength, with no great loss to ourselves. In essence, we might not be able to achieve total victory at that one stroke you plan, *Herr Admiral*, But in the eyes of the English they will have suffered a major tactical and strategic defeat. They will suffer greater casualties in ships than we do, and if we can reduce the size of their vaunted Grand Fleet to that of our High Seas Fleet, we will have much more freedom to use our ships in the North Sea.'

Hipper said (without too much conviction, von Bismarck could not help but think), 'That is the plan, sir.'

'Brilliant, Hipper.' He looked hard at the commander of the High Seas Fleet's battlecruisers. 'But may I ask you how exactly do you intend to draw off the bulk of the English fleet?'

Hipper, as afraid of the Kaiser's wrath as he was, still hesitated to give the notoriously boastful Kaiser, and through him his gossip shop of a court, the highly secret details of 'Plan X' on which everything depended. At that moment he cursed his superior Admiral von Scheer for being ill and therefore not present this day. Let his new chief, that firebrand von Scheer, decide what the Kaiser should and should not know about the great plan. Suddenly he had it. He turned to von Bismarck in the second row of the high-ranking officers.

The Kaiser tapped his right foot impatiently. He always tried to give the impression that his schedule was so full that he was in a tremendous hurry. Perhaps he thought this would impress his subjects; make them believe that he was as fully part of the war machine as any frontline soldier.

'Vice-Admiral von Bismarck has worked with Admiral von Scheer very closely on this matter, in particular on the intelligence side of it, sire. He can explain the details of the subterfuge, sire.'

The Emperor frowned when he heard the hated name of von Bismarck. He put on his fiercest look and stared at the vice-admiral. He wore his best uniform. Still it looked ill-fitting and slovenly on von Bismarck's flabby middle-aged frame and he lacked the stiff military bearing of the other admirals. The Kaiser told himself it was typical of the von Bismarcks. They felt no respect for the house of Hohenzollern. Otto von Bismarck had believed he had been the kingmaker back in 1870. He and his descendants had always believed that had given them special privileges. 'Ah, Herr von Bismarck!' he exclaimed as Klaus von Bismarck clicked to attention and gave a little bow, which showed no great respect. 'We have had no cognizance of your promotion to the rank of vice-admiral. Your superior should have informed us.'

'Sire, my chief, Admiral von Scheer, has been ill for some time.'

'Hm, well, we have heard of you, Herr von Bismarck.' The Emperor waved his good hand to indicate that the matter was dismissed and von Bismarck should get on with his report.

Inwardly von Bismarck shrugged. It was obvious that whatever the Kaiser had heard about him it wasn't very good. But it didn't worry him. There was no love lost between the von Bismarcks and the Hohenzollerns* with their decadent English blood, who had dismissed the great Otto von Bismarck as chancellor after he had founded an empire for the obscure Prussian aristocrats.

'*Majestät*, Admiral von Hipper has informed you of the general plan. Its basic aim is for our High Seas Fleet to break out of the Heligoland Triangle—'

'Yes, yes, get on with it!' the Kaiser said impatiently, though obviously he was enjoying taking a von Bismarck to task in this manner.

Von Bismarck remained unmoved. He kept calm. He went on with, 'Admiral von Schear, my chief, is planning to use a two-fold decoy to lure the English Grand Fleet out of its bases at Rosyth and Scapa Flow to do battle with our most modern ships. It will take the form of an operational and raiding cruise along the Danish coast by Admiral von Hipper's battlecruisers and some forty ships.'

Von Hipper looked very proud as his role in the forthcoming operation was mentioned by a von Bismarck, who, cynical as he was, knew that these self-important admirals, used to wielding absolute power from their quarterdecks, had to be flattered at all times. The Kaiser, much to von Hipper's chagrin, did not appear to notice. 'Yes, yes,' he urged. 'Get on with it, Herr von Bismarck. But how will this affect the strength of the British?'

'In this manner, sire. It is Admiral von Scheer's intention to reduce the strength of the Grand Fleet by that part that is drawn off by Admiral von Hipper's battlecruiser squadron.'

The Kaiser looked a little shocked. 'In battle, von Bismarck? I can't afford to lose a single one of my beautiful battlecruisers in the role of mere decoys.'

Von Bismarck could barely conceal his contempt at the Kaiser's retort. The man thought he was playing with toy ships

* The Hohenzollerns were the rulers of Prussia, a member of several states which made up today's Germany in the mid-nineteenth century. Otto von Bismarck had welded those states together by war and made William the Second's grandfather the first German Emperor at the end of the France-Prussian War of 1870.

like some silly schoolboy in a sailor's uniform pushing them about with a cane in his local pond. He didn't seem to realize that his 'beautiful battlecruisers' were weapons of war, manned by real flesh-and-blood men, designed to kill and be killed. 'No, Sire,' he said coldly, 'not by your battlecruisers, but by Admiral von Scheer's U-boats.'

'*U-boats!*' the Kaiser breathed, as if he could hardly believe his own ears, while his admirals stiffened. For all of them were big-ship men. The new-fangled U-boats were beneath their contempt, used so far to sink unarmed enemy merchantmen in coastal waters. Indeed, there were some of the high-ranking officers present that day who cursed the very existence of the underwater craft. The U-boat was an underhand sort of naval weapon, striking from the deep without warning against ships that could not defend themselves, and civilian ships at that. It went against their code of conduct and the reputation of the Imperial German Navy to number such craft among its ranks.

Von Bismarck ignored the looks on the Kaiser's face and those of his fellow naval officers. 'Sire, this is what is intended . . .'

When he was finished, von Bismarck could see that, despite their disdain for the U-boats, they were impressed, even the Kaiser. He flicked his upturned waxed moustache as if he were ascertaining that it was still looking fierce and suitably martial, before exclaiming, '*Genial* . . . brilliant, *absolut genial!*'

Von Bismarck was not impressed. No doubt, in due course, if the plan was successful, the Kaiser would be claiming that he had been its originator. But first von Bismarck told himself he had to ensure, one way or other, that the fool opposite him kept the secret 'Plan X' to himself. How, he didn't know at the moment, but somehow or other he would have to do it.

But half an hour later when the conference was over and the Kaiser and his lackeys were indulging themselves in the best French champagne the naval staff could provide for them, von Bismarck found that he, not the Kaiser, might well be the one who could be unintentionally giving away the details of 'Plan X' to the enemy.

For it was about that time that the urgent telephone call came through from Intelligence Headquarters in Hamburg-Wohltorf. It was his senior assistant, Leutnant zur See Dirksen, an obviously worried young man, who had also worked Holland and Dutch-speaking Belgium before the outbreak of war in August 1914.

Dirksen wasted no time. He knew his chief was supposed to be briefing the Kaiser and the senior admirals that day and he did not wish to ruffle any feathers at the conference. For, like his chief, Dirksen was a cynical realist. He felt no desire to find himself posted to the new U-Boat Army by some irate senior admiral. One didn't survive very long as an officer in those smelly sardine cans.

'*Herr Admiral*,' he said urgently. 'We have news of the girl – you know, sir?'

Von Bismarck did. He knew, too, just as Dirksen did, that the girl knew the rudiments of the great deception plan. Any astute intelligence officer could put together the details of what she knew and come up with all he would want to know about 'Plan X'.

'Yes,' he snapped. 'What? Fire away, Dirksen.'

The young officer did, 'She's been spotted again at Rotterdam. From there, according to what little we know, she's heading south.'

'South to where?'

'Don't know exactly. sir. But she's using the railway apparently, and the mainline heads straight for the Belgian border.'

Momentarily that puzzled von Bismarck. Most of Belgium had been occupied by the German Imperial Army since the autumn of 1914. There was only the narrow coastal strip still in Belgian hands, and those of the English, who had come to the aid of what they called, in their hypocritical English manner that always nauseated him, 'poor little Belgium'.

'Any reason why? Do you think she might attempt to cross the old border into Belgian Flanders? After all, she used the route often enough last year before our troops occpied it.'

'No, sir. If she did, she'd walk right into the hands of our

112

own people and they're always on the lookout for *Frontläufer*, or *'passeurs'*[*] as the French call them.'

Von Bismarck considered for a few moments, listening to the clink of champagne glasses and the noisy chatter and tipsy laughter of the admirals and the Emperor's fawning courtiers, all of them vying with each other to make their master feel that he was the greatest soldier ever born. Then he gave up trying to analyse Sussi's motives. *'Schon gut!'* he snapped curtly. 'Deal with her. She is a great danger to our cause now. Priority number one. Clear?'

'Clear, sir. But there's one other thing.'

'What?' von Bismark said, worried now about the girl and what she knew. 'More bad news?'

'I don't know. It's this, sir. The Englishmen you have already mentioned in that business of the Frisian Islands in nineteen thirteen. You remember, sir?'

'I do. What about them?'

'They've turned up again. In Holland.'

In the other room, they were crying, 'Hoch . . . hoch!' The shout by the assembled company was followed by the snap and crack of breaking glass. The high-ranking officers and the courtiers were celebrating the Kaiser's departure and presumably the coming victory over the English too. Inwardly von Bismarck cursed. Damned fools. There was many a slip between the cup and the lip, he told himself. They hadn't had their victory yet. What might happen now in Holland, with that young whore Sussi on the run and these young English naval officers turning up again, could well spoil things for that megalomaniac the Emperor and his toadies. 'And?' he queried sharply.

'They've appeared out of nowhere, sir, in a craft which has been badly shot up. They're now in Dordrecht south of Rotterdam. Are we to do anything about them, sir?'

Von Bismarck was playing it safe. There might well be some connection between the appearance of the English who had spied on him back in the Frisian Islands, and the

---

[*] Literally 'front-runners' and 'passers', agents carrying messages back and forth.

113

girl. At all events, he couldn't take the slightest chance. 'Eradicate them, too,' he snapped. '*Ende*.' With that he slammed the phone down, the decision made for better or worse.

# Two

For Freifrau von Hoofstra-Mecklenburg it had started as an act of desperation. After Rotterdam, she had been down to her last few cents, wet with the persistent Dutch drizzle and not a little hungry. But she had known she had to get away from the big port. So she had remained hungry, using her money to pay for the noisy old trains and trams, the only transportation she could now afford.

It had been an interminable journey, changing the local transportation time and time again, stiff from sitting on the hard wooden seats, watching with envy as her stout fellow passengers tucked into their cheese and hard-boiled eggs, accompanied by plenty of good country bread and butter, without a thought for the pretty pale girl next to them, her hungry stomach rumbling audibly.

Still, she knew that it was better than chancing her life any longer in a dangerous Rotterdam, not that she really knew exactly where she was going, save that it was southwards. She had travelled from the great port to Dordrecht. From there to Utrecht. She had skirted the unknown quantity of the Walcheren Peninsula, getting ever closer to the Dutch-Belgian frontier, an area that she knew fairly well.

She had run agents to and fro across that border in the early stages of the war, until the victorious Imperial German Army had conquered virtually all of Belgium and made her activities there unnecessary. Now she knew that Belgium's small army still held the coastal strip of their country up to the Dutch border marked by the Scheldt, but how far and in what depth – that was beyond her knowledge. She hoped, however, that the Belgian Army under their King Albert might be linked to the French in the Pas de Calais area, or, if not, there might

115

be some means of getting away from one of the small seaside ports, once the destination of rich tourists taking the sea air, that linked that part of Belgium with England just across the Channel.

For, as she travelled southwards at an incredibly slow pace in the blue-painted rusty Dutch trams, a rough-and-ready if dangerous plan was beginning to form in her still-confused mind. In the early days of the war, the frontier she was approaching so slowly had been a hive of hectic activity. German, French, British and Belgian agents, aided by Dutch smugglers and petty criminals, out to make more money than they had ever done smuggling coffee beans and the like, had passed to and fro nightly, risking their lives in doing so.

But she knew it had been a highly dangerous game even when the agent had reached the supposed safety of the country he was working for, mainly Belgium and the supposedly neutral country of Holland. Many an agent, she had learned, had ended up in a local canal with a knife in his back and bludgeoned to death.

Still, as she came ever closer to that disputed border, with the silent flashes of the heavy permanent barrage lighting up the dull grey sky, she told herself that she had to cross it come what may. It was her only chance. If she reached the Belgian lines, she might be able to contact the British Army authorities there. And this time, with a bit of luck, she might have a warmer welcome than the one she had received at the English Legation at the Hague.

But first she had to get close enough to the frontier to assess the best place to cross. She had little to offer a professional guide. Not that she was keen to do so. She'd heard they often took a fugitive's money and then quietly betrayed him to the authorities. That was too dangerous for her.

But as Sussi von Hoofstra-Mecklenburg, who had once been presented at the Dutch royal court, descended from the tram stiffly, chilled and hungry, to yet another cold damp shower, she realized that it was going to be much more difficult to get close enough to the Dutch-Belgian border to make her escape attempt than she had realized.

There were Dutch policemen in their strange square high

hats, and sloppily uniformed Dutch soldier conscripts everywhere, herding bewildered bunches of peasants in wooden shoes, carrying baskets of provisions, into wired-off enclosures to be questioned and perhaps even imprisoned, if they were proved to be agents and not humble peasants selling their goods on the Belgian black market on the other side of the border.

Despite her weariness, Sussi reacted immediately. With hardly a cent left in her pocket to pay for what she might purchase, she dodged into the nearest fish shop and began fussing around a barrel of cured herring as if she might be selecting some finer ones for the family dinner. The dodge worked. The policeman who had eyed her curiously a moment before, as if she might be someone he ought to question, turned his attention elsewhere, leaving her time to assess a new situation which she had not anticipated, but one she knew she'd have to solve soon, if she were going to get out of Holland in one piece . . .

Some eighty odd kilometres to the north, both de Vere and Dickie were also confronted with a totally unexpected problem that they, too, knew they had to deal with soon. It was the state of the battered Thorneycroft launch, which they had managed to land in the small harbour of Dordrecht instead of Rotterdam, as had been planned originally.

The British craft was in bad shape. Her bridgehouse was shattered, her mast still sprawled in the confused debris of the deck, while the hull was pock-marked with bomb splinters like the symptoms of some loathsome skin disease. It was all too clear that their once spanking-new ship had been recently engaged in a fire-fight with the German enemy. The fact that one of the first things that the two officers had been forced to do was to clear away the poor headless body under the eyes of the local civilian onlookers and the Dutch police didn't help much. As the local British consul, who had hurried to the quay in the centre of the coastal town on his cycle, had warned them, 'It's obvious, gentlemen, that you have recently been in a naval engagement. The Dutch know that, and as a nation that is leaning over backwards not to offend us or the Huns, they'll insist you leave their territorial waters within three days. If you don't, your crew and craft – or what's left of it – will be interned for the duration.' He looked at them sympathetically and added, 'I'm afraid you and your chaps are not going to enjoy the fleshpots of Rotterdam. It's back to sea as soon as you've made emergency repairs and provisioned. Otherwise –' he shrugged – 'it's barbed wire and Red Cross parcels for the rest of the war. Bugger, what, chaps.'

Bugger it was.

Now, however, they discussed their situation in the privacy of their little wardroom, which was in the same shambles as the rest of the ship. Outside, the curious Dutch civilians still lined the cobbled quay gawping at the ship as if it were one from another world, like one in an H. G. Wells novel, so popular that year. They kept their voices low – the civilians might hear them at that distance. And the consul had warned them, 'Don't trust the Dutch, they are a mercenary people, and the Huns pay well.'

'Let's assume that we accept this Dutch three day ruling,' de Vere ventured. 'What can we do to find the girl in that time? For two chaps who don't speak the lingo it's going to be a frightful job.'

'Even for two who do speak that awful Dutch, it'd be a helluva job, de Vere,' Dickie agreed. 'The question is, where do we start?'

'Let's put it like this first, Dickie . . . where don't we start?' He answered his own question. 'Not in the north, the Hague, Rotterdam and the like. Nor to the east with the border to Germany over there. It's got to be the south, if anywhere.'

'Agreed.' Dickie took a thoughtful and careful sip of his pink gin, savouring the precious liquid, for it was the last bottle, and though the consul had promised them more to replace their bomb-shattered supply, the crew's rum ration came first. 'So, putting ourselves in her shoes, what might we do under the given circumstances?'

'Try to make another approach to our authorities. It's her only chance, since the Huns tried to kill her, as the consul says.' He frowned, as if angry – which he was – at the way things were turning out. He was of an age when young men hate to fail; and C had sent them all this way at great expense

118

to find the girl, come what may. Now they were obviously making a mess of their mission. 'But where? According to the consul, there are no more representatives – officially – of His Majesty's government south of here.'

For what seemed an age, the two young officers tried to outguess the missing German girl. But, try as they may, they couldn't agree on a place where they should commence their search for her. In the end, as the light started to go and the crowd of onlookers began to disperse, they gave up. As de Vere said reluctantly, 'Somehow I don't think we're really cut out for this espionage business.' To which his old friend agreed. 'Perhaps the consul will have come up with something new when we go to dine with him this evening.' He said without too much conviction.

So the two of them busied themselves with ensuring that the crew had everything they needed after a day's hard work cleaning up the battered ship. For the consul had used some of the consulate's special emergency cash to buy beer and other delicacies long vanished from British wartime tables for the men – though as usual CPO Egan objected in his Calvinist fashion, maintaining, 'Yon consul's gonna make right Jessies of 'em, feeding 'em that kind of food, gentlemen. They'll be fat and soft by the time ye get 'em back to the old country.'

But CPO Egan was wrong. They wouldn't, for they would never see 'the old country' again, sadly enough.

The two young officers left their men, their ordeal of the previous day forgotten now that they had gotten some fiery 'Nelson's Blood', their rum ration, inside them, the delightful smell of plump Dutch goose (courtesy of the consul) wafting up from the tiny gallery, singing heartily as they waited to eat the feast, *'There's a long, long trail a-winding . . . Into the land of my dreams . . . Where the nightingale is singing . . . and a pale moon beams . . .'*

It was the last that Dickie and de Vere heard of them as they pedalled through the unfamiliar cobbled streets on their rented cycles, feeling a little out of place in their ill-fitting civilian clothes, as they headed for the consul's house in the centre of the little port. In the years to come, when they were hardened senior officers, the two of them would always fall

119

silent and somehow moody when they heard the old wartime song, 'There's a Long, Long Trail A-Winding'. It was as if it reminded them not only of the deaths, but also of their own innocent, unspoiled youth which never could return.

The consul was a widower whose children were back in England in a northern boarding school. All the same, he lived well and not without the 'comforts' of married life, in all senses of the words. He ate and drank well and both were served by a woman he called my 'dear housekeeper', Mevrouw de Groot, who certainly lived up to her name. For the Dutchwoman, with her blonde hair curled in a plait around her head like a halo, was bigger than all of them. Heavy with it too. Indeed, every time she bent to serve yet another dish of steaming succulent food, it seemed to the two young open-mouthed officers that her enormous breasts bulging through her dress might cause her to topple forward at any moment.

The consul was a good host. Not only did he provide excellent food and drink, and plenty of it at that, but he kept the two younger men entertained, trying to find subjects of conversation that would interest them and carefully avoiding any reference to the missing girl; for he knew that de Vere and Dickie had made no further progress in their search and would soon have to return to the UK if they didn't wish to be interned.

Instead he talked briefly about the war in Flanders, the certainty of the new offensive that Haig and Joffre, the British and French commanders, were planning, and when that subject was exhausted and the drink was beginning to have an effect, switching to his gramophone and the popular records of that year. Indeed, once he even danced a flushed and giggling Mevrouw de Groot around the room, her heavy footing making the petrol lanterns on the table rattle dangerously under her enormous weight.

Later, while she washed up, replete with the heavy Dutch meal and not a little drunk, flushed with pleasure, well-being and enjoyment at this time out from war, the three of them lolled on the overstuffed plush furniture, singing slightly bawdy songs.

They sang of that notorious French '*Madame from*

120

*Armentières, who'd never been fucked for twenty years . . .
inky-pinky parlez-vous'*; of that *'German officer who crossed
the Rhine, out to get some women and wine'* crying as he
marched into the first French village, *'Oh landlord, where is
your daughter fair? With the lily-white tits . . . skiboo . . .
skiboo . . .'*

But in the end, as the drink and weariness took over more
and more, the middle-aged man and his two young guests lost
their interest in randy German officers and landlords' daughters with 'lily-white tits'. Instead they returned to those sentimental ditties that even the most battle-hardened 'Tommies'
of the line sang as they waited for that tragic, inevitable death.
For the trite songs seemed to fulfil an unspoken longing for
that fabled 'Blighty' where all was sweetness and light.

But on that long evening, even in fat, self-satisfied, neutral
Holland, there was no real escaping the horror of war. They
had just finished their singing and were trying to force down
the cake and sweet wine that the consul's housekeeper mistress
had just brought into the salon when it happened, and they
realized instinctively that their time out of war had come to
an abrupt end.

There was a huge bang from the direction of the quays.
The windows rattled alarmingly. Dogs began to bark hyster-
ically. Abruptly the narrow cobbled streets were full of people
shouting and crying questions. There was the tingle of the
bells of the local voluntary fire brigade. The clatter of horses'
hooves going at speed. In an instant all was confused alarm,
and with sinking heart both de Vere and Dickie Bird knew it
all had something to do with them.

# Three

'Prepare yourselves for the worst,' the consul had cried breathlessly after talking on the phone. In the corner, Mevrouw de Groot had already thrown her starched white apron over her fat face and had commenced sobbing, as if she had already known without being told that something terrible had happened.

'In the name of God!' de Vere had gasped. 'What is it?'

'The most terrible of news . . . Your boat . . .' the consul had been overcome with emotion momentarily and had been unable to continue, while Dickie had pleaded, 'What *has* happened?'

A moment later the consul had pulled himself together and had told them. 'It's your boat. The Huns have blown it up . . . blown it completely out of the water. It's a mess of shattered wood . . .'

'The crew?' de Vere had interrupted him urgently, his voice thick with emotion. '*The crew?*'

'Dead . . . all dead,' the consul had quavered. 'I've just talked to the port authorities and the local ship doctor responsible for the port medical business – they confirm the deaths. Poor devils, not much left of them, the doctor says . . . However, if it's any consolation to you, de Vere, the doctor says they all died quickly . . .' His voice broke for a moment. On the chair opposite, Mevrouw de Groot started to cry even louder, her fat shoulders heaving mightily, as if she were heartbroken.

Dickie grabbed for his civilian cap. 'We must get to the harbour at once, de Vere,' he snapped.

The consul said urgently. 'No, that is impossible. You must stay here. I shall deal with—'

'Why man?' de Vere cried angrily. 'They are our people . . . It's our duty.'

'I understand,' the consul responded, his voice clearly indicating that the official was in control of himself again. 'But that would be too dangerous. You might be risking your lives to appear in public under the circumstances.'

'How do you mean?'

'It is obvious that you were part of the Huns' target, not only your poor chaps. They unfortunately were victims of a bomb that was really meant for you, de Vere. Do you understand now?'

Crestfallen and even humbled now, he had answered that he did, feeling a sudden sense of guilt that old CPO Egan and the 'Scouse git' Ferguson had given their lives for him. They and the rest, ordinary lower-deck ratings, had died for something that had been really beyond their ken. 'So, what can we do now?'

'Stay put. I shall work out something for the two of you, de Vere. But there is one thing you can know now. You must be clear of Dordrecht and on your way out of this country – I don't know how just at this moment – before a new dawn.' The two of them had been left staring at each other in blank bewilderment, while on her chair the fat housekeeper had sobbed, sobbed and sobbed . . .

Now, this new day, they were well on their way to Utrecht in a first-class compartment, well supplied with money from the consul's 'slush fund' and fitted up in new clothes, better suited to young men who could travel first class and eat an expensive Dutch breakfast of cheese, ham and freshly baked rolls, especially brought to the train from the station buffet by a uniformed railway employee.

Not that they did much justice to the typically hearty Dutch breakfast. They had little appetite. The shock of knowing that their whole crew had been murdered by unknown Huns was too great still. But already they *were* beginning to attempt to put two and two together.

The consul had been right, of course. The enemy agents had intended to kill them as well as the unsuspecting men of the lower deck. Why? Because obviously they were after the missing girl. It was clear, too, that the Germans were still after her too, and that they must have traced her progress southwards at least as far as Dordrecht. By blowing up the ship and her crew, they had hoped to prevent her making contact with them or vice versa.

'I have a rough-and-ready plan for you both,' the consul had said as he had parted from them in the taxi, its curtains drawn tightly as it parked by the rear entrance to the Dordrecht station. 'There are several little ports down along the coast, from which certain dubious characters ship people back and forth across the sea to England, or into Belgium or Northern France, in exchange for coin of the realm.' He had made the continental gesture of counting notes with his forefinger and thumb. 'With a bit of luck we can get you safely out of the country in the next forty-eight hours or so.'

'But what about the job for which we were sent to the Netherlands?' de Vere had objected. 'What about the girl?'

'Yes,' Dickie Bird had added stoutly. 'I mean, we owe that to the poor dead boys of our crew. Their lives were destroyed on account of your mission, consul. We can't just let them down like that. Nor can we let the damned murdering Huns frighten us off.'

'My concern is your safety,' the consul had answered softly, as if that was the end of the matter. 'Nothing else, gentlemen.'

But it wasn't the end of the matter for the two young men. As the train rolled slowly southwards along the coast and then inland after leaving Utrecht, their anger rose. It replaced the numbed sadness caused by the shock of the night's tragic event.

As de Vere expressed it, chewing idly on one of the Dutch cheese rolls and wondering how a civilized nation could eat so much cheese in the early hours – but then he told himself the Dutch seemed to eat raw herrings out of a barrel for the rest of the day, didn't they. 'Let's assume that the consul does find us a boat to get us out of the Netherlands, Dickie, and we've got the sovereigns from him to pay for it.' He touched his new money belt filled with the coins the consul had given him before they had parted. 'We can delay the departure of that boat as we wish.'

'I suppose so,' Dickie said without too much interest.

'Well then, if that's the case, why don't we take the girl with us. That would please C no end.'

Dickie sniffed. 'We've got to find her first, old bean.'

'I know,' de Vere answered a little miserably.

'And remember, we don't even speak the lingo.'

'My sainted aunt, Dickie, don't pile on the agony, please. But we have money now, remember, plenty of it. We can buy people who speak the language and we can buy information.'

'Agreed. In that sense we're better off. But where do we start with all our new resources, eh?'

'I've been thinking about that since we left Dordrecht, Dickie. This is what I've come up with. She can't go north – there's nowhere to go to. She can't go east for obvious reasons. She can't even go south-east, because of Imperial German conquests. That leaves south.'

'I'll buy that. Still, that's a large area all the same.'

'Certainly, Dickie. But we can narrow it down further. I am assuming that she'll have little money left, so she won't be in a position to use a boat and the coast for an escape like we are supposed to do. That leaves . . .?'

Dickie looked startled. 'That leaves Belgium, the strip that's not occupied by the Huns. But, de Vere, there she risks falling into the hands of the very people who are looking for her.'

'Exactly. But it means, too, that we can narrow down the places where she might take that risk.'

'How?'

'By the ways that these people who smuggle agents and the like back and forth use as secure routes. There cannot be too many of them.'

'All right, but still it's going to be difficult. I mean, you can't go up to anyone in the street and say, "I say, old chap, do you smuggle bodies across the frontier sort of thing" can you? You've got to find your smuggler first and I don't think that's going to be easy.'

'But we've got to try for the sake of those chaps of ours.' Suddenly de Vere, with his background and training not normally an emotional person, was overcome by a tremendous sense of grief. He closed his eyes swiftly in the middle of his sentence. But not quick enough for Dickie not to see the tears welling up in his eyes. Hurriedly Dickie looked away at the flat wet Dutch landscape passing slowly outside the carriage window. Thus they travelled the rest of the way in a kind of embarrassed silence, bound in an unspoken agreement not to mention the subject of what was to come until they were faced with it.

The little fishing and ferry port of Vlissingen on the peninsula of Zuid Beveland was packed. Although the former ferry line from the town the English knew as Flushing to Harwich across the North Sea was virtually closed – the German U-boats lurking off the British coast were too dangerous and the herring fishing was limited to Dutch territorial waters, there was plenty of shipping about. The ferries plying their trade across the Scheldt from Vlissingen to Breskens on the mainland some four miles away were still busy. For it was obvious to the two Englishmen who emerged from the little railway station, slightly puzzled about what they should do next, that a large number of civilians of all classes were eager to get to the opposite side of the great estuary. Some, like typical prosperous businessmen in suits, carrying the inevitable briefcases – which Dickie opined didn't carry important papers, 'but those damned cheese and ham sandwiches that the Dutch seem to eat all the time' – were obviously going about their legitimate business purposes.

Others, however, looked definitely shady: men in flashy suits carrying heavy bulging cheap cardboard suitcases, which obviously contained black-market goods to be smuggled into German-occupied Belgium. It was these individuals who the two Englishmen eyed curiously in the hope that one of them might turn out to be the local smuggler they needed. But both businessmen and crooks appeared to be in such a great hurry that they hesitated to stop one of them. In fact, as de Vere told himself, what would they say to anyone they picked out and stopped?

But in the event both classes hurrying towards the Scheldt ferries were outnumbered by the mass of what appeared to be refugees or locals from across the water who had been forced out of their homes by the police and brought to

Vlissingen in order not to offend the German occupiers of Belgium. Men, women and children, most of them wearing wooden clogs, their worldly goods carried in bags made of old carpets or in white pillowcases slung over their shoulders, these Dutch refugees wandered around aimlessly or watched idly as the brawny local fishwives, their skirts tucked into knee-length red bloomers, sleeves rolled up their stout arms as they gutted the newly caught herrings, pausing only to curse the gulls which shrieked and dived down on them, more often than not depositing white blobs of shit on the women and their fish.

Indeed, at first it seemed pretty hopeless to the newcomers to even start their mission. So they did what they would have done if they had been faced by a similar problem back in their own country: they went into the nearest bar, filled with fishermen drinking scalding tea punch, laced with rum, and ordered two *genevers*. And there they sat, a little miserably, listening to the organ music from outside, staring at nothing.

They had made the right choice. They hadn't long to wait in the crowded, smoke-filled bar with its blowsy barmaid serving hot punch as rapidly as she could keep the big black kettle on the stove in the corner boiling. Some five minutes after they had ventured inside, a small smiling man in a kind of purple tweed suit that had never been tailored on the other side of the North Sea approached their table, bowed and clicked his heels together in a manner totally out of place in the fisherman's bar and snapped, 'My card, English gentlemen.'

That 'English gentlemen' startled them somewhat. Later they would ask themselves if it had been so blindingly obvious that they were English? But then they had no time to consider the matter, for as they turned the grubby card over to read the name – '*Dirk Smits, Import–Export*' – the smiling little man in the purple tweed suit asked, 'How do I you help?'

Without thinking, Dickie answered, 'We're looking for a woman, Mr – er – Smits.'

The little man smiled broadly, revealing the two gold teeth at either side of his mouth, of which he was obviously proud, and said, 'Gentlemen, that is not heavy. I shall oblige you.'

Without further words, he sat down next to them and, snapping his fingers at the hard-pressed fat barmaid, cried, 'Three grogs for the Englishmen and me, myself . . .'

They had found their smuggler.

# Four

Twice Sussi von Hoofstra-Mecklenburg had dodged the tough Dutch police in their black uniforms trying to take the refugees from the frontier off the streets of the port and into the dreadful shanty towns, which were called grandly 'relocation camps'. However, she had managed to join the queues outside the soup kitchens and, without showing her Dutch identity card, which she thought would give her away, quell her hunger with a bowl of thick lentil soup and a hunk of bread, washed down with weak peppermint tea; for tea was becoming very expensive in that country.

Her money had virtually run out now, and the soup, twice a day, kept her going. She had discovered a rat-infested shed near the ferry docks, all but abandoned now, where she could sleep. She had learned too about the smuggling routes that led across the Scheldt to Breskens and from there to the former seaside resorts of Knokke-Heist, which weren't far from where the little Belgian Army under their soldier-king Albert still held out against the German invaders. From there, Sussi guessed, the Belgians would be supplied by the English over the water.

By now she knew it wouldn't be too difficult to stow away for the ten minute trip across the Scheldt in the ferry; it was always very crowded and no one seemed to worry about the fare. So that was no problem. Identity checks were slack too. The Dutch conscript soldiers were idle and time was too short for them to look at everyone's identity card. The problem was to work one's way from Knokke-Heist along the coastal road into the Belgian-held part of the coast. For although the details were unclear to her, it was pretty obvious that the Imperial German Army, which had failed to break through the survivors of the retreating Belgian Army in the centre, would be attempting to nibble their way forward on either flank. On the Belgians' left flank, the coastal road from Knokke-Heist was the obvious route, a main road along which they could deploy their massive, horse-drawn artillery. Indeed, the day before, she had seen an ambulance unit unloading wounded Belgian soldiers in Vlissingen from the other side of the Scheldt; and it was obvious how they had landed in Dutch territory, when the Dutch authorities were attempting to limit the numbers of their own people in the area. They had sought refuge in Holland and the Dutch had not been in a moral position to turn back wounded Belgian soldiers, who spoke the same language as they did, into the hands of the German invaders.

Now, as she ladled down her second potato soup of the day, wishing she could consume all the bread ration in one go, but knowing she'd have to save a hunk for the night, she only became aware of the little man in the purple tweed suit when it was too late to dodge him. Despite her shabby, unkempt appearance – she hadn't been able to take a bath for nearly a week now – he bowed like the men had done when she had been a regular at the Dutch royal court. He said first in Dutch and then – surprisingly – in heavily accented German, 'My name is Smits, *Gnädige Frau* . . . I have some English friends who would like to meet you . . . Over there in the Inn.' The little man raised a dirty forefinger and pointed to the noisy tavern opposite.

There, two young men in smart city suits sat on the chairs outside, obviously trying to escape the fug and noise of the interior, drinking glasses of beer.

For a moment their faces meant nothing to her. Then she remembered them from that foggy night on the Frisian island and her heart leapt with a strange mixture of apprehension and relief. They were the English agents and they wanted her. But for what purpose? Would it be to hand over her person to the Dutch authorities as an illegal immigrant? The Dutch weren't too fond of the English military, mainly because of the latter's activities against their cousins, the Dutch-speaking Boers, in the South African War of a decade and a half before.

130

Had they come to help her because they knew she had been prepared to give them information?

Before she had time to ponder the question more thoroughly, the man in the purple suit said, 'We must be off the streets before curfew, *Gnädige Frau.* Fear not,' he added with a bold look, as if he were prepared to defend her and her honour to the death, 'I shall protect you. *Bitte, meine Dame.*' He swept out his arm, revealing he was not wearing cuffs to his grubby white shirt, and bowed low. Hardly knowing that she was doing so, Sussi put down her metal soup bowl and followed him . . .

The meeting was awkward. It was not merely that the girl was German; it was that such a pretty girl had once attempted to kill them by luring the two young midshipmen of those pre-war days into a trap. Smits seemed, however, totally unaware of the awkwardness and the stilted conversation. He danced back and forth, bringing drinks, which she refused, and a thick cheese sandwich which she didn't; peering out of the window to check whether they were being observed; holding his dirty finger to his lips in warning if he felt they were talking too loudly.

It was only when they started to discuss her situation – and their participation in what would turn out really to be an escape from neutral Holland – that the little man in the purple tweed suit joined in the conversation. Without being asked, he sat down next to the great white tiled oven, took a drink from her untouched beer and said carefully. 'It will not be easy.'

The two young officers nodded their agreement, while she remained thoughtful and silent, head bent, as if she were thinking about what the little Dutchman, if he were a Dutchman, had just said.

'It will be difficult enough crossing the border,' Smits went on. 'But that is not the end, you understand, when you come to the Belgians.'

Dickie, now puzzled, as was his old comrade, asked, 'But why? Then we have reached the lines of our Allies, our friends. We are fighting on the same side. They will help us all to get to England.

For the first time, Smit's weaselly face showed something other than greed. A moment later they realized it was contempt, even anger at them. 'Allies . . . friends!' He spat on the sawdust-covered floor of the little inn. 'You are not safe with the Belgians . . . not with Belgian officers, *verdomme!*'

'How do you mean?' de Vere asked carefully.

'You English!' Smits hissed. 'You think that King Albert of *poor Belgium* –' he emphasized the words contemptuously, dark eyes blazing now – 'is so brave, fighting the *Moffen.*' He took a hearty drink of the fizzy weak beer and belched. 'Well, he isn't. If that brave Albert of yours had his way, he'd make peace with the Germans this day and sacrifice his Flemings to them.'

De Vere ignored the little smuggler's sudden eloquence. Later he told himself that the little man sounded at that moment like some 'frock' standing on a soapbox at the hustings. 'We think the Belgian King is brave, trying to hold back the German Army like he does.'

'Does?' Smits echoed, not caring just how loud he was now. 'Back in fourteen, he gave up the fight pretty damn quick. Now he lives at de Panne on the French frontier – the last house in Belgium. You English have protected him twice at Ypres. You lose many thousands of your soldiers. Did Albert help?' Again he spat scornfully in the sawdust. 'No, he did not. Since fourteen all he has done is to talk to the *Moffen* secretly through his German brother-in-law. He wants peace with the Germans. Your brave Albert, he don't like the English one bit. He—'

'All right; all right,' Dickie interrupted Smits' angry flow of words. 'Why are you telling us this, Herr Smits?'

The little man in the purple tweed suit drew himself up to his full five foot and answered, 'Because I am a Flemish patriot. This Albert of yours don't care about us. We are just – what you call them in that game, chess . . .?'

'Pawn,' Dickie volunteered. He flashed a quick look at de Vere and said out of the side of his mouth, 'Crikey, this is a turn-up for the books. A patriot and smuggler.'

The little man's English might well have been slightly fractured, but he caught the remark swiftly enough. He said

132

proudly, 'Yes, I am. I will help you because of money and because when – *if* – you get back to England you tell them what I tell you of that king.'

It was then that Sussi von Hoofstra-Mecklenburg took part in the conversation for the first time. Speaking in her excellent English, she said, 'I understand you, Herr Smits. But our position is this: we, officially enemies, are in danger, as you say, not from my own people, the Germans, but the supposed allies of these two young gentlemen-officers here?'

Smits gave a brief smile, showing those gold teeth of his, and said, 'Yes,' while de Vere and Dickie looked impressed at the way in which the girl had expressed the situation so succinctly. 'We shall trust no one?'

Again Smits answered, 'Yes.'

For a moment or two there was silence at the wooden table, broken only by the sound of a Dutch organ, all drums and cymbals, from outside on the quay.

In the end, de Vere broke it with, 'So we know now where we stand. Thank you, Fräulein.' He added one of his few words of German to make her feel more at ease. 'You expressed it well.' He turned to Smits. 'Well, Mr Smits, you are our guide, I hope.' He touched his money belt significantly. Smit's look brightened at the gesture; patriotism was all well and good, but obviously money was important to him as well.

'Yessir. I shall guide you.'

'So, when do we start?'

'This night, sir. We catch the last ferry across the Scheldt before the curfew.'

'Why at night?'

'Because by then the soldiers will be tired and want to be off-duty. And the police –' he made that gesture with finger and thumb, indicating money changing hands – 'they have bribes. They want *genever* and certain ladies.' Smits actually blushed and bowed slightly to Sussi. 'You forgive, gracious lady.'

'I forgive,' Sussi said, and for the first time since they had known her, Sussi von Hoofstra-Mecklenburg actually smiled, and de Vere realized that although she was the enemy, one who had tried to kill him, he liked her, perhaps more.

Swiftly the little man in the purple suit sketched in what his rough-and-ready plan for boarding the ferry to the other side of the Scheldt was to be, ending with the warning, 'You are not to be seen with me, gentlemen and gracious lady. I am known.'

De Vere told himself he probably was. By the police. But he kept his thoughts to himself. He nodded his understanding and took a handful of guilders to pay. Hastily Smits shook his head. 'Put away – quick!' he hissed. 'Dangerous. Let nobody see you with money here. You might not live.'

And with that curious warning, they parted, the two young men and the girl, while Smits paid their bill, for some reason known only to himself. After they disappeared around the door into the noisy quayside, now filling with stout, tipsy whores come to ply their trade with the sailors, the police and those of the shabby soldier conscripts who could afford to pay for a couple of minutes of hurried sexual excitement up against the nearest dark wall, Smits lingered in the waterfront cafe.

He did not linger long, however. Almost immediately a heavy-set figure busy doing up his flies came in from the outside '*cour*', the little bowl-shaped urinal attached to the back wall of the cafe. 'Well?' he demanded, picking up his glass of beer again. 'Is it her and the English?' His tone was that of someone used to giving orders and having them obeyed.

'*Jawohl, Herr Hauptmann!*' Smits replied in military style, as if he were some new recruit to the Imperial German Army.

'*Verfluchte Idiot!*' the German snapped. 'Not so loud. And don't speak German, for God's sake. *De Vlaams, ja?*'

Smits nodded hurriedly and continued the little conversation in his native Flemish. 'Yes, they are the people you are looking for. I knew that as soon as I spotted them. The English, they are so easy—'

'Your plan?' the German captain cut him off sharply.

'Take them across and lose them in your lines. It should not be difficult. And if they won't come voluntarily, well –' he rapped the bulge in the right pocket of that awful suit of his – 'I shall make them.'

'Good, Smits. You shall be rewarded. And remember, you

are doing this, not just for the money, but for the future of your native country, Flanders.'

Smits' eyes lit up. 'I remember, sir.'

'Well, you can go now.'

'Thank you, sir.'

For a little while the German captain toyed with his weak, fizzy beer thoughtfully. He had worked with Smits for a long while now. He knew the little Fleming as a petty crook, who maintained, however, that he was also a Flemish patriot who wanted to see his people 'freed' from the 'yoke' of the French-speaking ruling Walloons*. But still he didn't quite trust this self-proclaimed Flemish patriotism. One day the Fleming pack would be totally under German control and then those dirty peasants would really learn what German discipline and order meant. He drained the last of the rotten Belgian beer and decided there and then that Smits would have to be closely watched once he reached the other side of the Scheldt with his English and the German woman traitor.

---

* Belgium then was divided into a Flemish underclass and a ruling Walloon class.

# Five

They arrived on the other side of the great estuary without incident. By then it was completely dark, but to the east, where the German positions lay in front of the flooded lowlands which shielded the Belgian defenders from attack to a depth of a mile or so, the sky was lit up by the silent pink flashes of gunfire. Occasionally, too, where the two fronts were closer together, star shells rose into the sky, giving it a garish silver flickering hue. It was nervous sentries trying to ascertain whether the enemy out there in no-man's land was going to attack.

But the closeness of the frontier did not seem to disturb the black marketeers, some of them even pulling little carts piled high with their precious wares, or transporting them on the backs of great hulking dogs which had had their tongues severed to prevent them from barking. In one case, Dickie and de Vere were surprised to see a man herding a group of grunting pigs intended for some black marketeer's backyard.

'They go different ways,' Smits explained, as he waited for most of his fellow 'professionals' to disperse. 'It is better. Too many of them going one way.' He shrugged expressively. 'The *Moffen* –' he meant the Germans – 'catch. They know the ways well enough by now.'

'But we're not yet at the Dutch-Belgian border,' Dickie objected.

Smits pulled down the side of one eye in a kind of warning. 'Wooden eye, be careful the German, he say. They have their spies on this side of the border as well.'

De Vere nodded his head in understanding. 'That stands to reason. But what about us?'

'We have a special way,' Smits said, obviously pleased

136

with his own cunning. 'We go straight towards the *Moffen* front.'

In the darkness, de Vere felt the girl suddenly grip his upper arm tightly, as if in fear, and Dickie said, 'I say, old sport, that seems a bit thick. Ain't that a bit risky?'

'No, sir. The *Moffen* think we come to do dirty business with them. They can take us when they want. We are no problem.' He grinned again and, in the darkness, illuminated by the silver light of another burst of star shells over the front, they could see his gold teeth glittering.

'But when do we turn and head for the Belgies?' Dickie persisted. 'The front, they tell me back home, is always very confusing. No landmarks to speak of etc. People are always wandering off and getting lost.'

'Not Dirk Smits, sir,' the little man replied proudly. 'I know the front like back of my arm.'

'Well, if that's the case –' de Vere repressed a grin at the Fleming's fractured English – 'you'd better – like jolly old Shakespeare's McDuff – lead on. Time's a-passing.'

Smits obeyed with alacrity. He seemed to know what he was about. For the next hour or so, without rest, he led them down a series of narrow cobbled country roads, through sleeping white-painted villages, the shutters of the little one-story houses tightly closed and with no sound, human or animal, coming from them; though the smell of the raw minced beef the locals ate, and the sweet smell of cows told them that the places were still inhabited all right.

But gradually, as the tiny road gave way to muddy tracks between fields that hadn't been tended for a long time, and which were marked by great brown shell holes, they were approaching the frontier and the German line beyond. Indeed, by craning their heads into the cool night breeze, they could hear the faint rattle of machine guns to the south-east, and what might have been the obscene belch of trench mortars. It was clear that they were near enough to note some company action of one sort or another.

It was about then, with the luminous dial of Dickie's watch showing two o'clock, that Smits ordered a rest. He had obviously been this way before, because he stopped in

137

front of what they had taken for a haystack, but which was, in reality, a half-ruined barn, still smelling of the acrid burnt gunpowder which had taken most of its roof off. 'Half an hour,' he ordered. 'There is some water – good water – in the pail in the corner. Drink it. You will need liquid. Rest too. We won't stop after this.' He prepared to turn and head off up the rough farm track to the left of the barn. Hastily de Vere snapped, 'Where are you going, Herr Smits?'

'Do not worry,' Smits appeased him. 'I looky-looky . . . For *Moffen* before we start. The *Moffen* are cunning and dangerous.'

'You don't have to tell us that,' de Vere said. Then he remembered the girl, who had remained silent for most of the time since they had left the ferry. He pressed her hand hastily, hardly aware of what he was doing, but still wanting to reassure her that he didn't mean her in particular.

To his surprise, she returned the pressure. He felt himself flush with a mixture of embarrassment and sexual excitment, and tried to take his hand away. But she wouldn't let him. Thus they remained standing there in the glowing darkness hand in hand while de Vere wondered what he should – could – do about this strange turn of events.

Smits now vanished into the night, while they slumped gratefully into the mouldy, smelly hay of the barn, de Vere and Sussi still holding hands. Hardly had their heads touched the ground than they were asleep like lovers.

Smits, on the other hand, was fully awake and keenly alert as he ventured ever closer to the sound of the firing. He was playing a double game, a very dangerous one, and he knew it. Not only did he risk being shot by the *Moffen* for deceiving them, but also by his fellow Belgians, especially if they belonged to the hated Walloons and their haughty, arrogant aristocratic officers.

Smits had been recalled to his infantry regiment the day that the Germans had crossed the frontier into Belgium and breached the little kingdom's neutrality. He had returned to the old 18th barracks in Leuven – he had always refused to use the French name for the Flemish city, Louvain. Nothing had changed there, save that their officers, all Walloons, had seemed more arrogant than ever.

As before, when he had been an eighteen-year-old conscript there back in '12, a farm boy who had once been the proud possessor of real leather boots, he had been forced back into wearing wooden clogs, dressed in the shabby, ill-fitting uniform of the Belgian infantry and equipped with a rifle that dated back to the late nineteenth century. He could have tolerated all that, even the lousy food, for he was a poor farm boy from Flanders, used to hardship. But he had grown more politically aware since he had first been a soldier and now he could not bear the arrogance of the Walloon officers in their tailored uniforms and silver swords, plus the smell of expensive eau-de cologne that they always gave off.

From the *commandant* in charge of his company of fellow Flemings, down to the youngest, pimply *sous-leutnant* straight from Brussels University or the Sorbonne, not one of them seemed to speak *de Vlaams*. Instead they bellowed at the young soldiers in French, although they must have known their rank and file spoke no more than a word or two of the language. When the men didn't understand, the officers struck them with the scabbards of their swords and called them 'filthy Flemish clodhoppers', and the middle-aged *commandant*, who had learned his trade – and perversions – slaughtering and seducing blacks in the Belgian Congo, had summoned offenders to his quarters and had raped them with not a word being spoken.

On August 26th 1914, when the regiment had fallen back to Brussels, some twenty kilometres away, they had found the capital abandoned and King Albert and his staff in full flight westwards to the coast – and France as a final refuge. The empty capital had been full of rumours. It was said that King Albert would not join in the fight on the side of the Allies, who were now arriving in force to save 'poor little Belgium'. Indeed, a couple of days later the King had abandoned Ypres to its fate and the Tommies had been forced to re-take it for him at a cost of 50,000 casualties.

Smits, the Flemish patriot, had not been particularly concerned at King Albert's lack of resistance. What *had* concerned him that hot August had been the rumours

139

circulating in Brussels that the King was prepared to make peace with the Germans. But The *Moffen* had insisted that Flanders should come under their control. The King had baulked at that. Still, he had kept secret talks going with the Germans, even though the English, in particular, were fighting all out to save his kingdom for him. How could a king give away a people, or even contemplate doing so just like that, Smits had asked himself angrily. Were the Flemings simply animals to be given to the highest bidder?

That August, Smits had deserted like so many other Flemings, adopted the identity of a man from his village who had been killed in action, and had taken up the dirty business of smuggling in goods and human beings from Holland, while at the same time working actively to ensure that the Flemish people would gain their independence in one shape or form once the war was over.

He knew, naturally, that the Germans would offer them independence from the Walloons, at least for *now*. But they couldn't be trusted. The Germans simply wanted to weaken the little country which was now nominally on the Allied side. Once the *Moffen* had won the war, he knew things would be different. The Flemings would have exchanged one master who spoke a foreign tongue for another.

As the months and the years had passed, with the war dragging on miserably, Smits, when he had time to think of it, had started to conclude that perhaps the English might be a better bet, as far as his own people were concerned. They had been the ones back in the last century who had ensured Belgium's freedom. He was no particular friend of the English and their 'milords', and indeed their own royal house was related to Albert and his lot. Still, they did believe in liberty and freedom, at least as far as Europe was concerned. In the end, as 1914 had given way to 1915, he had decided that he ought to do his best for the English wherever he came across them, and in these last few months he had smuggled scores of English Tommies who had been left behind during the great retreat from Bergen[*].

[*] *Mons* in French.

Now he was helping two English milords who were obvi-ously more important than the humble Tommy. Why else should the Germans think them so important? Even German Intelligence, in the shape of Herr Hauptmann Scherz, whom he had met hours before, had been urging him to ever greater efforts to ensure that the English milords fell into their trap.

Abruptly, as the firing to the south grew ever louder and he realized that the Germans were putting in a large-scale night attack, one that might be the start of a new *Moffen* offensive against that traitor Albert, he made his decision.

He'd head for the Belgian front and contact the British Intelligence officers, who he knew were attached to Albert's force. Not only would they give him those precious 'Horsemen of St George' – he meant gold sovereigns – they would regard him as a friend of their native country; and in the years to come, he and his oppressed people would need all the friends they could find.

But there was no time to be lost. The level of noise was rising steadily, and the green and red distress flares were sailing into the sky over the Belgian positions. The Germans were on the move, and they could well be coming in his direction. He had to get himself and his 'clients' out of the way without further delay.

# Six

General der Infanterie Horst von Dung was an angry man. He had been trying for over a month now to get permission for his long-planned attack on the Belgian left flank along the coast. By attacking the enemy's left flank, he thought he could avoid a costly assault over the flooded meadows in front of the Belgian defences. A water assault would have involved not only more engineers, bridging equipment, even the assistance of the Imperial Navy etc, but it would have also meant warning the Belgians that his army was on the attack. And by now the paunchy, red-faced general knew from experience the effect a few well-sited and determined machine-gunners could have on a massed infantry attack.

Time and time again, however, his attack had been cancelled from Imperial Headquarters way back in the Belgian resort town of Spa. There the flunkies and staff officers had kept reassuring him that he might not have to attack at all. Negotiations were underway and it was highly likely that the Belgians under their King Albert of the German Saxe-Coburg dynasty would end this fraternal struggle by surrendering. In the meantime, von Dung had countered, the English were pouring more and more troops into the general area, including a battalion commanded by no less a person than that arch-enemy of Germany, the English politician Winston Churchill.

Now, when he had almost achieved fame by knocking Belgium, or what was left of it, out of the war (for, under the English pressure caused by the arrival of so many of their soldiers, Imperial HQ had sanctioned his attack), suddenly new restrictions had been placed on his army. He was to broaden and thus weaken the flank attack, all for the sake of some damned game of spies. As he had raged to his smart-

142

eyed chief-of-staff when the latter had brought him the latest signal from Imperial Headquarters, 'What have spies got to do with my infantry attack? And to cap it all, at the bequest of those boys in blue who have been sitting in the safety of their tin cans in harbour for most of the war?' For the signal had been countersigned by no less a person than the head of the German High Seas Fleet, Admiral von Scheer. 'They must be crazy up there at Spa.'

His chief-of-staff had sighed like a man sorely tried. 'Who knows what goes on in the heads of staff officers, general. Perhaps they read too many books,' he added.

'Or drink too much damned French champagne,' General der Infanterie von Dung had snorted. 'It addles their brains.'

In the end, however, the two of them had been forced to obey the strange and apparently very urgent directive. With his usual efficiency the chief-of-staff had extended the area of the left flank assault. But he hadn't used any of the army's storm battalions. Instead he had placed two battalions of *Landsturm* – middle-aged, second-class troops – in strung-out positions all the way up to within a hundred metres of the main coastal road to de Panne, held by the Belgians. As he had exclaimed to his angry commander, 'The two *Lendsturm* battle formations are no great loss, *Herr General*. Most of them will probably be busy at this very moment losing their false teeth and trusses so that they can't be forced to go into action. Or getting lost in some whore's bedroom.'

But if the chief-of-staff had hoped he'd make the general smile at his comment, he was mistaken. The general had instead snapped, 'If we catch anyone carrying on like that in my army, I'll have the bugger shot out of hand – without a shitting trial!'

Naturally, neither Smits nor the three fugitives knew anything of the German attack or the alteration to the enemy plan which would affect them. Even when they found out later, they could hardly believe that the Germans would change their intentions so drastically in order to catch the girl and themselves. As Dickie said, 'I know we're fully fledged sub-lieutenants in His Majesty's Royal Navy now, but we're not that important, are we?' No one answered that particular question.

But as the night progressed, and the marshy fields of Flanders seemed filled with strange noises, human and animal, Smits became increasingly worried, repeatedly saying, in that fractured English of his, 'There is something in the air . . . I smell.' And here he would sniff the night air.

Dickie repressed his desire to comment on Smits' assertion that 'I smell'. Then he thought the expression funny; later he wouldn't find it one bit funny.

Now it was four o'clock and they were slogging their way through a ploughed field turned into muddy quagmire by the rain and some previous artillery bombardment. The mud, glue-like and tenacious, clung to their boots and made every step hard work. Twice the girl lost her shoes and once de Vere had to carry her, shoes in hand, over a particularly difficult spot, feeling her warm body in his hands for the first time. Then for a few minutes he forgot the strain and enjoyed that delightful body contact, sensing a kind of sexual excitement, despite the danger and the physical hardship.

Half an hour later it became clear even to the novices of land warfare that they had found themselves in some kind of impending attack. Now flares were rising on all sides in profusion, colouring the night sky with their garish hues. Machine guns had commenced rattling to the south, and once they heard the whinnying of horses and an angry voice crying in German, '*He-rupp! Los, ihr Pferde!*' followed by the cracking of a whip and the rumble of some heavy cart or cannon being pulled out of mud and on to a cobbled country track. They didn't need Sussi's warning that 'They're German and they're going in the same direction as we are' to know what that meant. The Huns were attacking and they had become mixed in that attack.

Smits reacted at once. 'We must go faster,' he urged, voice lower. 'Soon there will be trouble.' And the little man in the purple tweed suit, now mired up to the knees in grey thick Flanders mud, was not wrong. That trouble was almost about to begin.

A tremendous roar. It was as if the door of some gigantic blast furnace had just been flung open. Immediately to the escapees' left, the sky turned a frightening scarlet. Even at that distance the tremendous heat made them gasp and fight for breath as it tore the very air out of their lungs. They stopped in their tracks. That man-made hellfire brooked no other reaction. In awed wonder they stared in silence at the transformed heavens. How was it possible? What had happened? Mesmerized, they didn't even have the strength to flee, though their minds told them urgently they should. Not for long, however.

A moment later that sudden hellfire was followed by a frightening hush. It was like an express rushing through a deserted midnight station at a hundred miles an hour. Abruptly the world fell apart. Shells screamed and whistled shrilly over the troops waiting in their trenches and dugouts, their fixed bayonets gleaming in that awesome light as if dipped in blood.

The shells burst along the Belgian frontline. Some missed their targets. Instead the shells plunged into the water defences, the flooded meadows in front of the Belgian trenches. Great geysers of whirling white water shot into the air. Others hit the reserve dumps of ammunition. The ammo exploded. Bullets and shells zig-zagged into the night sky in crazy profusion and burst green, red and silver. It was like some demented Guy Fawkes' fireworks display.

The din was tremendous. Smits shouted instructions at the others. They couldn't hear him. They could hardly breathe. The very air was sucked out of their lungs by the constant detonations. The hot blast whipped their shocked, ashen faces from side to side like blows from a flabby hand. Automatically the two sailors opened their mouths to prevent their eardrums from being burst. On and on the hell of that initial tremendous bombardment went.

De Vere grabbed the girl's hand hard. '*Run!*' he yelled at the top of his voice. Whether she heard or not he didn't know. But he pulled with all his strength, jerking her forward through the mud. She started to run, as if pursued by the Devil himself. The others followed suit. Now they were running for their lives. They zig-zagged to and fro, dodging the red-hot shards of gleaming shell fragments, jumping over fresh, smoking shell holes like the work of some gigantic mole. Once the four of them stumbled and fell into a smoking pit, filled with the acrid fumes of burnt cordite. For a moment they were blinded. The next their eyes cleared. The girl shrieked, '*Herr Gett!*' Smits breathed out sharply. Dickie recoiled with, 'Oh, in heaven's name!' There were dead Belgian soldiers plastered on the other side of the hole, bodies bloody and shattered, all of them minus their heads. Frantically they clawed their way out and went on running forward blindly, heading they knew not where, save to get away from the horrors of that pit of death and mutilation.

But there was no end to the horrors of that battlefield. Now the fugitives were scrambling through the rusty barbed wire of the Belgians' first line of defence. Fortunately, the German gunners' fire had been accurate. They had broken the wire virtually everywhere, ready for the assaulting infantry to follow through once that terrible barrage had moved on. Indeed, they had done their deadly work all too well. There were dead Belgian observers and forward artillery spotters spiked on the shattered wire everywhere. They were attached to the rusting strands, arms outstretched on the bloody, cruel barbs like latterday Christs on a cross.

But the men knew there was no time to be squeamish, though the girl recoiled in horror at having to brush by those crucified men. Every moment they spent out on the open battlefield spelled danger, perhaps sudden death. De Vere pushed her forward. She brushed by a dead Belgian and repressed a scream just in time, as he seemed to come alive again and slowly started to sink from the wire which held him.

But now, after what seemed an eternity, the barrage began to lift. It was creeping forward, its progress marked every fifty metres or so by a signal shell exploding in a burst of bright yellow smoke to indicate to the German gunners that they had reached the end of that particular objective. Now the rain of death hit the Belgians' second support trench, where they kept their reserves. In the quietening of the barrage they could hear the yells and fierce cries of the German infantry, the shrill whistles of their officers, the trumpet calls of their buglers as they went over the top and charged forward. Believing that the first Belgian line of defence would have been wiped out by that tremendous bombardment, and wild with a bellyful of cheap schnapps, they ran happily to their deaths.

For, as always in these attacks, some of the defenders had survived that rain of steel from the sky. They had had months to build their fortifications. Now, from the deep dugouts which had survived, the machine-gunners sprang to their parapets. Faces fierce, almost animal in their desire for revenge for this cruel indignity which had been forced upon their minds and bodies and had slaughtered so many of their comrades, they swung their machine guns back and forth.

There was no need to aim. The German infantry were stumbling and staggering forward in tight-packed lines, urged on by their officers and NCOs wielding their swords and ceremonial dirks, crying, '*Deutschland über Alles!*' – straight into that murderous fire. The whole first Line vanished in an instant, as if it had never even existed. Still the second one came on, stumbling and falling over the twitching bodies of their dying comrades. At close range the Belgian bullets smacked into their bodies, the impact twirling them round like clumsy ballet dancers, the fronts of their field-grey tunics flushed an instant scarlet. Scores of them, hundreds, piled up in front of the machine-gun pits like mounds of human offal, so that the crazed Belgian gunners had to reach out and push away the bodies in order to keep their fields of fire free.

But now the flight of the escapees slackened. They still had to contend with the Germans' creeping barrage smacking into the line to their front. But they no longer needed to fear the German follow-up. The enemy was being held. Their rear was free.

Still Smits, now in the lead, was cautious. He guessed that the men holding the second line and waiting tensely for the German infantry to appear would be trigger-happy. Their motto under such circumstances would be: shoot first and ask questions afterwards. And he, the Flemish patriot, didn't want to be killed by one of his fellow Flemings. So, slightly ahead of the others, cupping his hands around his mouth, he yelled at intervals, '*Jongs, de Koffie is klaar!*' It was a banal phrase, meaning no more than 'boys, the coffee's ready'. But it was

147

one that his fellow countrymen would recognize, one that in better times their wives and mothers had called out to them at home. With the phrase and the way he spoke it in the true accent of a Fleming from East Flanders, he could appear, he hoped fervently, nothing else but one of them.

So they advanced, crouched low, bodies tensed for the first impact of hard steel striking them, with Smits repeating his homely but silly phrase time and time again in any break in the ear-splitting noise of that horrific barrage.

Now they were less than twenty-five metres or so from the Belgian line. The defenders were observing fire discipline well enough, save for here and there, where some nervous soldier fired his rifle. The rest obviously knew that to fire prematurely would give their position away to the advancing *Moffen*, once they had cleared the first line of defence.

Smits grew more confident. A couple of times, he raised himself to his full five foot and, standing there boldly with the German shells whistling dangerously above his head, to explode in a brown geyser of mud, stones and earth only yards to his front, he yelled his foolish little phrase and waited, head cocked to one side for the answer that would confirm he was safe.

Then it came. To his left a helmeted head popped itself over the edge of the parapet. A rifle was levelled in the little man's direction. '*Wat?*' a voice enquired in some kind of Flemish dialect.

'*Geen Deutsche,*' Smits yelled back swiftly. '*Vlaams. Ik ben*—'

It was just then that tragedy struck. From somewhere to the right of the little group crouching there, an old-fashioned machine gun opened up slowly like an irate woodpecker pocking away at a stubborn piece of hard wood. Smits went down immediately in a wild flurry of flailing arms and legs, yelling out in unbearable agony. Dickie followed. 'Holy cow!' he cried. 'They've hit me in the knee . . .' The next moment he collapsed on his face. The girl shrieked. A sudden scarlet flame seared the front of her dress. De Vere tried to grab her before she fell. To no avail. In that same moment, he too was struck. It was as if someone had just thrust a red-hot poker

148

into his stomach. Blood flooded his mouth and choked him. An instant later he was falling, unconscious or dead before he hit the ground.

# One

That winter, Portsmouth Naval Hospital was packed with wounded. They were everywhere, in their blue hospital uniform, hobbling around on their sticks and crutches or trying to balance now that they had lost their arms and parts of their upper bodies. But all, on the whole, cheerful, for they had received their 'Blighty'. They had fought honourably for their country and, for the time being, they were out of the slaughter. They included Marines, who were now mostly fighting on the land as ordinary infantry in the trenches.

But there were those who would probably never leave their beds. They lay in rigid lines of white metal cots, with enamel chamberpots below and a plain wooden cupboard holding their pathetic bits and pieces. They waited for death: men infected with gangrene, whose wounds stank and for whom nothing much could be done save amputate another chunk of flesh in front of the creeping killer. Here few would venture into the stinking wards, save those who were on duty there, the Red Cross nurses and worn, pale-faced doctors who were working flat out already trying to cope with the flood of casualties from torpedoed ships and land battlefronts from Gallipoli to Flanders.

Indeed, when Dickie, de Vere and Sussi had been unloaded on their stretchers at Newhaven, with Sussi still unconscious, there had been attempts to transfer them to a rural cottage hospital somewhere in the wilds of Kent. C, who had personally made the journey from London to receive them, had put his foot down. Dressed in the uniform of a full colonel, complete with the bright-red tabs of the staff and green ones of Intelligence, he had bellowed to the receiving medical officer, 'These poor people are going to the Royal Naval Hospital at Haslar. They need skilled treatment.'

153

The harassed doctor in his bloodstained white apron had given in until he had turned back the red blanket which covered Sussi's slim body to discover she was not a wounded serviceman and had exclaimed, 'But sir, this patient is a woman!'

It had been a pretty foolish thing to say, especially to someone with C's hair-trigger temper. 'Why, of course she's a woman!' C had yelled above the moans and pleas of the wounded lying everywhere on the quay while the good women of the port fed them tea and bits of chocolate. 'I would think even a doctor of your calibre would be able to see that.'

'But sir, we can't have a woman in a male naval hospital!' the MO had protested. 'It wouldn't be right,' he had added somewhat lamely.

C had looked at him scornfully. 'Don't be a damned fool, man. Take a look at these poor chaps on the stretchers. I think it's hardly likely they'll be up to any sexual high jinks in their current state of health, do you now?'

Thus they had been transferred with the girl – 'the German spy', as the nurses came to call the poor wounded girl, who had an armed Marines sentry posted outside her hospital room, where all three of them received the attention of top Harley Street specialists, whom C paid personally to come down from London to examine them twice a week.

Dickie was the first to recover. Within a couple of weeks, his leg encased in plaster to the hip, he was hobbling around in his hospital blues, even managing to get into Portsmouth itself, after which he regaled an envious, but still quite sick, de Vere with his tall tales of cocktails, the new American fashionable drink and the high-born ladies who paid for them and seemingly were prepared to offer even more exciting things for 'a poor wounded young officer', also without payment, if he so required.

It was about the second time that Dickie took one of his 'jaunts' into the port that C came to see the two young officers. But this time he was not entirely concerned about their health. He had other, more military, things on his mind. As he explained, things were going badly for the Allies at the front. The Middle East had been a disaster and, as C told it,

154

the French were on their last legs at Verdun, with their battered Army seemingly on the verge of mutiny. There was a rumour going the rounds in Whitehall that now Field Marshal Haig's British Army, the one raised by Lord Kitchener, would have to take up the slack soon, as the weather got better, in order to avoid a disaster. In the meantime it was clear that the German High Seas Fleet was up to something that boded no good for the Royal Navy.

'In essence, young Dickie, we're clutching at straws as far as the German Imperial Navy's intentions are concerned.' He looked at a still very pale de Vere, who was recovering more slowly from his bad shoulder wound – twice he had been laid low by a sudden infection of the wound where cloth had been forced into it by the Belgian bullets. Luckily it hadn't developed into the fatal gangrene which so often carried off the wounded. But de Vere didn't respond. C guessed why.

'The German girl,' C ventured, a little hesitantly for him, for he had already learned from his own sources in the great naval hospital that the two young officers were half in love with their 'Sussi', especially de Vere. 'She must know something – anything that might help us would be like a gift from the gods at the moment.'

Dickie said, 'I know that, sir. But she's in a bad way. She has been severely wounded in the left lung, as you know, sir. But the wound really refuses to clear properly.'

C knew. His specialists from Harley Street reported directly to him in Queen Anne's Gate immediately they returned from Portsmouth on their twice weekly visits. 'Can I have a peep at her?' he asked.

Under other circumstances, Dickie would have been amused at C asking him, a humble sub-lieutenant, for his permission to have a look at the sick girl – the Cs of this world, he knew, didn't ask, they took. 'Yessir. Just a peep. The last time de Vere and I looked in she was sleeping a little, thank God.' He looked down at de Vere, who had been forced to use one of the hospital's wheelchairs this day. 'All right, de Vere?'

His old comrade nodded, but said nothing. So, with Dickie pushing de Vere's wheelchair, followed by C, who for some reason looked embarrassed, they moved down the corridor

155

smelling of ether, Jeyes fluid and human misery, to where the immaculate Marines sentry stood with his fixed bayonet outside the door to the sick girl's room.

'Don't knock,' Dickie commanded after the Marine had examined their passes. 'Just open the door quietly and peep in. We don't want her waking. They've got to give her morphia now and again so that she can sleep when she's really in pain, sir, you see.'

Gingerly C did as he was ordered, his usual blustering, sometimes even bullying, manner vanished. He could see immediately that the German girl was really very sick. She lay on her side, a tube attached to her back, which led to a great demijohn of a bottle at the foot of the bed. From the wound, a thin red mix looking like a weak rose wine filtered into the bottle, while she breathed harshly, even in her sleep, like people did, as C knew, who had been badly wounded in the lungs. He couldn't see too much of her face, framed by hair that was matted and damp with perspiration. But what he could see of it told him, the veteran of the old colonial wars in Africa and on India's North-West Frontier, that she was in a bad way. Her face was very pale, with sunken cheeks, and there were dark circles, almost like bruises, under her closed eyes.

He shut the door gently and as they moved back down the corridor and the Marines sentry took his post up once again, C broke the heavy silence to say quietly, 'I see what you mean.'

'They keep draining the wound, sir, as you see. But they can't seem to clear it up once and for all. The lung fills up again and then she faces another emergency.'

'Once I heard her cry out, "*Ich ertrinke!*"' de Vere broke in. 'I asked one of the Hun prisoners here what it meant.'

'And?' C asked softly.

'It means, I am drowning . . . Drowning in her own blood.' He stopped short as if he couldn't go on any more.

It was when they were outside once more in the pale winter sunshine that C spoke again. 'You may think me heartless,' he said slowly, as if he were considering his every word. 'Believe you me, I feel tremendously sorry for your friend.

156

But please understand me. I have the responsibility for trying to save the lives, not of one person such as your Sussi von Hoofstra-Mecklenburg, but thousands upon thousands of our own poor chaps. In a nutshell, gentlemen, it's one for the price of thousands – and remember that one *was* an enemy of this country.'

'What's that supposed to mean, sir?' Dickie asked in an unusually cold tone for him, with his normally sunny nature. Next to him de Vere clutched the sides of his wheelchair with knuckles that had suddenly turned white with suppressed tension.

Again C looked embarrassed. 'The girl . . . I – well, we – think she knows something of importance about the Imperial Navy's future plans. After all, she worked closely with that Hun swine Klaus von Bismarck. We know that she was his mis—' C caught himself in time when he saw the look of anger on de Vere's face, and added quickly, 'Now it is of the utmost importance, in the light of our military situation, to know what she probably knows, even if her information is somewhat outdated. W—'

'They can't expect to get anything out of her,' de Vere butted in, his eyes blazing. 'Not in the condition in which she finds herself. I mean, there have been times that Freifrau von Hoofstra-Mecklenburg has been next to death's door. Those specialists you send down regularly from Harley Street must have told you that.'

C actually blushed. He had been found out. At any other time he would have been furious with this young whipper-snapper talking back to him like this. But the youth had suffered for his country and he guessed, though he had long forgotten the emotion himself, de Vere was probably a bit in love with the sick German girl. 'So what do you suggest, de Vere?' he asked, forcing himself to keep calm, knowing that when he got back to Whitehall, his superiors and his colleagues would be gasping for the latest that he might have obtained from de Vere's 'Sussi'.

The question caught de Vere off guard. He didn't know the answer to it, and for the moment he had no idea of what to say. But Dickie Bird did. He said, 'We can't force her to speak, even if she was well enough to do so. We're not Huns, who might well torture anything she might know out of her. I suggest, sir, we are given another week till she has got over her present crisis and is fit enough. Then we'll ask her straight out what she knows, if she knows anything.'

'A week's a long time,' C said reluctantly.

'It might be,' Dickie answered. 'But at this time of the year we can't expect any great military operations. Field Marshal Haig will be taking his new army into action for the very first time. He'll need the best weather conditions possible to do so successfully. It has to be pretty much the same with the Hun High Seas Fleet. The German ships have been bottled up in their ports since their bombardment of the North Sea coast. Their ships and crews will need working up for any new action, and their admirals will want the best possible weather conditions. A week more or less won't make much difference, I suggest.'

C gave in. 'All right!' He reached for his gold-braided, red-trimmed cap and his brown swagger stick. 'Let's say a week then. And I hope you're right.' He nodded to de Vere. 'Look after yourself, young man. The country needs fine young men like you.'

De Vere didn't respond.

Dickie did. 'And what about me, sir?' he asked with his normal cheeky grin back on his face. 'Does the country need me, too?'

C responded with a smile of his own, relieved that he hadn't lost the two of them altogether. 'Of course, it does, young Bird. Now come on, you can see me out to my car.'

Obediently Bird followed, noting how the wounded soldiers pressed themselves to the side when they saw C approaching. Unlike the sailors, they were impressed by the 'brass hat', perhaps they even feared these officers of the staff with their red tabs, who had attempted to send them to their deaths and perhaps would do so again when they were healed and sent back to the front, crying out for bodies to sacrifice to the insatiable God of War, Mars.

But as they passed out into the open where C's staff car was waiting to take him to Portsmouth main staion to catch

158

the train back to London, there was one group of soldiers who were not impressed by this particular 'brass hat'. It was not surprising, for they wore the field-grey of the German Army and the insignia of the Prussian Guard, the Imperial Army's elite.

C frowned and pointed at them with his stick, as if they were particularly repulsive animals. 'What are those Huns doing here?' he demanded of his companion.

'German POWs, sir. All been badly hit and won't be able to fight any more. They're to be exchanged for our own chaps over there in Hun POW camps who are similarly badly injured and *hers de combat*.'

C sniffed, as one of the German exchanges shook his fist – he only had one – and declared loudly, '*Gott strafe England!*' Next to him a little soldier acting as a guard nudged him in the ribs and said politely enough, 'Come on, Fritz, move on. You ain't gonna to be strafing anybody no more now, are yer?'

C shook his head at the little guard's reaction. 'When will we English ever learn to hate like that big German swine obviously does.' Then he dismissed the German POWs, soon to return to their homeland. 'Watch Lieutenant de Vere for me, Bird. He's obviously upset, and, you know . . .'

Dickie knew what the head of the Secret Service meant, but he didn't comment. One way or another, whatever de Vere felt about Sussi, the relationship would have to come to an end sooner or later. After all, she had been an enemy agent and it was obvious that C still regarded her with suspicion, and as a person really only useful as a source of information. So he came to attention, raised his hand to his battered naval cap in salute and waited till C's Rolls Royce started to draw away. Then he turned and began to make his way back to the wards, his mind full of many things.

Behind him the Prussian Guardsman who had cursed C stared at his back in undisguised hatred.

# Two

'*D*e Vere, please.'
It was two nights later. As had been his custom ever since he had begun to heal and was no longer confined to his bed, de Vere had stationed himself outside Sussi's room for an hour or so before lights out to reassure himself that she was all right and that if she needed something – he didn't quite know what – he'd be there to help. After all, the nurses were really worked off their feet, especially at night when they brought the wounded in under cover of darkness so that the local civilians couldn't see the mounting cost of the war on land and sea.

Immediately he seized his cane and with a slight knock at her door entered, ignoring the smell coming from her still suppurating wound. But now, for a change, she had raised herself a little more from the pillow on which she normally slept to help her lung drain. There was a light tinge of colour in her thin cheeks, too, as if finally she was beginning to recover. He hobbled across to her and seized her hand, which had lost its customary icy coldness, and said lovingly, 'Sussi, do you need help?'

She shook her head and said, 'No, darling, I need you.'

His heart went out to her, and if she hadn't been so ill, he would have seized her and kissed her passionately.

'I heard what that general said the other day,' she continued.

'General?' he exclaimed, then he remembered and said, 'C, you mean.'

She nodded. 'He doesn't like me because I'm German,' she added simply. 'But that doesn't matter. I am German, but I feel nothing for that country. Germans tried to kill me – and you. Why should I be loyal?' She coughed suddenly and he

160

could hear the thick wheeze of her wounded lung; it was like the awful sound dying old men made. Hastily he said, 'Don't worry about it. We must be concerned with ourselves, whether we are German or English. It doesn't matter. We're important, that's all.' He pressed her hand again.

'Thank you, darling. But I don't want you to have trouble because of me. I have to help you, if I can.'

Again he tried to reassure her that it didn't matter, but she stopped him short with, 'I only know the little I heard from Klaus – Kapitan von Bismarck. How the High Seas Fleet might beat the English in some future battle. He was always trying to think up clever schemes that would get him promoted. He was mad about promotion and he would try those schemes out on me, de Vere.'

For an instant de Vere felt a nasty pang of jealousy. She had lain in that swine von Bismarck's arms. They had made love together, done things in bed his young mind dare not even think about, she had writhed in passion, gasped words . . . He stopped himself thinking of her naked body in the older man's arms with an effort of sheer will power. That was the past, he told himself. He couldn't change the past; it had to be forgotten. It was the future that was now important – for the two of them. Even as he thought the words – 'the two of them' – he knew that somehow or other Sussi and he would find a new life together when the damned war was over.

Again she pressed his hand weakly, as if she guessed what might be going through his mind at that moment, and said, 'I must help you, darling. Let me tell you what bit I do know.'

He forgot his doubts and jealousy. 'If it's not too much of a strain, Sussi.'

'Last year Klaus – von Bismarck,' she corrected herself hastily, 'had a new plan which he told me a little about. It was in connection with the High Seas Fleet and how it might trick you English into a battle where you couldn't use all your ships.'

'Yes,' de Vere, said. 'We have numerical superiority over your fleet. But please go on, dear Sussi.'

She did and he listened with growing interest and excitement as she gave a rough outline of the same plan that Klaus

161

von Bismarck had explained to the Kaiser and the august collection of senior German admirals. More than once he wanted to stop her and ask for an explanation or further details. But he could see she was wearying fast, using up what remained of her new-found strength, and decided against it. He'd be able to fill in the odds and ends later, and, if he couldn't, he was sure that C would be able to do so. Thus he let her continue, listening as he did so to the laboured pumping of her lungs. They were beginning to fill up with fluid once more. In a few minutes he'd have to call the sawbones to insert that damned long needle through the hole in her side and draw off the fluid before it choked her.

Then she coughed, thick and nasty. A thin trickle of blood ebbed from the side of her mouth. She had done enough. Hastily he grabbed his stick and hobbled as quickly as he could to the alarm button next to her bed. Already her thin face was being covered by a lather of sweat. He hit the button hard and kept his finger pressed down on it until he heard the hurried pad of rubber-soled shoes hurrying down the corridor outside. It was the staff coming to deal with the emergency. He breathed a sigh of relief and allowed himself to be escorted outside as the MO started to strip down her sweat-soaked nightgown to reveal the wound that disfigured her emaciated pale-white body, seeing her breasts for the first time now, reduced to the size of those of some girl in puberty. As they closed the door behind him, he started as she moaned with pain. They were thrusting that long cruel needle inside her once more. Just in time, Dickie, alerted by the shrill persistent tone of the alarm, caught him and said, 'Steady on, old chap. They know what they're doing, de Vere. She'll be all right, take it from me.'

But Dickie Bird was wrong. Sussi von Hoofstra-Mecklenburg would not be all right.

The next two days passed in a confusing mix of travel, conferences and what would eventually amount to a slanging match between senior members of the Royal Navy, so that, worried as he was, de Vere had little time to think of Sussi. Within an hour of his telephoning C to inform him of what the girl had told him, C's own Rolls Royce had appeared at the Portsmouth Hospital. Together with Dickie and a senior medical orderly, just in case he needed help, he was on his way back to London.

Despite the earliness of the hour, C was waiting for him in that eerie room of his at the top of Queen Anne's Gate, fully dressed, washed and shaven, and visibly impatient to hear more details. For, as he informed the two young officers, 'You've certainly set the cat among the pigeons, de Vere. Not only here in Whitehall, but also up north. Both Beatty and Jellicoe –' he meant Admiral Sir David Beatty and Admiral Jellicoe – 'are on their way south at this very moment in a special train to hear what you say. And,' C sighed, 'by what I've already heard, they're going to be very sceptical. Opinion here in Whitehall is that the Huns won't risk their ships at this juncture. They are preoccupied with the land battle at Verdun against the French and are, according to our intelligence, expecting some action by Haig's army in France to try to take the pressure off the French under Petain.'

Bewildered as they were by this sudden dramatic turn of events, the two of them nodded their heads, as if they understood – which they didn't – and waited for C's further orders. They were simple. 'Get yourselves to Claridge's. You've got a suite there. Get as much shut-eye as you can, and the best breakfast my slush fund can afford. That's important. For this is going to be a long, and I'm afraid, for you two in your present condition, a trying day.'

It was.

First they were quizzed by the officers of Naval Intelligence, all of whom were senior in rank to them, including the supercilious 'wavy navy' officers*, mostly Oxbridge men brought on account of their language and coding expertise. They weren't impressed by Dickie's and de Vere's efforts to put

---

* Royal Navy Voluntary Reserve, known thus due to the wavy arm stripes that distinguished their service from the regular Royal Navy officer, who wore straight ones.

across what they had learned from Sussi before she had been taken ill again. As one of the Oxbridge men, who affected a monocle, of all things, and had a pink silk handkerchief tucked up in the cuff of his tunic, said, having difficulty in pronouncing his 'r's, 'Weally, gentlemen, can we weally accept the wamblings of a women who was once a Fwitz spy!'

The two of them fared little better when they had their preliminary meeting with members of Navy's staff later that day. A staff captain asked what he thought was a leading question, and one for which they had no answer. He wasted no time and said, 'I'm going to read a letter to you which I received a day or so ago from Admiral Beatty himself. He wrote, and I quote, "The German submarines are a very serious danger to our merchant ships and those of the neutral countries plying their trade with us. So far our losses have been kept within reason."' He had looked up and added sharply, '*Just*. "But in the future, if they keep rising, they will jeopardize the fate of our nation and seriously interfere with our successful prosecution of the war."' He placed the letter on the table in front of him and added solemnly, 'Now then, young men, why should the Huns risk their capital ships with large crews aboard against our own fleet, which is superior, when they can inflict grievous losses on us with submarines crewed by a score or so of their sailors – subs, to boot, that can be manu-factured cheaply and swiftly, something one cannot do with large capital ships?'

When they had been unable to answer his question, he had picked up his briefcase and turned to the rest of the committee, saying, 'I don't think we ought to waste any more time on this business, gentlemen, do you? Let's leave for the club and have some lunch, eh?' With that they had filed out in order of seniority, leaving the two young officers feeling embar-rassed and somewhat of a failure.

It was not much different with the others of what C called contemptuously 'the Hall Admirals'* whom they met during the course of the rest of that frustrating day. De Vere and

* Pun on 'Whitehall admirals.'

164

Dickie had known naturally that Britain's 'senior service', The Royal Navy, was conservative, and perhaps rightly so. But until now, meeting such illustrious officers, they had not been aware of just how set the senior people were in their ways.

All the senior officers they met were so hidebound and old-fashioned that they believed that when their fleet sallied out to fight the enemy, it would be a kind of glorified Trafalgar. Their dreadnoughts and battlecruisers would fight other enemy ships of the same type, which they would defeat in short order, just as Nelson had done a century before. After all, their ships outnumbered the enemy's three to one.

Seemingly these 'Hall Admirals' didn't take into account the new revolutionary weapons of war, now being used: the aeroplane, the submarine, wireless telegraphy and the like. Nor did they appear to realize that the Germans, with the newest navy of all the great continental powers, didn't play the game according to the antiquated rules of the nineteenth century, based on the sailing ship: those rules by which Nelson and his great captains had fought Trafalgar, which had allowed the British Navy to dominate the oceans for a hundred years.

As the two of them slumped in their splendid Claridges apartment, exhausted by that long frustrating day, they felt defeated and not a little pessimistic about convincing no less a person than Sir David Beatty himself on the morrow. C had earlier told them they would have to go it alone with that dominant figure. The Admiral, who commanded Britain's battlecruisers, the most dashing arm of the British fleet, had little time for soldiers like himself. His life was centred on the Royal Navy and his fast battlecruisers, which would lead any attack on the German High Seas Fleet once they came out to fight.

As a deflated C said over yet another double scotch, paid for by that mysterious 'slush fund' of his,[*] 'Convince Beatty, difficult as he is, and you'll have the rest of those Hall Admirals eating out of your hands, chaps. Don't convince

[*] A secret fund that had not to be accounted for by Parliament or the Treasury.

him and . . . He shrugged and left the rest of his sentence unsaid, but they knew what he meant even if he didn't put his thoughts into words.

# Three

Beatty had left his fleet up in Scapa Flow and journeyed all the way down the whole of the British Isles to meet them. Still, the little admiral, with his tough red face and white cap tilted cockily to one side – in no way conforming to naval regulations – seemed as fresh as if he had just enjoyed ten hours' sleep. He stepped jauntily into the room, full of pompous naval brass hats, and snapped, hands stuck in his tunic pockets, as if he were back on the quarterdeck of his flagship, *HMS Lion*. 'Morning, gentlemen,' he snapped briskly, and then to the surprise of the 'Hall Admirals' in their stiff upright white collars, whipped off his gold-braided cap and flung it neatly at the nearest hatstand. He beamed at his aim. 'The old hand hasn't lost its cunning, what!' he exclaimed to no one in particular.

Without further ado, he strode to the tall window over-looking the parade ground, hands behind his back, and said, 'Well, I suppose we ought to see them, eh. Should we wheel 'em in?' It was as if he were talking about two defaulters who were being brought before him on the 'rattle'.

The First Sea Lord, Admiral Sir H. B. Jackson, frowned severely. Vice-Admiral Sir W. F. Oliver, Chief of the War Staff, cleared his throat, and when the First Lord didn't speak, said, 'Don't you think we ought to discuss this thing first, Beatty?'

'No time, no time, old chap. Have to get back to the Fleet. Heaps of work. Wheel 'em in, what?' He smiled at Oliver, but his eyes didn't light up. He thought the Chief of the War Staff was a slow-minded bumbler and Beatty had no time for slow-minded bumblers, whatever their exalted rank was. He nodded to the elegant flag-lieutenant at the door.

167

The officer acted at once. He swung the great eighteenth century door open and called, 'Smith and Bird.'

Slowly the two friends, feeling totally out of place in their crumpled blue hospital gear, came in. They had asked C for naval uniform. He had turned them down with, 'Let the bugger see that you are wounded heroes, not some pasty-faced idiot fighting the war from behind a desk. You're going in your hospital togs.'

Without their caps they were unable even to salute, but they did attempt to come stiffly to attention, though in de Vere's case it was not only difficult but also painful. He winced.

Beatty saw it. He barked, 'All right, you two young heroes, stand easy. In fact, you'd better take the weight off your feet. Jenkins –' he indicated the elegant flag-lieutenant with his shining lanyard – 'get these officers a chair.'

Feeling even more embarrassed in the presence of all these high-ranking officers who were still standing, they sat down, while Beatty took a hard look at them momentarily before remarking, 'You've done well. I've heard about your escape through the Hun lines. Fine work. I hear the King is going to award you something for your bravery.' His tone changed and was very businesslike now. 'I hear from you know who that you've come up with some notion that the Huns are going to lure our ships into a trap of some kind or other, eh.'

'Yessir,' de Vere said hesitantly, and Dickie, deadly serious now, added daringly, 'I don't think it's really a notion, sir.'

Beatty took what the other admirals might well have regarded as insubordination in his stride. He said, 'Well said, young man. Like a chap who sticks to his principles, even if they're wrong.'

De Vere's heart sank a little. That last sentence was the first indication that Beatty might well turn out to be like the other hidebound admirals, though his manner appeared to be so bright and breezy.

'Now,' Beatty continued, apparently not noticing the look on de Vere's face. 'Tell me what you think of the Huns' supposed fiendish plan?' He smiled momentarily at the other admirals, as if he were telling them that he was humouring these two brave but naive young officers.

168

Again, Dickie did the talking, for de Vere felt suddenly that it was pointless going through the whole bloody business once again; for Beatty was not going to believe them either.

'So, as you see it – and have heard from this German lady,' Beatty said after he was finished, 'the Huns are going to attempt by their plan to separate our two fleets, Sir John Jellicoe's from mine, and then, when they have achieved equal numbers with one of us, and the score is even, set about blasting our ships out of the sea, eh? That's it in a nutshell.'

'Yessir,' Dickie said, his voice faltering now that he had realized that Admiral Beatty was really playing him along; that he didn't believe his account one bit.

Beatty sniffed. 'I know you are both loyal, decent officers, who have the best interests of our service at heart. But has it ever occurred to you that this Klaus von Bismarck of Hun Intelligence might be more devious than you think. Everyone on this side of the German Ocean –' he meant the North Sea – 'seems to think that the Hun is wooden-headed and without imagination. But that has not been my experience. The Hun is as cunning as they come. So I put this to you. The girl once worked for German Intelligence, you must admit.'

They nodded.

'Well then, why shouldn't she *still* be working for that same organization, eh? What if she has been stringing you along now in the present as she once did in the past? What if the Huns are planning something totally different than what she has made you two believe they intend . . .? And being young and, if I may say, somewhat green, you've fallen for it hook, line and sinker?' He cast a triumphant glance at his fellow admirals.

De Vere felt himself blush an angry red. Next to him Dickie clenched his fists. With difficulty, trying to control his temper, de Vere answered, 'Sir, the girl in question was seriously injured trying to help us to escape. Besides, that same Klaus von Bismarck had attempted more than once to have her murdered since she defected from the German service.'

Beatty didn't seem to hear his explanation. Perhaps he didn't want to. Instead he said, 'Why isn't this German woman here, complete with interpreter, if one is needed? I'm sure, gentlemen,' he added, addressing his fellow admirals and ignoring the two visibly angry young men, 'we could get the real truth out of her in a few minutes, what?'

There was a rumble of agreement from the others and Admiral Sir Henry Jackson said in that sombre manner of his, as if he were used to speaking only in official cliches, 'There must have been an oversight, Beatty. The matter must be rectified. At once.' He raised his voice and addressed the young, elegant flag-lieutenant. 'See what you can find out about this woman. Ascertain if she can be brought from Portsmouth this very day.'

De Vere couldn't contain himself any longer. He recalled Sussi on her hospital bed only a couple of days before, her emaciated body racked with pain, the bloody fluid trickling out of the side of her gaping mouth. 'But you can't do that, sir,' he objected hotly. 'The girl is next to death's door.' Later he bitterly regretted he had uttered that phrase; it became for him a kind of an omen that should not have been spoken aloud.

Beatty shot him a cold look, but said nothing. Though his look said everything. It read: *What do we care about the fate of this Hun woman, who is probably up to no good?*

The flag-lieutenant departed on his mission, while the admirals chatted among themselves, totally ignoring the two young men in their wrinkled, stained hospital blues; it was as if they suddenly didn't exist. They felt that abrupt isolation. In later years, when de Vere was older and wiser and used to the ways of those who wielded the power in Britain, he realized that it had always been thus and always would be. There were those in his native country who could display a coldness of heart that cut them off from the greater mass of ordinary citizens. For those who walked the corridors of power in Whitehall and such places, their own positions, personal power and plans were the only things that counted. The greater mass of the nation was merely there to further their own aims.

The flag-lieutenant seemed to be taking longer than they had anticipated. The admirals' gossip died away to nothing. Some lit cigarettes. Others stared in obvious boredom out of the great windows of the admiralty at the little parade outside.

170

The guardsmen no longer wore their red coats and busbies. Instead they were dressed in the khaki of the front. But their drill was still the three-hundred-years-old drill of the Regular Army. It, too, seemed to de Vere to symbolize the continuing power of those who had always run the country and always would.

Down below a sergeant was bellowing, 'Old Guard will present arms . . . New Guard will take up their duties,' when the great door opened suddenly and the flag-lieutenant rushed in, face red and flustered, no longer the smooth young flunkey he had seemed a few minutes before.

The Admirals turned, a little startled. 'Well?' Beatty demanded harshly. 'Where's the fire?'

The young officer licked his lips, as if they were suddenly very dry. 'Sir,' he stuttered.

'Get on with it.'

'Sir, something terrible has happened.'

De Vere sat bolt upright.

Next to him, Dickie did the same, jerked out of his reverie, seized by a sudden sense of foreboding.

'The woman, the German woman, sir,' the flag-lieutenant answered Beatty directly. 'She's dead.'

Somewhat stupidly Admiral Beatty asked, 'How do you mean *dead*?'

The young officer licked his lips. 'They say in Portsmouth that she's been . . . murdered.'

'*Murdered?*'

'Yessir. My informant says that one of the other patients went beserk. He took his razor and slit her throat.'

Dickie groaned out loud. De Vere clutched his head in despair. 'Oh no!' he moaned. '*No . . . no!*'

The admirals stared first at the bringer of these terrible tidings and then at the two young officers, faces a mixture of disbelief and almost unbearable grief.

Even Beatty, so bluff and hearty, master of every situation, however bizarre, was taken aback. 'But . . . but,' he stuttered a little. 'How could anything like that happen?'

The flag-lieutenant fumbled for words. 'Apparently, sir,' he blurted out, 'it was one of the prisoners who did it.'

171

'Prisoners?'

'Yes sir,' he answered. 'Germans bound for repatriation because they were so badly wounded that they would never be able to fight again. This one was a bit cracked. Well, sir, for some reason known only to himself, he must have decided to kill the German woman.'

'Go on, get on with it, man,' Beatty urged impatiently.

'Well, he dodged his guards, knocked out the Royal Marines sentry guarding the woman's room and . . . er, slit her throat with his cut-throat razor and . . .' He couldn't go on, stopping in mid-sentence. Opposite him, de Vere gagged and fought back the hot bile which flooded his throat, as he visualized what that act had meant. His poor beloved Sussi with her neck slit open.

'The German madman?' Beatty demanded, his voice not quite steady either.

'Shot while trying to escape, sir,' the flag-lieutenant managed to explain.

'Dead on the spot, sir. We—'

He broke off suddenly. De Vere couldn't contain himself. He retched and began to vomit, his shoulders heaving with the effort, like those of some heartbroken child. Next to him, Dickie Bird said, as Beatty jumped back hastily, 'Hold on, de Vere . . . For God's sake, hold on . . .'

# Four

De Vere did hold on. Dickie Bird, too.
The resilience of youth helped. The war, too. For now, the plan that C had feared so much ever since he had guessed that Klaus von Bismarck had worked out some sort of devilish scheme to defeat the greatest navy in the world did not materialize.

Indeed, French Intelligence reports from the Verdun front indicated that German sailors from their fleet still bottled up in their northern ports were being formed up into infantry battalions to take part in the terrible war of attrition being fought at that city on the River Meuse. C interpreted that to mean that German admirals were not going to use their capital ships in the foreseeable future.

As far as he could see, the only German naval activity of any importance was their increased use of their submarines. The U-boats were now ranging beyond the 'German Ocean' into the Mediterranean, and the Atlantic even, to reap a rich harvest in sunken Allied merchant ships. Even the hidebound traditionalist 'Hall Admirals' were becoming more worried about the U-boat threat than that posed by the German High Seas Fleet. They were trying desperately to combat this new underwater menace which was threatening the very lifeblood of the British Isles – and British troops in France. Thus it was that, for a while, C forgot the two young officers, de Vere and Dickie, back at their old base in the shadow of Scarborough Castle in Yorkshire.

In a way, the two young officers, now promoted to first lieutenants and wearing the ribbon of the DSC, presented to them personally by the King-Emperor George V, were glad that they had been forgotten by C and the powers that be.

173

They had had enough of the 'Hall Admirals' and everything and everyone connected with them.

Back in those terrible days after Sussi had been murdered, they had discovered just how little she or they counted in the scheme of things. The authorities in Portsmouth had even refused to have the poor girl buried by one of the great port's many churches. The two of them were informed that it might outrage the local population – most of whom had relatives fighting with the 'Senior Service' – to have a 'German spy' buried in their midst. They had protested hotly at the decision, with de Vere writing personally to the new Prime Minister, the so-called 'Welsh Wizard', Lloyd George. To no avail. They had received a cold formal reply from Number Ten informing them that the 'Prime Minister cannot see his way to interfere in this minor dispute.'

*'Minor dispute!'* They had raged for a day or more at the term, as they considered what to do next. Their anger and frustration had increased even more when they had received a telegram from one of Portsmouth's leading undertakers stating that he could not carry out the funeral of the 'German lady'. The local authorities in the great naval port would not allow the body to be cremated in the municipal crematorium.

Feeling was running high in the city, in which there were so many naval families and those who had connections with the Royal Navy. The situation had not been helped by the fact that a German had been murdered by one of her crazy fellow countrymen. As the local paper, the *Portsmouth Post*, had headlined it: *'MAD HUN SLAUGHTERS FELLOW FEMALE HUN!'*

In the end they had given up on Portsmouth, where she had died so cruelly. They had taken a week's leave and spent a month's pay to make arrangements to bring poor Sussi's body up to Scarborough, where they felt they could find a place to bury her. They did. The elderly and gentle vicar of All Saints' Church had agreed to carry out the ceremony and have Sussi buried in his own church graveyard. Although his church had been damaged during the German bombardment of the place in 1914, and there was bound to be some sort of outcry, he

174

wasn't afraid to carry out what he called 'my sacred duty as a Christian'.

Both of them had sat by her plain wooden coffin in the guards' van on the long journey from King's Cross to Scarborough. They had said little to each other. They were drained of emotion and had little to say. But when Dickie had gone to the dining-car to buy a sandwich and have a drink, de Vere hadn't been able to resist the temptation to have one last look at Sussi. She looked too frail, wan and pale in death. But he had done something which, in a way, had made him feel guilty. He had taken her ring. He had to have something to remember her by; he simply had to have it!'

Thus she was buried. In a drizzle. The two of them, the vicar and his burial party. It had been the briefest of ceremonies and there she now lay, buried with the brief details of her life inscribed on a simple gravestone. In German, whether the locals liked it or not: a language that neither of them understood. In a way it seemed a fitting memorial to a dead young girl from an alien culture who had entered so briefly into their lives and had departed in such a strange and alien manner.

As winter gave way to spring that second year of war, an astute observer would have noticed a change in the two officers, who once had been so light-hearted and without any apparent cares. Their faces had hardened and they had little time for any failings on the part of their now even younger crews, mostly eighteen-year-old new recruits. Their orders were barked now, and they made a very clear distinction between the upper and lower decks, even though officers and ratings were living cheek-by-jowl on their small fast craft. Whenever they had a chance, they'd apply for CPOs and POs from the pre-war regular navy, who still believed in the rope's end and would put any young matelot who appeared in the slightest way to be 'cheeky' 'on the rattle' immediately. It meant another barrier between them and the ratings of the lower deck.

Even their speech patterns seemed to have changed. No longer did they use the silly phrases of 1914 – 'the old bird' . . . 'my sainted aunt' and all the rest of them. Even de Vere's tendency to slur his *R*s, turning them into *W*s had vanished.

Now when he heard Army officers of the old silly school speaking in that pre-war style, he would turn up his nose and snort to Dickie, 'What a damn lot of bloody fools those Army types are. No wonder we're losing the war in France.'

In the North Sea, de Vere, Dickie and the rest of those hard-boiled officer survivors of the sea battles were certainly not losing their relentless search for and destruction of the new German naval weapon, the U-boat. Now they had no time for the affections of 1914. There were no silk mufflers or ladies' silk stockings tied round their necks as they roared into the attack with a triumphant 'tally-ho, chaps!' as if it were all some glorified fox hunt. Now they hunted the U-boats, which the German Naval High Command were using in an attempt to starve Britain into pleading for peace – with deadly purpose, showing little mercy whenever they managed to send another of their victims to the bottom of the sea. If they felt safe enough to do so, they'd stop engines and pull the gasping, oil-soaked U-boat survivors out of the waves. If they didn't, they'd let them drown. Sometimes when there had been a series of local ships sunk by their U-boat enemies, they might even machine-gun any German survivors of a sunken sub in the water. Back home some of the more tender-hearted members of the public might have regarded such conduct as cold-blooded murder. But not de Vere and Dickie. As they told their fellow officers when they were drunk on pink gin in the wardroom after a successful patrol, 'It's kill or be killed, chaps. We're only giving the Hun a taste of his own medicine.' And if at such moments they remembered the 'Hun' who they had both loved, each in his own way, they showed no sign of it.

But in a way they were justified in their attitude. The war had brutalized them. They expected to die young, and by the way they were being pushed by their seniors into ever riskier naval action, the admirals and commodores in command of their fates thought the same. Now their patrols were being steadily extended.

There were few British aircraft available that could take the war to the North German coast in the manner that the German zeppelins could range deep into British territory.

Instead their superiors expected them to do the job that an aeroplane could have carried out more safely if it had had the range.

Weekly their light craft, armed only with torpedoes, machine guns and, quite recently, with a 20mm quick-firer, ventured out of Scarborough harbour, headed out on a south-easterly course to fool any unwanted observer – or directly east in the direction of neutral Holland – before changing course when they were far out to sea and darkness had fallen, sailing towards the Danish coast and the exit from the Baltic.

There it was their objective to find and sink the German U-boats before they left the confines of the coast and ventured into deeper water. It was a risky operation. For not only did surface craft risk being spotted by patrolling German aircraft and zeppelins, they also faced betrayal – for money – by the many small Danish fishing craft and coastal freighters that operated in that same narrow area. The Danes, who had fought the Germans back in the mid-nineteenth century and had had some of their territory taken from them by the victorious Prussians, felt no great love for the Huns. But money was tight in wartime Denmark, and even the most patriotic Danish skipper would forget his dislike of the enemy for hard German marks.

But Dickie and De Vere, just like the other hardened young skippers of the fast light craft, were prepared to risk detection by German aerial reconnaissance, and betrayal by treacherous Danish skippers. If one of them 'bagged' a U-boat, even if it was one for the whole of the flotilla, it made the danger and hardship of a voyage spent mostly in hiding, dodging in and out of Danish waters, worthwhile.

Naturally the Germans knew they were operating from somewhere off the Danish or Norwegian coasts, and they did their utmost to discover and destroy the English intruders. But that fact seemed only to make the young skippers even more determined to 'tag' a U-boat before their fuel and food ran out. All of them took incredible risks in the hunt. Once de Vere took his boat into the midst of a German submarine wolf pack about to submerge as they left the shallow water of the area. There, with U-boats on the surface all around him, he

177

succeeded in torpedoing the central boat and then fled with half a dozen of the Germans firing point-blank at his craft.

Dickie Bird was equally daring. He breached neutral Danish waters to crawl behind a Danish freighter, whose skipper he suspected was going to betray the presence of the British flotilla to a German submarine waiting just outside territorial waters. His guess had been right. Just when the Dane started to close with the U-boat, which had surfaced and was waiting motionless on the surface, he had given her the benefit of two of his precious torpedoes and, even as the German had begun to sink, he had ordered his quick-firer to rip the Dane's superstructure to shreds as a warning. Afterwards, when the Admiralty had signalled a complaint about attacking a neutral ship, he had signalled back, '*Nelson . . . blind eye . . . Copenhagen.*' It was a reference to Nelson's unauthorized attack on the Danish fleet during the Napoleonic Wars back at the beginning of the nineteenth century. That time the Admiralty had let him get away with this grave breach of neutrality. He had even received a mention in dispatches, plus a warning.

It had meant nothing to Dickie. At the young officers' customary gathering over several bottles of pink gin, with which they celebrated the end of each long patrol, he had raised his glass a little drunkenly and said, 'Here's perdition to all Hall Admirals and their bloody Mary Anns of flunkeys!' It was a toast with which all of them agreed; for as they would say when it was all over, 'Back in sixteen we were all bolshy – absolutely unbelievably bolshy.'

Yet, 'bolshy' or not, it seemed that the Admiralty and their 'bloody Mary Anns of flunkeys' were becoming worried by the sheer number of submarines passing through into the German Ocean via the coast of neutral Denmark. As April 1916 gave way to a red-hot May, and in France, Earl Haig prepared for his greatest British offensive, the light craft flotilla received even more requests from above for more detailed accounts of what was going on in that particular area of Northern Europe.

The requests reminded Dickie and de Vere of what poor, dear, dead Sussi had told them. As Dickie said, one late May afternoon after they had been to place flowers on Sussi's simple grave – a custom they kept up after every patrol – 'Where subs can go with impunity, de Vere, so can warships, capital ships. Now the Huns realize that we are concentrating on that same area off Denmark, what if they sent capital ships there instead of their U-boats, knowing just how our people in London would react at the news?'

De Vere nodded thoughtfully. 'I see what you mean. They'd react by sending some of our own capital ships to intercept them, Dickie.'

'Yes, and as she told us, poor Sussi, those ships might well be just a decoy which we'd fall for. Thereupon they'd make war-like noises and we send the rest of the Grand Fleet, which the Hun just might equal in numbers – and, with a bit of luck for them, defeat. What a hell of a blow that would be for us.'

For a moment or two, they paused to watch a cricket match being played out by a lot of farm labourers rigged out in khaki – new cannonfodder for the Western Front – against fit-looking local shopkeepers and the like who were obviously determined to live to be old men who would die in their own beds and not in some rat-infested Flanders trench. Both of them remembered how desperately they had tried to convince the Hall-Admirals that this was roughly what the Germans intended, and how it all had ended in the tragedy of Sussi's cruel murder by her mad fellow countryman.

Then, as they walked on slowly down to the docks, Dickie broke their heavy brooding silence with, 'But what can we do about it, de Vere?'

To which the latter shrugged and said, 'Nothing . . . exactly nothing, Dickie.'

Behind them on the cricket field there was a burst of clapping and someone cried excitedly, 'All out for eighty four . . .!'

# Five

'*Herr Kapellmeister!*'

*H* The portly band conductor in a flash uniform of his own design, his moustache generously waxed and swept upwards in the fashion of his Imperial Majesty, a masterpiece of his barber's curling tongs, turned stiffly, baton in hand, and bowed. '*Jawohl, Herr Admiral.* I stand at your service.'

Klaus von Bismarck, quite drunk now, his stiff collar open, as if he had just avoided being choked by it, ash drooping unnoticed from his cigar, said thickly, 'Music, Maestro,' and narrowly avoided being swamped by vomit from his second-in-command, who next moment slumped on the table, face forward, with the rest of the 'beer corpses', as they were called in the Imperial Navy at such drunken orgies. '*Schweinerei,*' von Biswarck cursed, but there was no malice in his voice for a change; the new Admiral was happy, this last night ashore. After all, with nearly two years of planning behind him, everything was working out splendidly, as he had always hoped it would. '*Preussens Gloria!*' he bellowed over the racket in the smoke-filled ballroom of Hamburg's largest brothel just off the *Jungfernstieg*.

As if he were leading a military band instead of a bunch of cracked-lunged, old fat men, each with a litre of beer placed carefully on the stage between their feet, the Kapellmeister launched into the Kaiser's favourite march. Suddenly the room was filled with the blare of trumpets and the rattle of kettledrums. Even the worst of the 'bear corpses' stirred at the noise, and the young flag-lieutenant, hanging by his tunic collar from the hatstand peg in the corner, murmured weakly, '*Noch ein Bier Herr Ober*', before beginning to snore drunkenly once more.

But no one had eyes for him. Their gaze was fixed on the great door at the back of the ballroom. It had been flung open. From without there came the harsh stamp of marching feet. The spectators tensed. This was going to be the high point of their last night on shore. Abruptly they erupted into a wild burst of applause and crazy clapping. *'Donnerwetter!'* the older naval officers gasped at the sight. 'They're worthy of belonging to the Imperial Guard. *Donnerwetter nochmal!'*

The whores who now came stamping in, their booted feet working up and down in perfect unison in the goosestep, did indeed rival the Kaiser's Imperial Foot Guards. Every one of the women was well over the minimum height for the elite regiment and well built with it, their naked breasts flopping back and forth to the music of the march. Their heads bore the silver-burnished helmets of the guards and, save for a short skirt, which revealed easily that they were without bloomers, they were totally naked. But it was the female drum major who caught a delighted von Bismarck's attention. She was even taller than the rest – indeed, taller than most of the Naval Intelligence officers in the room; and to make her appear even taller she wore the winged silver helmet of the Garde du Corps on her blonde head.

She caught von Bismarck eyeing her and, as she swung round, thrusting her silver drum-major's mace back and forth in an obvious sexual gesture, she raised her jackbooted legs even higher, so that von Bismarck caught an excellent glimpse of what lay beneath her short skirt. Old lecher that he was, with experience of all types, creeds and colours of women – 'Black, brown, yellow, comrades,' as he was wont to boast, 'I've had 'em all!' – he gasped with surprise. Her pubic hairs, trimmed nicely, had been dyed yellow to match her blonde mop.

'Heaven, arse and cloudburst!' he breathed in admiration to himself. 'That one will be mine before the hour's out.'

Next to him, his second-in-command lifted his head from the drink-sodden table and said thickly, 'That one's worth a sin or two, Herr Admiral.'

Next moment he collapsed back into a drunken sleep as von Bismarck agreed. 'Worth a whole damned churchful of sins, my dear fellow.'

On the raised dais, as the Kapellmeister brought the stirring Prussian Army march to an end with a loud flourish, the blonde with the dyed pubic hair raised her hand to her helmet in salute, bellowing over the noise, 'Honour guard will now present weapons. *Present!*'

As one, the girls, as stiff as ramrods, raised the front of their tiny skirts to reveal their naked loins as the big whore stood there, hand to helmet, face set and stern, as if she were really a Guards drum major on the parade ground at the Kaiser's Palace of Sans Souci. Then she stamped her mace down on the floor three times. 'The music corps,' she bellowed above the clapping of her delighted audience, 'will now fall out . . . a brief rest for refreshments before recall to duty.' To make her meaning quite clear, she did something very obscene with her mace. The girls broke ranks immediately. Squealing and shrieking with delight, they headed for the tables, where von Bismarck's happy, if drunken, officers waited for them eagerly, arms outstretched in anticipation.

Hastily von Bismarck, already feeling that familiar splendid stirring in his loins, clicked his fingers urgently at the line of waiters, standing patiently at the far wall behind their trolleys piled high with silver buckets containing iced champagne. '*Champus!*' he ordered. '*Herr Ober Champagner!*'

As on the stage the Kapellmeister raised his baton once more and the band swung into a fast Viennese waltz, the whores squealed with delight at the thought of champagne. Von Bismarck crooked his finger at the blonde with the dyed pubic hair.

She knew her officers, especially when they were rich and drunk, as these were, or even worse, belonged to the Prussian aristocracy like Admiral von Bismarck. They needed to be shown their place. Otherwise they would indulge themselves in all sorts of disgusting piggeries and then forget conveniently to pay for services renderered. They had to be put in their place right from the start.

So she turned swiftly, bent and threw up her tiny skirt once more to reveal her plump dimpled buttocks. 'Kiss that, *Herr Admiral*,' she cried contemptuously.

Von Bismarck was not offended. He'd make the whore pay

182

for her cheek afterwards. He knew these working-class pave-ment pounders. As his mother had often said in her native Pomerian peasant dialect, 'There's many a big tatie rotten.' With what he'd got between his legs, she'd soon learn who was master and who was maid. But first, he had to make his final decision after all these years of planning. Should he sail with the High Seas Fleet or not?

It could be dangerous, naturally. The English would fight, of course, and fight hard. He didn't want to die now. Now he had achieved the rank the Kaiser had deigned to bestow on him, he wanted to enjoy it. For that he must stay alive. All the same, as the author of the intelligence basis to the great plan, he wanted to be part of the action, with his photograph taken on some great – and safe – ship, so that the public back home would know that he was a true von Bismarck, a worthy successor to his great uncle, the Iron Chancellor. Why, he might retire from the Imperial Navy and go into politics. There would be enough Jews and nouveau riche industrialists only too eager to grease his palms for business favours and honours at court. Half the damned rich Polack and Russian Jews in Berlin these days now called themselves 'von this' and 'von that'.

But it was the big blonde in the Garde du Corps who made his mind up for von Bismarck. Hands on hips, legs spread wide apart, she looked down upon him and said with a cocky sneer on her broad Hamburg face, 'Well, sailor boy, you want a bit? Or do you prefer the five-fingered widow instead?' She jerked her right hand up and down rapidly, the sneer turning to an obscene leer.

He hesitated, but she wouldn't let up. 'But perhaps the sailor boy would prefer something like that.' She indicated the flag-lieutenant hanging from the hatstand by his collar, snoring loudly. 'They tell me you sailor boys favour that more than a good woman's bits and pieces. I'll buy you a tube of vaseline if you do.'

'*Bitch!*' he exploded suddenly, losing his temper and forgetting totally the decision he had to make this night before the fleet sailed at dawn. 'I'll show you what *I* want!' With a surprising display of agility for his age and state of

183

intoxication, he sprang from his seat and grabbed the whore by her broad hips. Taken completely off guard, she tumbled backwards and fell to the floor on her face, her little skirt up to reveal all the ample charms of her massive dimpled bottom. 'Now, whore,' he rasped through gritted teeth, as he fumbled with his flies with one hand. 'Now see what you think about trying this one on for size!' Next moment he thrust himself inside her with all his strength. Caught totally by surprise, she let it happen, screaming with pain and outrage as she felt him enter her in a way that normally she would not have allowed without a great deal of money.

'You rotten, perverted pig!' she shrieked and tried to escape from his grip on her broad hips. To no avail. He held her like a vice, working himself up and down on her fat buttocks, pumping her body as if his very life depended upon it, making throaty unintelligible, almost animal noises as he did so. Behind them on the stage, the middle-aged bandsmen, controlled by the warning look of the Kapellmeister, did not dare look in the direction of the two humans copulating before their very eyes. Instead the tempo of their music increased by the second, so that in the end, just as von Bismarck gave a great sigh of sexual relief, they were playing Strauss at a speed the old Viennese composer would never have thought possible.

In the ballroom, those who were still sober enough to realize what was going on ceased their drinking and their fondling of the nearly naked whores. The women, too, had stopped their silly giggling. Instead, both male and female, they gazed at the spectacle taking place before them in open-mouthed wonder, until one of the whores cried angrily, '*Pfui Teufel!* Leave our Elli alone, you pig-dog! And you a shitting admiral at that! Shame on you!'

'*Shame on you!*' the women took up her cry of rage and disgust on all sides, while the Kapellmeister, puzzled by it all, let his baton droop. The music faltered to a stop. But the sweating bandsmen were too overcome by the sight of an admiral rising slowly to his feet, his trousers around his ankles, that they forgot even to reach for their mugs of beer.

For what seemed a long time, Klaus von Bismarck appeared

unable to move, even to think, while at his feet the big whore pulled at her short skirt as if she was some prudish little virgin who was afraid of showing too much of her untouched body. Her helmet rolled from her dishevelled hair. It seemed to act as a signal for von Bismarck.

Abruptly he realized what he had done. Naturally he knew a man could do virtually anything to a whore – they were paid for that kind of thing. But he had done it in public in 'red' Hamburg, in front of a bunch of tough dockside whores who, just like their working-class pimps and lovers, hated the officers. Von Bismarck could just imagine what would happen on the morrow. The tale of how a von Bismarck had anally raped a local woman would be all over the port, right up to the rich business area around the two inner lakes, the Alster, even out to the wealthy suburban towns of Reinbek and Aumuhle. The local socialist rags, which masqueraded under the name of newspapers, would see to that; they had always hated his uncle on account of his anti-socialist point of view. God Almighty, what was he going to do?

In the event it was his second-in-command, as drunk as he was, who made the decision for him. He staggered over to where the flag-lieutenant hung from the hatstand and grabbed the Admiral's greatcoat and sword. 'Pull up your pants – *in heaven's name!*' he commanded roughly.

Numbly von Bismarck did as he was ordered, ignoring the big whore who had now risen and was trying to hold on to his left leg. The whores seemed to sense what the second-in-command intended. They tried to bar his way, a mass of flailing arms and wobbling fat breasts, crying and spitting at him. Red-faced and harassed beyond measure, he drew the Admiral's sword and wielded it threateningly to left and right. That cleared a path for him. He threw the greatcoat over von Bismarck's naked shoulders and cried to the perplexed *Kappellmeister*, 'Play, man. Play something, for God's sake.' Holding von Bismarck close to him, sword upraised, he started to push his way through the crowd of angry, excited women, while the band struck up a loud polka by Lehar.

'Where are we going?' von Bismarck managed to gasp.

'To sea. We're ducking out of sight. We're sailing with the

185

High Seas Fleet at dawn. By the time we come home victorious, all this mess will be forgotten.' He thrust his sword at a whore in black silk stockings and nothing else, who had tried to stop their progress. She staggered back, broad face blanched with fear.

'To sea?'

'Yes, we'll sail with the *Lützow* with von Hipper. Come on.' He swung the Admiral's sword once again and then they were outside in the misty night, shouting urgently for a horse cab before the crowd of angry whores caught up with them.

Hanging from his peg on the hatstand, the drunken young flag-lieutenant came to momentarily to catch the gleam of the admiral's sword as the second-in-command wielded it one last time. For no obvious reason, he laughed crazily and cried, *'He who lives by the sword shall perish by the sword!'* Next moment he had lapsed into unconsciousness once more, snoring heavily in his drunken sleep. He would survive . . .

# The Battle of Jutland

Dawn had come reluctantly this May morning. It had been cold, grey and with a hint of showers. But visibility was dropping and the wind was freshening. On the bridge of the fast vessel, de Vere guessed that there'd be the usual coastal fog for a while before the wind blew it away. Not that visibility mattered much. He and Dickie, in his own boat, had been patrolling these coastal waters for over a month now and had seen little action. Once or twice they had been overflown by German aircraft from Emden, but they had taken little interest in the two British ships below. The area was apparently of no real importance to the enemy and they left it to the Danish coastal shipping which was sailing regularly to and fro. Perhaps, Dickie and de Vere had reasoned, the Germans didn't want to offend the neutral Danes, who were important to their economy, especially as they supplied the blockaded Germans with a great deal of their eggs, pork and bacon.

De Vere licked his lips. At this moment he could pay justice to a plate of bacon and eggs, especially at the end of a long 'graveyard watch'. Below, the cook was singing away lustily. It was the old song of the men in the trenches, *'Don't cry-ee . . . sigh-ee . . . There's a silver lining in the sky-ee . . . Cheerio, chin-chin, napoo . . . toodle-oo . . . Goodbye-ee.'*

De Vere frowned and wished the cook would forget that 'silver lining in the sky-ee' and get on with breakfast. One of the petty officers must have felt the same, for there came a harsh cry from below, 'Put a frigging sock in it, Dusty . . . or I'll put something frigging else in yer frigging eye-ee!'

De Vere grinned momentarily and then forgot his rumbling stomach. Instead he lifted his brass-bound old-fashioned

189

telescope and stared at the Danish coast and the nearest strand.

Perhaps it was too early for the Danes. But there seemed little going on out there. A couple of fishing smacks with red sails, still trailing their nets behind them as they headed for port with their catch; a small freighter, its hull painted with the Danish national colours, and the legend '*DANMARK*' – and what looked like some sort of tug of uncertain nationality, though de Vere guessed from its silhouette it was probably Danish too. For a while he focused on the shore lights, intrigued by them after the years the British coasts had been blacked out. To their centre there was a lighthouse, painted a brilliant white, its beam swinging round in a 180 degree arc at regular intervals, as was customary.

De Vere gasped abruptly. Hastily he adjusted the focus. Yes, there was no mistaking that long shape to his right, outlined a stark menacing black in the flash of hard white light. It was of the *Nassau* class, one of the Imperial German High Seas Fleet's four dreadnoughts. For a moment he didn't seem able to move. But there was no mistaking the German battleship as the beam swung away from it, leaving him still gasping. After all these years of plotting and planning, death and disappointment, C's hunch had come true. The Huns had had a plan all along for tricking the British fleet into an action where the odds would be evened out and the numerically inferior High Seas Fleet would have a good chance of winning the battle.

De Vere shook his head like a boxer attempting to wake up and recover from a punch before the referee counted him out for ten. He had to inform the authorities what was going on, though he suspected that British Naval Intelligence would have already alerted the fleet that after two years the Germans had left the security of their northern ports at last.

Now, out of the corner of his eye, he saw in the distance that Dickie had already tumbled to what was going on. His craft was gathering speed rapidly. With a white bone of foam at the prow, she was heading straight in de Vere's direction. But there was something else, too. Behind Dickie's boat, unseen German craft were ranging in on him. Shots were

190

throwing up spouts of angry seawater to left and right of Dickie's boat, and already he was beginning to zig-zag wildly to avoid the falling shells.

'Good for you, Dickie, old chap!' he yelled to no one in particular, and inreased the speed of his own craft as, below, the alarm bells started to ring urgently, and the off-duty watch tumbled up on deck, pulling on their oilskins and asbestos face masks ready to meet the German challenge.

But already new enemy vessels were entering the one-sided contest, and yet another of the Nassau dreadnoughts appeared out of the increasing mist, her forward turrets swinging round to blast them out of the water. Two subs, an alarmed de Vere saw, had appeared off the port bow. Within minutes, as slow as they were on the surface, the Hun U-boats would be between him and any chance of escaping from Danish waters. He knew they wouldn't observe the rules of neutrality. They couldn't afford to let the British ships escape and sound their warning.

Wildly de Vere flashed a look around for some means of escape. But Dickie Bird had found it already. From below, their 'Sparks' yelled frantically, 'Sir, morse from Mr Bird . . . Danish fishing smacks to our starboard. Head for them, sir. *Urgent.*'

De Vere didn't need to be told that. Dickie had sent his signal in clear. Very likely the Germans in their submarines had picked up the message too, and were feverishly trying to translate it into their own language at this very moment. He had only minutes to spare to get into the cover provided by the Danish fishing boats. For he, like Dickie, guessed the Huns wouldn't fire upon them and breach Danish neutrality.

He gave the craft all the power she possessed. She seemed to leap out of the water. He felt that old nauseating sensation in his guts as the sharp prow began to hit each wave as if cleaving through a solid brick wall. He fought back the hot vomit which flooded his throat, his hands holding the wheel in a vice-like grip, willing his and Dickie's vessels to reach the protection of the Danish fishing smacks before the Germans changed course and intercepted them. If he failed, he knew that the British fleet might well sail into the trap unwarned.

That could mean a fatal defeat that would affect not only the war but perhaps the whole future of the British Empire . . .

'*Marine bugler!*' the officer of the watch in his stiff upturned collar snapped, as if he were back on some ceremonial review of the Grand Fleet in front of the King-Emperor. 'Sound the alarm!'

The Marine, ramrod-straight, clad in an immaculate pre-war full uniform of the Royal Corps of Marines, raised the gleaming silver bugle to his lips. He paused there in front of the public address system, took a breath, spat out a little, wet his lips and started playing the traditional call to arms.

High above him on the bridge of the *Iron Duke*, his flag-ship, Sir John Jellicoe, Commander-in-Chief of the Grand Fleet, nodded his approval gravely. 'Gentlemen,' he said solemnly to his staff. 'I feel, as I hear that bugle, that Admiral Nelson would approve. We are going into whatever comes, just as his Lordship would have done over a century ago.'

There was a solemn murmur of approval from his staff officers, as the battleship's captain, Captain Dryer, watched anxiously as his crew tumbled out to their duty stations, the gunners pulling on their anti-flash masks; the deck officers already thrusting up their telescopes to view the grey sea on either side, hoping to be the first officer to spot the approaching German fleet; the air sentries spreading out on the huge, highly polished deck just in case the enemy had launched his feared Zeppelin. All was controlled chaos and Jellicoe was pleased, as was the captain of the *Iron Duke* at just how well the crew was handling the sudden emergency.

He flung a glance to aft. There was a slight fog over the sea and visibility was poor, yet he could see his dreadnoughts, the capital ships of the greatest fleet in the world, were forming up in perfect line as he expected them to do. Again he was pleased, especially as he'd had such short notice of the fact that the Hun High Seas Fleet had sailed from its lairs on the German coast to do battle at last.

Fortunately his battlecruiser squadrons had been engaged in one of their periodic sweeps through the North Sea the previous afternoon when the signal had come through from the Admiralty in far-off London. Intelligence had just

192

reported that the German fleet had sailed. That could mean one of two things, Jellicoe had told his staff officers at the conference and briefing he had called immediately, 'Either the Hun is prepared to do battle with us, gentlemen. Or he wishes to draw us into some sort of a trap, baited with ships he can afford to lose. Then he'll scuttle back to the Fatherland and let those damned U-boats of his line up to sink as many of our capital ships as they can.' He had hesitated before adding finally, 'In my personal opinion, the Hun is attempting to set a trap for us.' That afternoon, as his fleet had sailed from Rosyth and Beatty's had done the same from Scapa Flow, Jellicoe had been right about the trap – only it had been a different kind of Hun trap. Now the divided fleet, the most powerful in the whole world, was heading straight for disaster . . .

In the same instant that a burst of twenty-millimetre shells from the leading German dreadnought ripped the length of de Vere's craft, bringing the superstructure tumbling down everywhere, the young skipper slipped in behind the last of the Danish fishing smacks, the sweat dripping down his forehead in opaque pearls. Behind him, Dickie Bird fought to get the last bit of power out of the great Thorneycroft engines, still zig-zagging crazily as the German gunners pursued him relentlessly with their shells. For the enemy knew that once he reached the cover of the neutral ships, they were powerless. The C-in-C, Admiral Reinhardt von Scheer, had ordered that they must not fire on the Danish ships. He didn't want to cause an international incident, especially with such a close neighbour as Denmark.

But the enemy gunners had not reckoned with the cunning and daring of the young British skipper. Suddenly, startlingly, Dickie did something that was completely unexpected and caught the Germans off guard. He swung the fast craft round. In a great comb of mast-high water, the vessel headed straight back in the direction from which it had just come. Watching open-mouthed, hands formed into tense claws as he stuck close to the last Danish fishing boat, de Vere prayed that his old comrade's bold manoeuvre would succeed. For now he was heading straight for the German dreadnought, while behind him, the enemy shells were falling harmlessly into the sea.

For a moment de Vere was puzzled. He had anticipated Dickie breaking off his daring trick at this stage and, before the German gunners could line up their guns on him, turning about and racing hell-for-leather for the cover of the Danish fishing smacks. But that was not Dickie's intention at all, it seemed. 'Christ Almighty!' he yelled, though he knew that his comrade could not possibly hear him. 'Turn about . . . *turn about, will you, you bloody fool!'*

But Dickie had no such intention. He continued his daring attack on the great grey dreadnought towering out of the sea above the speeding craft like a solid cliff of steel. De Vere groaned in despair, his whole body damp and sticky with a sweat of apprehension. Suddenly the little craft appeared to shudder and stop momentarily. A dull grey sausage of steel slapped into the water at her bow, bubbles burst to the surface to both sides of the steel object. Next instant it was speeding towards the German dreadnought. 'Oh, my God! He's trying to torpedo the big bastard!' de Vere yelled.

Dickie was. As machine guns lined the whole length of the battleship's port side, forming a wall of vicious white tracer, Dickie turned and broke at last, leaving the torpedo to do its deadly work. Five minutes later, his vessel riddled and ripped with shell fragments, most of its superstructure hanging down in a chaotic mess of tangled, distorted steel, Dickie too reached the safety of the Danish fishing boats. Behind him he left the *Nassau* class dreadnought limping along slowly, flame flickering greedily around her aft, her speed suddenly reduced to a snail's pace. David had won his first round with Goliath . . .

But already the British battlecruisers under the command of Admiral Sir David Beatty were in trouble. The fifty-two ships of all classes and sizes under his orders had sailed all-out to meet the Germans. 'The Hun,' Beatty had proclaimed in that cocky, confident manner of his, his white cap set at an even jauntier angle than ever, 'is about to slit his own throat! We outnumber him and we outgun him. The Germans are in for the worst defeat of the whole war!' Soon Beatty was to be proved wrong.

Now, erect on the quarterdeck of his flagship, he looked

the very epitome of the fighting sailor in the Nelson style, ready for anything – and everything – knowing that, come what may, *he'd* defeat the foe. Unfortunately, he was short of intelligence. He possessed no aeroplanes and no submarines to do his advance scouting. All he really knew was that he was ordered to join Jellicoe and his Grand Fleet. Not that it worried him if he missed his senior officer. Jellicoe was a bit of a 'nervous Nelly', not inclined to take risks, and visibility was becoming worse, so that if his ships were out there somewhere, within sighting range, he'd have difficulty spotting them under these conditions. Still, he was sure he could tackle and see off the enemy by himself.

Now it was three forty-five on that afternoon when the fate of the British Navy was at stake – and perhaps even more. High above the cocky little admiral, the lookouts scoured the horizon for the first sight of the Germans. And then, quite surprisingly it seemed, there they were, coming out of the fog. They were in a line, the High Seas Fleet's latest ships – the *Von der Tann*, the *Elbing* and the like, under the command of Admiral von Hipper. Beatty smiled, pleased with what he saw. His opponent didn't seem to have ordered his fleet into the usual battle formation. In line like that, unable to fire ahead, just in case they hit another of their ships, they'd have to deploy pretty sharpish to tackle his own fleet. Swiftly he rapped out his orders before the Huns started to disperse ready for the coming engagement.

On board Hipper's *Von der Tann*, a still miserable von Bismarck prepared to swallow his *'Lutt un' Lutt'*, as the sailors called the fiery mixture in their native Hamburg dialect. His head throbbed and his tongue felt like dried leather; he would have dearly loved simply to lie down and sleep. But he knew, after his disgraceful conduct of the night before, he daren't. He must show the Admiral that he was busily engaged in the action of the day. After all, senior officers had already come up to him and congratulated him for having volunteered for this action. They maintained staff officers, especially those of Intelligence, didn't customarily risk their necks in battle if they could avoid doing so.

He lifted the small glass of schnapps with a hand that trembled badly. '*Ein, zwei, drei . . .*' he breathed to himself. '*Ex!*' With a flourish he downed the whole glass and felt the liquid hit the back of his throat like a blast of fire. Hastily he followed the schnapps with a swallow of the ice-cold beer, which made up the second part of the sailors' drink. In an instant he felt new life coursing through his body and he was part of the battle scene, as, at a range of fifteen kilometres, the *Von der Tann*'s big guns thundered into life, sending her shells in the direction of the English battlecruiser *Indefatigable*, barely seen through the haze and the fog of war.

Von Bismarck allowed himself a smile. The battlecruiser was straddled accurately by that first German salvo. The next one could not fail to hit her directly. The British ships might have bigger guns, but the Germans' were more accurate and their gunners far better than those of the decadent English. 'Pig-dogs!' he yelled. 'Now where's your talk of Nelson and his damned Battle of Trafalgar? *Die, you arrogant swine . . .*'

Closer than Beatty's ships to the Danish coast and still sheltered by the fishing smacks, Dickie and de Vere tried desperately to ensure that von Bismarck's wish was not fulfilled. For already they had spotted the lean, frightening shapes just over a sea mile away which indicated that the Germans were about to spring their trap on the unsuspecting battlecruisers, now pinned down in battle with von Hipper's ships. *Submarines!*

Like grey wolves they were heading for the still unsuspecting British battlecruisers, also using the cover of the Danish fishing boats. But as he watched them approach like predatory killers seeking out their prey, he realized two things. The Germans had seen neither of the two British vessels, nor had his friend Dickie seen them. He bit his bottom lip till the blood came. Was he to warn Dickie of their approach and give the game away – for the Huns would naturally pick up his signal – or should he tackle the U-boats by himself? But if he did and failed, who would alert Beatty's battlecruisers that they were sailing into the trap posed by the submarines?

He focused his telescope, still covered by the red sail of

the nearest Danish fishing boat, while, on the deck, his crew worked feverishly to remove the wreckage and prepare for action again. For they knew their young skipper. He would not run for it in the face of a massed U-boat attack – and there were already four of the underwater killers within range. Some skippers would have done so and felt justified in running. Not de Vere Smith. His class and their traditions would not allow him to save himself, even if it meant sacrificing his old comrade. He would rather die in the one-sided battle soon to come than flee.

De Vere made his decision. 'Stand by the torpedoes,' he ordered in a voice that he hardly recognized as his own. 'Gunners close up to your guns.' The crew, even the youngest and greenest recruits, obeyed immediately, all fears thrown to the winds now. Hastily they doubled across the debris-littered deck, ignoring the bloodstains here and there. 'England expects!' a young and keen petty officer started to shout, as the gun-layer at the quick-firer began to shout out his orders, 'Zero-five-green . . .'

'*Ballocks to that!*' a grizzled old three-striper cut into the petty officer's patriotic slogan. 'We'd rather fuck than fight!'

But the old sailor was wrong. Coward and would-be hero alike, the crew of de Vere's battered little craft were going to fight . . .

The *Indefatigable* had been hit five times now. Her speed had slowed. Everywhere her superstructure was a mass of twisted, grotesquely contorted derricks, masts and the like. Already she was beginning to list badly to port, trailing thick black smoke behind her as she limped on bravely. Still the *Von der Tann* pounded the battered British ship relentlessly, while von Bismarck watched almost greedily, his hangover and the shame of the previous night's business with the big whore forgotten now. He told himself that everything was going according to plan, or even better. The sinking *Indefatigable* would slow Beatty's ships down – the cocky British admiral couldn't afford to leave the battlecruiser behind the rest of his fleet. Thus the U-boats now lurking off the Danish coast would have even more time to reach their British targets and begin the slaughter. Once they were engaged in

197

action against the U-boats, von Scheer would take up the battle with the most modern ships of the High Seas Fleet, and the British Admiral Sir John Jellicoe would find that he would be facing an enemy who equalled him in numbers. No longer would the British be able to rely on their superior numbers to beat the Germans. This time, a triumphant von Bismarck told himself, the world would witness a Battle of Trafalgar in reverse. It would be the German heavy ships that would blast the enemy off the face of the ocean, just as Nelson's three-deckers had done the Spaniards and the French back in 1805.

He signalled the wardroom steward in his starched white jacket, who he had ordered to leave his duty station as a stretcher-bearer to attend to his wishes. 'Steward,' he commanded. 'Chill the champagne . . . Half a bottle for every officer of my staff . . . And none of that Moselle German muck,' he added. 'Real French champus.'

'But, *Herr Admiral*,' the steward protested. 'We are fighting a battle. I won't be able to get to the liquor locker—' He never ended his objection. At that moment the *Indefatigable* was hit by a full German salvo in its magazine. There was a tremendous roar. Even at that distance, the Germans could hear the explosion as scores of shells went up in one terrific furious blast. Von Bismarck threw a swift glance through the porthole. The *Indefatigable* had split in half. Her stern reared straight up into the air like a massive steel cliff, her screws thrashing the air purposelessly. She was sinking rapidly, and he imagined with glee the hundreds of English sailors who had survived that initial explosion throwing themselves panic-stricken into the freezing water to perish there sooner or later. He smiled at the nonplussed young steward. 'I don't think you need to worry about such formalities, young man. The Tommies are already well on their way to being defeated. We'll need that champus soon, I'll be bound. Now move it.'

The steward moved it . . .

'Square up, gun crew!' the young petty officer yelled in response to de Vere's command. Hastily the quick-firer swung round to target the still unsuspecting U-boat, approaching steadily, as if it had all the time in the world before the killing commenced.

Up on the shattered bridge, de Vere swung his telescope round. He focused on Dickie's boat. The latter still hadn't spotted the U-boats. For an instant he prayed that his old comrade would be alerted by his opening shot and take evasive measures. Then he dismissed Dickie. He took a deep breath and then roared at the top of his voice, 'Commence firing . . . *Fire!*'

The gunners at the quick-firer and the Lewis machine guns needed no urging. As one, they opened up. *Crack!* A hush of air. The first stream of shells, accompanied by bursts of Lewis gunfire, sped low across the grey-green water towards the nearest U-boat.

The Germans were caught completely by surprise. Shells and slugs ripped the length of the U-boat's hull, Immediately it was scarred by the gleaming silver of the hits. Almost melo-dramatically, the sub's deck-gun crew reeled back to left and right in a welter of flailing arms and bloody wrecked bodies. The machine-gunner behind the bridge was struck, his chest ripped apart by the cruel fire. He slammed back against his stanchion, the machine gun firing purposelessly right into the grey sky.

'Adjust your range!' de Vere yelled above the racket, as, on the U-boat's deck, others of the watch started returning fire. Again the gun-layer snapped into action. With eager fingers he lowered the range, right eye glued to the rubber eyepiece of the sight. '*Fire!*' de Vere cried.

The quick-firer burst into chattering frenetic activity. Even as the panicked U-boat skipper started to flood his tanks in order to submerge – great bubbles of compressed air exploding on the surface with obscene fartlike sounds – the quick-firer's salvo ripped the length of the conning tower, with the last shells slamming into the hull below.

In an instant the submarine was listing or sinking rapidly. Panic-stricken sailors started to throw themselves over the sides before it was too late. Oil escaping from the stricken U-boat's diesels began to flood the surface, dragging the escapers under as they fought to avoid its clogging clutches. Someone

199

began to wave a white flag on the conning tower. De Vere no longer had any time for the courtesies of war. He wanted to sink one of the detested U-boats and wipe out all aboard her. There'd be no surrender this day. Face set in a grimace of animal-like rage and the lust to kill, he rasped, 'Keep firing, you men. Don't stop now. Sink the bastard!'

Now Dickie Bird was alerted to the danger he was in. It was as he heard the firing close by that the horizon was illuminated by the flash of ugly red flame followed by the hollow boom of a major explosion. Dickie didn't know it then, but he had just witnessed the sinking of the second of Beatty's gigantic battlecruisers. It was the *Queen Mary*. One by one, von Hipper's fleet was picking off the British ships.

But Dickie had no time for the fate of others. He knew he had perhaps only minutes to save his own command. Already he could see the line of ripples hurrying faster and faster towards him. It was a German torpedo launched at his midships. Sweating with sudden apprehension, he twisted the wheel round with all his strength. The vessel answered perfectly. The torpedo flashed by with feet to spare and ran on into the unknown.

Now he surged forward at top speed, ignoring the submarine's fire, which flashed towards him in what seemed a solid white wall, great founts of water being thrown up on either side of his vessel, drenching the deck crew over and over again.

To his front, the submarine seemed to stop, as far as Dickie could judge through the crazy fog of war. Perhaps the German skipper was considering whether he should crash-dive or not while there was still time. But he hesitated a fraction of a minute too long. As the electric klaxons sounded the order to dive and the skipper began to flood the U-boat's tanks, Dickie's craft hit her admidships. The U-boat reeled violently. Her mast almost touched the water before she righted herself. But not totally. Already diesel oil was leaking copiously from her shattered tanks. Plates groaned. A first gunner flung himself overboard in panic. The gun commander drew his pistol to try to stop the rot. To no avail. The U-boat was sinking and the gun crew didn't want to go down with her. The other gunners followed the first, bobbing up and down in the water, gasping and choking for breath, their faces already blackened with the escaping oil.

But Dickie had no time to concern himself with the fate of the doomed U-boat's crew. He was in trouble – serious trouble – himself. That impact which had wrecked the submarine had torn a great hole in his own bows. He was sinking too, slowly, and he had to get his craft away from the U-boat before she dragged him under as well. Desperately, as the U-boat sank lower and lower, with the men from below pushing by the skipper in the conning tower to throw themselves over the sides in an attempt to save their lives, he tried to reverse his craft.

There was a terrible rending, tearing sound. Metal gave. Still he remained trapped where he was. He applied the last of his power. His screws thrashed the water into a white fury. The sweat poured down his contorted face. 'Come on, come on,' he urged, willing the damaged boat to come free. 'For Chrissake, *move!*'

From the safety of his position behind the slow-moving Danish fishing fleet, whose skippers had still not decided whether Denmark's neutrality was enough to save them in the midst of this great naval battle between Britain and Germany, de Vere saw that Dickie was in serious danger of sinking at any moment. There was a great jagged gleaming hole in his hull and, tied as he was to the sinking U-boat, there was a big chance he'd be dragged below the surface by the larger vessel. He had to act – *now!*

'Stand by your piece, petty officer!' he yelled at the gawping deck-gun crew. 'Torpedo mate, prepare to fire.'

'Ay, ay sir,' the answers came back confidently enough. All of his crew had faith in their young skipper, despite the perilous situation in which they found themselves, with at least three other German submarines within range and the whole of the German fleet behind them.

De Vere gave her full power. The craft's sharp prow rose out of the water at a steep angle. Once again bright white water combed to left and right of her bow. Beneath his feet on the bridge, the boards pulsated and vibrated like a live

201

thing. It took all his strength for de Vere to keep control of the steering. Water flung up by the bow deluged the windscreen in front of him time and time again. Yet when it cleared momentarily, he saw to his alarm that Dickie's position was growing worse by the instant. Already flames were flickering up greedily the whole length of the U-boat. Any moment now she'd go up in flames or sink. Time was running out fast for Dickie Bird and his trapped boat . . .

Admiral Beatty was now worried about time, too. His usual cockiness and self-assurance had vanished. The Germans were inflicting too many casualties on his battlecruisers for his liking. Naturally he had anticipated casualties among his ships, but not this many. Already he had lost two of his capital ships, and in a brief engagement between his destroyers and a large force of German destroyers and light cruisers, he had lost the destroyer *Nestor* and suffered serious damage to two others of the destroyer fleet. Although he would never report this to Whitehall and the new critical Prime Minister – the 'Welsh Wizard', Lloyd George – his ships, part of the greatest fleet in the world, which had ruled the waves since Trafalgar, had been plagued by initial bad positioning, sloppy signalling, lack of initiative – and bad luck.

But if these failings would never reach the 'frock coats' – the detested politicians, the bane of the soliders' and sailors' lives – they would become known within the Navy itself. In due course heads would roll as a consequence – and he didn't want his, in particular, to join those unfortunate heads.

In the final analysis, it would be up to Jellicoe, somewhere to the rear, to make the decision on what should be done next. The Commander-in-Chief of the British fleet bore the ultimate responsibility. But before Jellicoe, who was inclined to be too cautious, in Beatty's opinion, made his final decision, he would continue to carry the war to the enemy. As he said to his staff, raising his voice above the roar of another salvo of shells heading for the enemy. 'Gentlemen, we have to show the enemy the traditional British 'Nelson touch' – but not only the Huns, our nation too. Our people must retain their belief that, although the Army might fail now and again

– after all, it is an army of conscripts and the like now – the regulars of the Senior Service never fail. We shall continue to fight the enemy even if we have suffered severe casualties and may suffer more. The honour of the Royal Navy demands it.'

'But what if the Hun use their subs . . .? We may be sailing straight into a trap,' a staff member objected.

All around him, his fellow staff officers looked severe. One didn't ask such questions of 'Battling' Beatty. It wasn't cricket.

Beatty, as worried as he was privately, took the question in his stride. 'Did Lord Nelson ask such questions at the Battle of the Nile . . . at Copenhagen, even at Trafalgar?' Beatty demanded. 'Of course he didn't. Captain, let us worry about Hun subs when we spot them. Signal to all . . . *Continue the attack!*'

Another explosion racked the doomed U-boat. De Vere, at the controls on the shattered bridge, gasped. The very air seemed to be dragged from his lungs, leaving him choking for breath. It wouldn't be more than a few minutes before the U-boat went up – or down – completely. Desperately he turned in a great swerve of water, ignoring the lone German machine-gunner still firing when the rest of the frenzied crew were trying to save themselves before the inevitable happened.

He grabbed the loudhailer the best he could with one hand, and yelled, voice echoing back and forth across that deadful scene of impending death, 'Abandon ship . . . Hell's bells, Dickie, abandon ship . . . You've done your bit, Dickie!'

He waited, lowering his speed, ready to take on board the survivors of his comrade's boat before it was too late.

Now that the U-boat presented no further danger, de Vere's crew abandoned their weapons. They seized boat hooks, flung Carley floats as far as they could into the oil-scummed water, dotted here and there by the still corpses of the floating dead, unhooked the guard rails, each man as anxious as the skipper to save their comrades. Now the war was forgotten; now they were fighting the matelot's age-old enemy, the sea itself.

'*Dickie!*' de Vere bellowed frantically, knowing that Dickie clung to the old Royal Navy tradition of not abandoning his ship until every man of his crew had done so. '*Abandon ship!*'

The rest of his frantic plea was drowned. Suddenly the submarine reeled violently. There was the grating, rending sound of tearing metal. With a crunch, Dickie's craft freed itself and started to sink immediately as red, angry flame exploded out of the interior of the conning tower, sending up what seemed like a gigantic smoke ring into the lowering sky. That did it. Dickie had no alternative now but to drop into the water as, all around him, his crew did the same.

Not a moment too soon. Like a great fiery blowtorch, flame seared the length of the doomed U-boat. The paintwork bubbled and exploded like the symptoms of some loathsome skin disease. The submarine was racked time and time again by great explosions. The conning tower crumpled as if it were made of cardboard. Here and there, sailors racing along the red-hot glowing deck were caught by that all-consuming flame. Unable to run any further, they lay there, gasping their last frantic breath, turning rapidly into shrunken pygmies, parodies of the fit young men they had once been.

To de Vere's front, the water was filled now with survivors, British and German, caked in oil, fighting desperately to get away before the diesel which flooded out of the sinking U-boat's tanks ignited too. To the rear, those closest to the sub had already been caught by those greedy flames. They lay burning and screaming on the surface of the water, black skeletal arms, which through the bone gleamed like polished ivory, thrashing impotently.

The rest swam for safety like they had never swum before. Behind them the burning oil raced to catch up with them. Like some primeval monster of the deep, scenting its prey, it caught yet another desperate victim. A sailor, British or German. He started to burn immediately. Before the eyes of the horrified rescuers, his head above the water was transformed into a charred death's head. Still screaming hideously he disappeared beneath the surface in a hiss of steam.

But now the ones who would live were being hauled aboard de Vere's boat, gasping and spluttering, trying weakly to remove the oil sludge from their blinded eyes, pulling it out of their gasping, crimson-lipped mouths before they choked.

Here and there sailors could accept rum from their rescuers, but it only caused them to gasp and cough and vomit over the men who had fed them the fiery spirits.

De Vere, seeing that Dickie was now aboard, and knowing that the sub would go up at any moment, yelled, 'Get on with it . . . Petty officer, cut the lines—'

He never finished. With a great roar the U-boat exploded. Its back broke immediately. The stern rose for a moment, straight into the air. But next it came slamming down in a great fountain of water and disappeared immediately, followed by the rest of the sub. One second it was there, the next it had vanished totally, leaving nothing to mark its passing save for the still dead, drifting back and forth on the wavelets aimlessly . . .

'*Ein Hoch!*' von Bismarck cried triumphantly, already a little drunk from the '*lutt un' lutt*' . He raised his glass of ice-cold champagne to the other members of his intelligence staff. 'A toast to your victory, gentlemen.'

As one, the other officers raised their glasses, arms set at the regulation forty-five degree angle, parallel with the third button of their tunic. 'To victory,' they echoed.

'*Ex!*' von Bismarck commanded.

'Ex!' they repeated, and drained their glasses. Immediately the white-coated steward set about refilling the tall glasses. The officers didn't seem to notice the men, but then that was customary in the Imperial Navy: lower-deck ratings were never noticed by their officers. They were there simply to carry out their duties and die obediently and without complaint whenever necessary.

Von Bismarck said, face flushed an excited red. 'Victory is ours, gentlemen. We have sunk two battlecruisers of Beatty's fleet, five cruisers and seven destroyers. Our own losses have been modest in comparison. Admiral Hipper is now about to return home. Beatty will naturally follow. He'll want revenge, of course.' He shrugged cynically. 'He won't get it. Instead, our fine English admiral will suffer a defeat. The trap is set. The U-boats will be waiting for him, and –' he emphasized the words – 'the plan has been realized. How?'

He didn't give them a chance to answer his rhetorical question. 'I shall tell you. We have just deciphered a signal from Jellicoe with the main British fleet. He has turned south. It seems he is wavering . . . indecisive. Perhaps the losses are too much for him. However, von Scheer will be waiting for him – and this time the two fleets will be equal, and I don't need to tell you, gentlemen, that our German superiority in men, spirit and modern vessels will win the day. For the first time since the damned English Royal Navy set out to dominate the oceans after their famous Lord Nelson won the battle at Trafalgar, it will be defeated. And by whom? Need I tell you?' His voice rose in triumph. 'By the German Imperial Na—'

His cry of victory was drowned by the battleship's klaxons sounding the call to battle stations once more. Crew members ran up and down the decks, beating the gongs to call the off-duty watches from their bunks and hammocks to their divisions. Everywhere there was haste and noise, interspersed by the sound of the starboard machine guns abruptly firing full out, and the hoarse cries of the petty officers cursing their underlings for being so slow. At the door of the wardroom, the suddenly pale young steward dropped the silver tray holding the newly filled glasses of champagne to celebrate their victory. Even as he did so, von Bismarck experienced a sudden sensation of alarm, already aware that something had gone wrong with his great plan; that there might not be a great victory after all . . .

De Vere, at the wheel with a battered, oil-smeared Dickie holding his wounded arm next to him, forgot the danger. Now he was carried away by a wild, unreasoning euphoria: the unreasoning bloodlust of battle. Squeezing every last ounce of power from his wreck of a craft, he headed straight for the German dreadnought.

Minutes before, the two of them had managed to gain wireless contact with Jellicoe's flagship the *Iron Duke*. The best they could, with the power failing by the second, they had sent their vital message, warning the admiral of what the Germans had waiting for him and his fleet. Jellicoe was a slow, careful man, but this time he had reacted swiftly enough. In clear, his signaller had replied. 'Splendid work. Will comply. Give me a small victory.'

That last phrase had puzzled the two of them for a few moments, until Dickie Bird had snapped excitedly, 'He means sink one of the bastards. He wants a delay so that he can alter course and head for safety.'

De Vere had caught on immediately. His exhaustion had vanished, as if it had never even existed. '*Small victory!*' he had cried. 'Let's show the Lord Admiral what our little craft can do. We won't give him a *small* victory.'

'What do you mean, de Vere?' Dickie had asked, wiping yet more diesel from his face.

'Mean? Why, Dickie, we'll give him a bloody great *big* victory . . . Look over there, me lucky lad.' He pointed to the south. 'What do your glassy orbs see there?'

'God bless us and save us, yer honour,' Dickie had exclaimed in what he thought was an Irish accent. 'It's the Jerry dreadnought – and bad cess on him, too, your honour.' He had dropped the fake accent on the spot as he had realized what de Vere intended. 'You think we can, de Vere?'

'Of course we can. After what you and I have been through these last years, Dickie, nothing can stop us now. Come hell or high water, we're going to give Jellicoe his victory . . .

Now, as they came in for the kill, the revs on the machometers started to mount rapidly. A white wave combed to both sides of the prow. The noise of the engines grew and grew. It was deafening. Now they had to shout at each other to make themselves understood. Not that they spoke. Both their gazes – and minds – were focused exclusively on the great steel wall of the German dreadnought to their front.

'*One thousand yards!*' Dickie yelled at the top of his voice.

At the wildly swaying bow, the two torpedo men, hanging on for all they were worth as the deck heaved and bucked beneath them, tensed over their deadly fish.

'I'm taking evasive action,' De Vere cried as tracer erupted in a white fury to their front. The whole hull of the German dreadnought seemed aflame with it. He flung the flying craft to left and right. The tracer peppered the water all around them.

'*Seven hundred and fifty!*'

Now the steel monster seemed to fill their whole world, blocking out the light. Shells were falling all around them. Still the two crazy young men, hair flying in the breeze, didn't seem to notice. Nothing mattered now. There was no past, no future, just the wild mad present – the overwhelming desire to kill the gigantic steel monster which had become the most powerful thing in their world.

'*Five hundred!*'

It was time. De Vere knew he could wait no longer. Their luck had to run out in a second or two more. With all his strength, he yelled to the soaked torpedo mates, 'Fire . . . fire . . . fire . . .'

The torpedo men waited no more. They fired one and then two. The flying craft shuddered violently. A thick asthmatic cough. A yellow flash. The first tube of death, packed with a ton of high explosive, slid into the water. The next followed. '*Running true, sir!*' the torpedo mate yelled, his face dripping with sea spray.

De Vere still surged forward. Eager to be in at the kill, he resisted the urge to break to left and right and get out of the way of that deadly hail of fire coming from the battleship. To his front the two torpedoes fanned out to left and right. Like steel sharks, they headed straight for their target. And there was no hope for the great dreadnought now. She was too cumbersome and unwieldly to turn swiftly out of the way of the two torpedoes.

At the very last moment, when the deck watch had tensed in dread expectancy, thinking their young skipper would never change course and they would smash into the side of the great ship, de Vere broke to the right. As a last desperate burst of machine-gun fire swept the bridge, hitting both Dickie and de Vere, the tin fish exploded.

The sky was torn apart by that tremendous explosion, which seemed to go on and on for ever. Water shot as high as the masts of the stricken ship in a great whirling-white mass. An instant later it was followed by the blinding orange flash of a boiler exploding below. Parts of the superstructure came tumbling down like metal rain. Almost immediately the dreadnought started to slow, as its rudder failed and it began to circle powerlessly.

As de Vere began to sink to his knees, gasping for breath, like a gravely hurt boxer valiantly refusing to go down for the count, and Dickie slumped, already unconscious, over the shattered wheel, less than a hundred yards or so away, Klaus von Bismarck was dying. Not that he knew it. Nor would he have believed it if anyone had told him that. He was a von Bismarck, the scion of a family of *Realpolitiker* who had always survived – won through. For years now he had planned this victory, not for Prussia, nor for the new Germany that his famous uncle had created, but for himself.

Was that the only real reason for living, the secret of power: the power to maintain one's self in a world of one's own creation? But something had gone wrong. He knew that, at least. He could see it, as he lay in the shattered wardroom among the dead and the broken bottles of champagne and broken glasses, the blood seeping from his guts as they uncurled from his torn stomach like the coils of some slimy grey-pink snake.

Of course, it would all come right in the end. It always had for him. Didn't he deserve it, as a member of the family which had created the New Germany? He gave a laugh at his own stupidity at believing that anything really serious could happen to *him*. The laugh ended in a throaty cough as the thick, hot copper-tasting blood which signified the end he didn't believe in filled his throat.

Outside, there was the sound of heavy boots crunching over the debris. The ship lurched alarmingly, as a frightened voice called, 'Anybody there?'

Another voice answered, 'Ner, only a dead officer. Got pissed on champagne and didn't even know what frigging hit him, the classy arse-with-ears.'

The boots began to crunch away again. Once more the ship lurched and set off a frightening creaking and moaning, as the ship's plates began to buckle under the pressure of the water flooding in through the gaping holes made by de Vere's torpedoes. 'No!' von Bismarck croaked, or thought he did. In reality he made no sound; he couldn't. 'Please . . . please, don't leave me here . . . I'm Klaus von Bismarck. You know . . . von Bismarck, friend.'

But no one was listening and, if there had been anyone there to hear him mention that proud name and title, they wouldn't have taken any notice. They were abandoning ship. Now it was every man for himself, from rating to admiral. Von Bismarck started to cry noiselessly, overcome by self-pity, and died with silent tears trickling down his raddled, evil face . . .

There was a muddled, muffled mixture of voices all around them. Half-conscious, Dickie and de Vere, being fixed into the bosun's chairs to carry them across to the *Iron Duke*, were only dimly aware of them, and the gentle hands adjusting the straps. '*Hay una urgencia. Donde esta el medici?*' a voice demanded in Spanish. Why Spanish they never found out. Another said, 'Now, take it easy. The two officers are badly hurt. You ratings just fix 'em securely!' There was a creak and the rattle of the tackle. Instinctively, de Vere caught hold of the support with his right hand. In his other he clutched his talisman, her ring. It had brought him through safely so far. Now it would continue to do the same.

There was the hiss of taut rope. He started to move forward. The bosun's chair swayed to left and right above the waves. He didn't see it. He was still half doped with morphia to ease the pain of his wounds. Behind him Dickie started to follow. Under the command of a first lieutenant from the flagship, someone of de Vere's crew cried, 'Three cheers for Mr Smith and Mr Bird . . . *Hip, hip, hurrah!*'

De Vere smiled wanly, vaguely aware of the cheering. He told himself they all deserved a cheer. Indirectly they had helped to save the day. By now the Germans must have scut-tled back to their lairs in North Germany. Somehow he doubted they'd ever come out again.

Drugged as he was, he forgot his loyal fellows almost immediately. Now all he wanted to do was to sleep and sleep and sleep and blot the whole bloody business of this May day out. Still, even now, afflicted as he was by utter weariness, he held on to that precious ring, as the bosun's chair reached the rail of Admiral Jellicoe's flagship and once again caring hands reached out to unbuckle him from the wooden seat, with officers ordering, 'Stand by there, sick-bay attendants!' and, 'Petty officer, remember the two officers are badly wounded . . . treat 'em gently, will you?'

Carefully, very carefully, he was lowered to the wet deck of the great battleship, followed a few minutes later by Dickie, who was placed next to him. Someone started to roll up his left sleeve. Half-blinded, he couldn't see who it was, but for one drugged moment he thought it was someone attempting to steal his precious ring. 'Don't,' he breathed. 'Don't you dare—'

His protest gave way to a little yelp of pain, as the sick-bay attendant plunged his needle into the wounded officer's arm and gave him another injection of morphia. De Vere sighed and the pain started to vanish again almost immediately.

'All right, lads,' the officer in charge commanded as soon as Dickie had received his injection too. 'Get 'em to the sick bay. The surgeon-lieutenant's waiting to clean 'em up before you know who comes to see 'em. Smartish now.'

Five minutes later they were both naked, stretched out on the sick bay's tables being fussed over by the attendants, while the surgeon cleaned their bodies, tut-tutting a little when he saw their wounds, talking to himself as he did so in the fashion of doctors engrossed in their treatment. Once he attempted to force open de Vere's hand holding the ring, until the latter muttered something and he said, 'All right, old chap, I'll deal with that later. Don't want to be seen fighting with the patients when the big nobs arrive.'

Then the medical personnel were finished. Hastily the doctor changed his gown for one not stained with fresh blood, patted his hair into place and checked if his staff were ready to receive the most important person in the Royal Navy. On their tables in the sick bay, which smelt of ether and Jeyes fluid, the two wounded young men closed their eyes, ready to slip into a drugged sleep at any moment. But not just yet.

Vaguely de Vere became aware of the stamp of heavy boots,

the commands, the movement of many feet. A breeze came through an open bulkhead into the warmth of the sick bay. He stirred uneasily. Next to him, Dickie murmured something unintelligible.

Someone leaned over him. His nostrils were assailed by the smell of expensive talcum powder. A voice, used to shouting commands, said softly, 'Can you hear me, Smith?'

He felt like not answering. He simply wanted to sleep, to fall into the blessed oblivion of sleep and forget the misery. But the voice went on, a little more loudly now, 'I'm Admiral Jellicoe.'

He forced himself to nod his head. 'Sir?'

'I'd just like to say to you, Smith – and you, too Bird, if you can hear me – thank you . . . thank you both a great deal. You have helped to save my fleet this May day. The Hun has fled and has left the field of battle to us . . . Thank you . . .' The voice receded into the background and later de Vere thought he heard the C-in-C order the Surgeon-Lieutenant to take great care of these two young officers, because 'they deserve everything that our country can give them'. But then he might have imagined the order. For later, when the criticism of the C-in-C and his part in the Battle of Jutland began, no one really wanted to know what had happened in fact. Everything, even their part in it, had to be censored, hushed up.

Once more the boots stamped down hard. A few commands. Cool air entered the sick bay momentarily and they were alone with the MO. He fiddled with his two wounded patients for a few more minutes. Then, surprisingly for a doctor, he smoothed De Vere's brow gently, whispering, 'It's all over. That's the end of the bullshit for you two heroes. Sleep.'

De Vere didn't even have the strength to nod his appreciation. Instead he gripped *her* ring weakly for a few moments before relaxing his hold. An instant later he was fast asleep, snoring harshly with the morphia they had pumped into him, as the *Iron Duke* turned and started the long journey home. It was all over at last. They had won. At least they believed they had . . .

# Duncan Harding

Dear Reader, have you ever ventured past the Watford Gap and on to that remote wilderness known as Yorkshire? No? Good for you. You are wise to stay where you are in the civilized south. You see, I have experienced the nameless horrors of that wild place. Twice. Even with a relatively large publisher's advance in my pocket and a bottle of Haig – '*Don't Be Vague. Ask For Haig*' as they used to say – I ended my last visit to the place with my nervcs almost totally shattcrcd.

Why did you go? you may ask, gentle reader. Well, I had some sort of stupid idea that maybe I might still find some sort of confirmation all these years later of my two toffs' story. I know . . . I know. I should have had my head examined by the blokes in white overalls, armed with rubber hammers.

But I did have that large advance, and the current lady in my life – 'Miss three for the price of two', as I call her (behind her back naturally) – was thinking of applying for a Marks and Sparks credit card.

So, damned fool that I am, I journeyed to that northern county on this silly whim. To a place called Scarborough to be precise, where my two toffs started their long path to the Battle of Jutland. 'The pearl of the North-East coast', the local literature call it. Some pearl!

Yes, I know, I know, dear reader, whoever would go there when there's Butlins or Pontin's available? Only basket cases, who dribble from every orifice and can't even remember what thcy had for breakfast, borne there from what are laughingly called 'care homes', perhaps? Even Yorkshiremen, it is rumoured up there, avoid the place like the plague.

Well, there I was, muffled up in my overcoat with two pullovers on underneath – *in July* – enjoying the 'bracing

213

ozone', as the local travel literature calls it. To my sensitive nose, it seemed more redolent of burger an' fries and stale bitter. Anyway, enough nit-picking. Once out of the station yard and thrust into the merry throng of geriatrics on their Zimmer frames, I took a sip from my bottle – concealed in a brown paper bag, as is apparently the native custom – and was ready to delve into the heroic past.

There wasn't one! The locals didn't think so, apparently. Perhaps they'd lost it. One couldn't really call the ones I spoke to locals. Some were obviously illegal immigrants – 'English I speak little. You from council?' Many were 'Yorkshire folk', as they called themselves, but not from Scarborough. The women were dyed blondes, showing plenty of meat in their blouses, and 'our Pete' or 'our 'Arry' wore a blue blazer with highly polished buttons. They weren't unhelpful, I have to admit that – well, for 'Yorkshire folk' they'd stop and 'pass the time of day' with you, as they called it. It was simply they didn't know anything. History had started for them when they'd sold up in Halifax or Rotherham and moved to the pearl of the North-East coast. Just like most of the true locals, they'd never heard of the 'Great War'. 'Was it summat to do with yon Hitler bloke?' Anyway, they were all eventually moving to Spain. They'd had enough of the pearl's 'bracing ozone'. They were heading for Spain, sun and sangria, presumably to die of booze and boredom within a couple of years there.

In the end I gave up on my sentimental journey into the past. If there were any traces of my two young toffs – and naturally that poor, ill-fated Sussi von Hoofstra-Mecklenburg – they'd long vanished. So, while I waited for the next train to bear me southwards and back to civilization as we know it, I repaired to the nearest 'eaterie', as they call the former 'boozers' up north. In truth there was little there that reminded me of the traditional 'boozer'. The days of cloth caps and whippets had long vanished, apparently. So had 'knife and fork suppers'.

In these 'eateries' they sat around little tables, eating 'continental specials' and actually drinking wine – 'Red or white, luv?' There wasn't a black pudding or pint of 'Old Peculiar' in sight. So I pushed to the bar, ignoring the continental special (scampi and chips, to be exact) and slumped in the corner out of the way. Next to me there was a tall old geezer with what looked like a gammy foot. It was wrapped in a huge, dirty bandage which was coming loose at the back, though he didn't seem to notice. There he leaned on his metal NHS stick with its adjustable notches, brooding over a small glass of beer.

'Sad and sick at heart?' he queried, totally out of the blue, looking at himself in the mirror behind the bar. His voice was rough and rasping, like that of an old established toper who had sunk too much cheap sauce down his gullet.

He caught me completely off guard, I must admit. Old hacks like yours truly are not much surprised usually. But the old geezer's outburst did. It was, in a way – what can I say? – philosophical. Before I knew what I was doing, I was answering in the affirmative. I know I shouldn't have; you usually get stung for a free drink by lonely old geezers sitting at bars. With my kind of 'advances' from that publisher in London who drinks the expensive '*Mouton*' red stuff with the dosh I earn for him, you don't throw your money about 'like a man with no arms', as Stoker Harding might have put it all those years ago.

'I'm not surprised,' the old geezer said, He gestured around the room, noisy with the clicking of knives and forks and false teeth. 'Anybody living in this place *would* be sad and sick at heart . . . Yer know what they say about Manchester?'

I didn't, but the old geezer soon told me.

'The quickest way out of Manchester on a rainy day is a bottle of gin.' He didn't laugh. 'Scarborough isn't much different, even when it's *flaming* July.'

That did it. I liked it, especially that bit about 'flaming July'. I bought him a drink. A double to be exact, and even in moments of extreme elation or drunkenness, old Duncan Harding doesn't often buy strangers doubles. In fact, I bought him several doubles, and naturally several for yours truly as well. I had my ticket back to the 'Big Smoke' and enough whisky in the paper bag to see me through till at least Peterborough. So I could afford to be generous with my publisher's advance. Besides, if I didn't spend it, Miss three for the price of two would.

The old geezer turned out to be some sort of local chronicler. Donkey's years before, he'd even written a history of the North Sea coast – 'When I was still full o' piss an' vinegar! I thought, stupidly, people would be interested in that sort of thing. Nowadays, if they can't do it on the History Channel or turn it into frigging Disneyland, nobody's interested.' Here he'd looked morosely down into his empty glass and I'd signalled, fool that I am, to the lad with the bow tie behind the bar for yet another double.

A few more doubles later and we were on first-name basis – 'Dunc' and 'Chuck'. By then we were a couple of first-class moaners, growing ever more cynical about our 'island race', as Chuck was now calling them after he'd pulled off his bloody, dirty bandage to display his 'gammy' foot. 'None of that exposing yersen in here!' the lad in the bow tie behind the bar had snapped angrily. 'Or yer out.' For a moment I'd expected him to pull his baseball bat from beneath the bar and lam into us. Posh 'eaterie' or not, they're like that in Yorkshire.

About that time, Chuck said, 'I don't see why you give a frig about history, Dunc. Give 'em a tale, forget the fact, ditch our history altogether. All the punters want is to be entertained. Bread and frigging circuses, yer know, old lad.'

In a half-hearted way, I objected, 'But Chuck, somebody's got to remember them.'

'You mean the blokes in the blazers and berets, with the polished medals,' he retorted scornfully. 'Come off it, Dunc. Silly old farts like that. They're just bullshitting and getting their pix in the local rag . . . waiting till they turn up their toes and they sound the 'Last Post' at the British Legion for 'em.'

Here Chuck had staggered to his feet, nearly overbalancing in the attempt. Then he sounded the 'Last Post', blowing through his fingers. Actually, it sounded more like an extended wet fart.

'That's done it!' the lad behind the bar snapped angrily, his bow tie all askew. '*Out!* And don't come back here . . . Drunken old sods. Ought to be bloody ashamed of yersens – at your age!'

216

Thus rejected and ejected we staggered out into the blinding July sunshine. Well, there were a couple of weak rays about, and over the sea the rainclouds were gathering. But it seemed 'blinding' to us after all those doubles.

Now people were looking at us. Not that it mattered much to Chuck. He limped at my side to the station, trailing a dirty bandage behind him, his NHS stick over his shoulder like a rifle (naturally, in his state, the stick was on the wrong shoulder). For some reason he was warbling 'Land of Hope and Glory'.

I decided to leave him at the station's entrance. I had an awful premonition that, in his state, Chuck might fall beneath the wheels of the departing train. I suspect he wouldn't have minded particularly. That way he could have said goodbye to 'our island race', as he liked to call us.

Me, I wouldn't have liked it one bit. It would have meant I might have been stuck in the 'pearl of the North-East' for days, and there wasn't enough whisky in the place to stop me going mad in that eventuality.

Before I left, Chuck said, 'Don't take on, Dunc. It's a mistake to visit old battlefields – they've always changed the scenery'. They had in a way. I'd achieved nothing except to meet poor, cynical, dying Chuck (I never for the life of me remember his last name). I'd found not a trace of Grandad Harding's toffs or poor Sussi, or even of those six thousand odd 'matelots' of Beatty's and Jellicoe's fleets who had been killed in action that day in 1916 – and a lot of them had been from this self-same North-East coast.

As I'd predicted, I woke up at Peterborough. I had a headache and naturally all the Haig had gone. I licked my parched lips and noticed that someone getting out there had left behind the Leeds paper, the *Yorkshire Post*. I turned to the obituaries straight away. All us old farts do that.

And there it was. 'LAST SURVIVOR OF THE BATTLE OF JUTLAND DIED, AGED 111'. If I'd been in the right mood, I would have given a little whistle of surprise at the coincidence. But I wasn't. So I desisted. But there it was. No one now was left alive who had been present there that May day. The Battle of Jutland was finally closed. Now it was all

217

the dead past. History. Well, it meant something, though God knows what. Forty-five minutes later I was back in the 'Old Smoke' and I was thinking of my next 'exciting epic', as my publisher likes to call my books, and more importantly the next advance . . .